MARKED OFF

Don Cameron

NEW ISLAND

MARKED OFF
First published in 2015
By New Island Books,
16 Priory Hall Office Park,
Stillorgan,
County Dublin.
Republic of Ireland.

www.newisland.ie

PRINT ISBN: 978-1-84840-415-1
EPUB ISBN: 978-1-84840-417-5
MOBI ISBN: 978-1-84840-416-8

British Library Cataloguing Data.
A CIP catalogue record for this book is available from the British
Library.

Typeset by JVR Creative India
Cover design by Taisiya Putova
Printed by ScandBook AB

New Island received financial assistance from The Arts Council (*An
Chomhairle Ealaíon*), 70 Merrion Square, Dublin 2, Ireland.

10 9 8 7 6 5 4 3 2 1

For Mum & Dad

who always believed

Acknowledgements

I would like to thank everyone who helped me write this book, From Don Egremont's early encouragement to write, to Wendy Conroy's first red-pencilled corrections, there were always many helpful voices. Also to Brendan Hayes, who has read the book more times than I have, for his observations. Without them, life, and the writing of this book, would have been a lot less interesting.

Big thanks to the RTÉ *Today Show* & New Island Books for creating the prize that was to have this book published. I am eternally grateful for the opportunity. And a heartfelt thanks to the professionals at New Island, especially to Shauna Daly for her insight and enthusiasm.

Lots of love to Millie, Niall and all my family and friends for their generous and continued support – it is invaluable.

A lucky boy.

1

A flash of lightning lit up the sky as the rain lashed against the windscreen. The crack of thunder that immediately followed made his heart jump. 'That was close,' he said, and watched dark clouds roll out to sea.

Across the bay, the sky above Howth was an unbroken blue canvas. David shook his head. Not for long, he thought, and feared that their planned barbecue would have to wait for another day.

Another curtain of rain danced along the road.

He got out of the car, grabbed his briefcase, and holding it over his head, ran to the front door.

He stepped inside.

'Hello, love, I'm home!' he called out. He put his briefcase down, and slipped off his wet jacket. He could hear music playing in the kitchen and knew that Barbara was listening to Lyric FM. It was Mozart, her favourite composer.

'Hello!' he called, a little louder.

The music didn't seem any louder that it usually did, so Barbara should have heard him. Maybe the thunder and heavy rain had made it impossible.

'Barbara, where are you?'

He stopped, listening to hear if she was upstairs, but there was nothing. She was probably in the garden, rescuing clothes from the clothesline. Where else could she be?

'Barbara!' he called, stepping into the kitchen.

The empty wine bottle was on the counter, exactly where it had been when he had left for the office. 'Shit,' he muttered, as he touched the hot iron. Barbara's golf shirt was lying on the ironing board.

That's odd, he thought, when he saw the unemptied shopping bags on the table, and the upturned flower vase.

His heart skipped a beat.

A stream of water had made its way over the edge and onto the floor. Something sparkled in the water, like a little star, and he squinted to get a better picture before bending down and touching it with his finger.

It was a small piece of glass and it turned over when he pushed it with his fingernail. He saw other bits of glass and wondered what was going on.

Maybe Barbara had hurt herself and had gone into their neighbours for help.

He was now aware of the creepy stillness in the house. It touched him like a cold hand – he was scared.

'Barbara?' he called out again.

He could feel the blood pounding in his ears as his call was again answered with an eerie silence.

The door between the kitchen and the dining room was ajar, and beyond the door was the patio.

Then he saw her, and his heart froze in his chest.

Barbara was lying face down on the cream-coloured carpet. Her head was against a chair leg, her left arm outstretched with her fingers touching the patio door.

'Jesus, Barbara.'

She didn't move when he nervously reached down and touched her cheek. It was cold. Deathly cold.

'Oh fuck!' he cried, and staggered to the middle of the room, unable to look away from his wife's lifeless body. Moments later his legs went from beneath him, and he collapsed heavily onto the floor.

2

It was almost seven o'clock when Bob Nolan leaned forward in his chair and picked up the telephone. 'Yes?'

'Detective Nolan, I've got an emergency call,' said the receptionist. 'I'll put it through.'

A moment later Nolan was listening intently and making notes on his pad. The humming of the tall fan in the corner was the only sound in the room as he wrote and asked questions.

'Who found her?' he asked.

'Barry Hayes, a neighbour.'

'A neighbour. How?'

Holmes cleared his throat. 'Well, her husband came to the neighbour's door, and he was covered in sick. He was a mess, mumbling about his wife being dead. So the neighbour went to the house, found her, and called it in. He's scared shitless.'

Nolan closed his eyes and then shook his head in disbelief. 'Okay, cordon the place off and don't let anyone in. Nobody, absolutely nobody!'

'Will do, sir.'

'Good man, Holmes. I'll tell the boss and be back in touch in a few minutes.'

He ended the call and sat back in his chair. 'Christ, that's all we need. That's *all* we fucking need.' He shook his head again, got up and went to see the boss. He stretched his right leg, it was painful – too much sitting behind a desk was never good. He winced and let out a low whistle as the muscles relaxed.

Could have been worse, he thought, and slipped a pen into his shirt pocket.

The boss, Chief Inspector Eddie Doyle, was working his way through a tray of mail when Nolan broke the news.

Doyle was not one for overreacting, and he waited for Nolan to finish before standing up and walking to the window. Beyond the harbour, Dublin Bay shimmered in the evening sunshine, where numerous sailboats were riding the warm breeze. Above, a few puffy clouds eased their way across the clear sky.

'So what have we got, murder?'

Nolan coughed, a nervous habit. 'That's what the lads reckon, but we'll know better when someone takes a proper look at the scene, sir.'

Doyle nodded. 'Who's available?'

Nolan touched his thumb against his index finger, and began counting. First choice. 'Dave Conroy was called out about an hour ago. A robbery in Sandyford.'

'Robbery?'

'Somebody snatched a van stuffed with televisions and cameras, and hit the driver. He's been taken to hospital but he'll be okay.'

Doyle waited.

Second finger.

'Brendan Murray went on holiday yesterday, and Pat Brady is at a course in Athlone. He won't be back until tomorrow.'

'That just leaves Danny O'Neill.'

Nolan nodded.

Doyle turned and looked out at the pleasant scene beyond the window. No trouble out there, he thought, and took a deep breath. 'Okay, get O'Neill.'

'I'll call him right away, sir.'

'And Bob, tell him to contact me as soon as possible. I want to hear from him tonight, not tomorrow. Is that clear?'

'Loud and clear, sir.'

Nolan headed for the door. 'Bob, I see you're limping. Is there something I should know?'

'No, it's just the old hip injury, sir. It stiffens up if I sit down for too long.' He shrugged. 'I'll walk it off, it'll be fine in a few minutes.'

Doyle nodded his understanding.

Nolan left, and Doyle continued looking out to sea, beyond Dun Laoghaire harbour, and wondered what drove someone to kill. It was an impossible question. He went back to his desk and dealt with more mundane matters.

★

He could feel the sweat running down his back as he pushed hard along the beach. The sand was firm by the water's edge and he splashed noisily as he ran towards his target, the old baths. 'Faster, faster,' he urged himself, and dug his toes into the sand, sprinting for his personal finishing line. Moments later, he reached the baths and slowly came to a stop, hands on thighs and gulping in lungfuls of air. His fingers touched the scar on his lower stomach, an uneven ripple, and a reminder of his fight with a robber. He was eventually subdued with a head butt, but not before his knife had left its mark. It was an occupational hazard and could have been much worse. Shit happens.

Around him people walked easily on Sandymount Strand, while out to sea sail boats bobbed across Dublin Bay. The sun was a large orange ball descending slowly into the blue waters as overhead, gulls swooped and cawed in the summer breeze.

He was still breathing heavily, but easier, when he heard his phone ringing. 'Yes?' he panted, and wiped a hand across his face.

'Danny, it's Bob Nolan.'

He knew from his tone that it was going to be bad news. 'What's up?'

'It looks like we have a murder, and the boss wants you to handle it.'

Further along the strand, a young guy was flying a kite with real expertise. It moved up and down and then suddenly it twisted, headed for the sea, and twisted again into the sky. O'Neill was transfixed.

'Danny, can you hear me?' said Nolan.

'Yes, I've heard everything, Bob. I'll be there as soon as I can … and I will call Doyle afterwards. Don't get your knickers in a twist!'

'Fine. And best of luck.'

O'Neill nodded. 'Thanks, Bob, I'll be in touch.'

Forty minutes later he parked his car near the house and noted the small group of interested onlookers on the green, watching the proceedings. Members of the Forensics Unit, dressed in white boiler suits, ducked under the flapping yellow tape, going about their grim business. It was quiet, and in the near distance a dog barked, making heads turn.

'So you're the lucky boy, eh, Danny?' said Gary O'Connell, leaning against a Forensics Unit van.

'Yeah, the winner alright, Gary, that's me.' He had known O'Connell for almost ten, or maybe eleven years, and liked him. He was head of the Forensics Unit, the 'FU' as some referred to it, and a top investigator. O'Neill had thanked Gary on at least three occasions for producing information that was vital in securing convictions. He was definitely somebody you wanted on your side and it helped that they actually liked each other.

O'Connell handed O'Neill a pair of plastic booties and gloves. 'Can't have the detective in charge of the case contaminating the crime scene, eh? That would make *me* look bad, Danny, and I can't have that.'

O'Neill didn't respond and slipped on his booties. Across the road there was much incoherent mumbling and muttering as the onlookers watched him duck under the tape and follow O'Connell.

'In my steps, okay?'

O'Neill nodded. He'd done this many times before, and grinned when he looked down at the improbable footwear.

'Very fetching, but no good for dancing,' said O'Connell.

'Or so *you're* told.'

O'Connell made a face. 'Or so *I'm* told. Now, follow me.'

O'Neill saw a young policeman at the front door, a nervous look on his face. 'Where's Holmes?' he asked.

'Inside, sir. Back room.' He said it like he was happy to be where he was, firmly outside the crime scene.

O'Neill understood. It was probably the first murder scene he had attended and that was never easy. 'Good. Keep an eye out, and don't let any photographers or journalists near the place. We don't want any silly reporting, do we?'

The policeman grimaced. 'No, sir.'

O'Connell led the way into the hall. O'Neill noted an elegant table against a wall on which were a bunch of keys and some unopened post. Above, a mirror, at least five feet long, hung opposite the stairs, which were covered in a deep red carpet. A painting of a white house in a busy harbour beneath a blue sky, suggesting better times, was slightly off centre.

O'Connell pointed under the table. 'Look, Danny, the telephone cable has been cut.'

O'Neill saw the spliced cable. 'Recent?'

O'Connell nodded. 'Yeah, fresh as a daisy.' He looked at O'Neill. 'It wasn't an accident, Danny, it was deliberate.'

O'Neill hunkered down for a better look and got a bad feeling in his stomach. Two forensics officers came down the stairs, past the pretty scene, and headed for the door.

'Anything?' said O'Connell.

'Nothing so far, sir, but we've still two rooms and the attic to check.'

'Let me know if you find anything.'

They knew the routine, and they would.

A sudden flash caught O'Neill by surprise and he rubbed his eyes in response. 'What the fu ...'.

'Sorry 'bout that,' said the photographer as the camera's flash hummed, recharging.

'You okay?' asked O'Connell.

O'Neill rubbed his eyes, and scrunched them before opening. 'Jesus, I thought for a minute I was blinded.'

O'Connell turned and took a few long steps on the carpeted floor and stepped into the kitchen. He was well over six feet tall, maybe six-three, and all his men looked up to him. Very few didn't.

O'Neill looked around the room and spotted the black marks on the doors, bottles, glasses and cups left by O'Connell's men looking for fingerprints. One of them was dusting a door handle while another stood above him and took photographs. O'Neill closed his eyes again and turned his head away.

'Right lads, take a break – ten minutes,' said O'Connell. The two officers went outside.

'Any ideas, Gary?'

O'Connell stepped backwards, allowing O'Neill a view of the table, the adjoining door to the dining room, and the crime scene. 'So far my lads have no signs of breaking and entering.'

'What about the patio door?'

O'Connell nodded. 'It was the first one we checked. There's nothing. We've checked it for fingerprints and there's no sign of any broken glass or scratches on the lock. So?'

'She must have let the killer, *her* killer, in,' offered O'Neill.

O'Connell nodded.

'Why?'

O'Connell looked into the room where the body lay. 'Don't know, Danny, but you feel that she must have known him. There's no way, or reason, for that matter, to let someone you don't know into your house.'

'Unless they're expected.'

'Yeah, like the TV repairman or someone like that.'

'Exactly.'

O'Connell pointed to the corner. 'The the iron was still hot when we arrived…'.

'So she was interrupted,' added O'Neill, looking at the now unplugged iron.

'And … the shopping bags are still on the table. She never got a chance to put the stuff away.'

O'Neill looked into the bags and realised that a barbecue was probably in the offing. Jesus, he thought, and scrunched his lips.

The room was tidy except for the upturned vase and the small pieces of glass on the floor. Both men had been to many murder scenes, and although they were all different, they had a sameness they recognised. Some places had been completely trashed while others, like this one, were almost undisturbed.

O'Neill felt a sneer twisting his lip, but he couldn't stop it. It was a gut reaction to the thought that had drifted into his mind. The killer was methodical, no crazy person lashing out at the friendly woman who opened the door and invited him in. No, she must have known and trusted her killer – that was different.

'There are no marks, you know scuffle marks, in the hall,' added O'Connell. 'So whatever happened kicked off here.'

'So she opens the door, recognises him and invites him in. She, or he, closes the front door, and seconds later he attacks her in the kitchen. It was almost immediate.'

'So it was planned.'

'I think so,' O'Neill said, looking into the garden.

O'Connell's eyes followed his gaze.

O'Neill rubbed his chin in his hand, the stubble rough in his fingers. He shrugged his shoulders and looked at O'Connell.

'What time is it?'

O'Connell checked his watch. 'It's almost nine – eighteen minutes to.'

'It's still bright outside. When the killer came here he did so in broad daylight, right?'

'Right.'

O'Neill was doing his best to hold onto the idea and closed his eyes. 'Our man didn't mind, didn't care, that it was broad daylight.'

'You think he knew something?'

O'Neill tapped his knuckles against his chin, thinking. 'He must have known that she was on her own; otherwise he would never knock on the door. And that's why he's a dangerous man. No crazy here. This guy's a planner.'

O'Connell made a face. 'Jesus, Danny, I don't like where you're going.'

'Nor do I, Gary. Now let's see the victim.'

A dark halo of blood surrounded Barbara Ryan's head and there were scratch marks on the back of her hands. She must have struggled, thought O'Neill, leaning down to get a closer look, and a cold dead eye stared though him. 'What's all the glass about?'

'From a fruit bowl, sir,' said a voice behind O'Neill.

Holmes stepped forward. 'There were three big pieces of glass on the floor when I arrived. The forensics lads have taken them away.'

'They need to give it a close look back in the lab,' said O'Connell.

O'Neill stood up and turned to Holmes. 'Tell me what happened, will you? And don't leave anything out.'

O'Connell went outside as O'Neill looked around the smartly appointed room. A large flat-screen television sat in a corner opposite a leather sofa and matching armchair. A glass-fronted bookcase took up most of a wall and a painting of ballet dancers hung in the alcove by the fireplace.

'The neighbour called it in after he found the body. He said Ryan knocked on his door and seemed to have lost his mind. He told him to wait there while he came over and checked the house.'

'And this is what he saw?'

'Yes, sir, a right mess.' Holmes took a deep breath, settled himself, and continued. 'The neighbour, Barry Hayes, then phoned 999, and that's when I got the call.'

'Thank God for good neighbours.' In this age, when most people kept their distance, it was good to know that there were still some good guys out there.

O'Neill got down onto his hunkers for another close look at Barbara Ryan. Judging from her photograph on the mantelpiece, she was an attractive woman. Had been. What a waste. 'Carry on, Holmes.'

'He went back to his house and tried to comfort David Ryan who was still dumbstruck. They sat on the bonnet of his car and that's where I met them. After me and Carter found the victim I phoned the station and the sergeant told me to tape the place off and wait for his call. I thought I should wait in here, especially as Carter wasn't very keen.'

'Fine, well done. And tell me about the broken glass – the bowl.'

Holmes swallowed before continuing. 'I almost stepped on the biggest piece but Carter stopped me in the nick of time. It was lying about a foot away from her right shoulder. The other pieces were lying further away – one was between her knees and the other near her left ankle. I took photos of their position on my mobile phone. Do you want to see them?'

'No, not now, but download them and send them to Paul Grant, our technical guy. That was good thinking to do that.'

'Thank you, sir, I'll transfer them as soon as I get back to the station.'

Gary O'Connell came back into the room. 'Danny, I've someone here to see you.'

O'Neill stood up and felt both surprised and uncomfortable to see Shelly Tobin. He knew someone from the Coroner's Office would show up, but he had hoped that it was not going to be her.

'Hello, Danny, thought I'd see you here!' she said, and set her metal case on the floor. 'You get all the good ones!'

Holmes blushed and tried to hide his face in his hand.

Shelly Tobin knelt down, opened the steel case and took out a pair of rubber gloves that she expertly rolled on. She looked up at the three men. 'Well, is one of you gentlemen going to tell me what happened? Or at least what you think happened? It might be helpful.'

O'Connell told her about his team's findings and O'Neill told Holmes to tell his story. She listened intently and nodded here and there confirming what was an important point. 'Okay, so you think that there was a scuffle of some sort, which started in the kitchen, continued through the adjoining door into this room where she was killed by a blow to the head. Most likely with the vase. Seems reasonable,' she said, kneeling down closer to the victim.

She slipped her fingers under the blonde hair and felt for a pulse. There was none, and the body was stiff to the touch. Rigor mortis had set in – that would help in establishing a time for the murder. She'd know more when she got the body back to the lab, but that would have to wait.

As she moved her fingers along the victim's shoulders, the blonde hair rippled in a macabre, bloodied response. The men were all straining to get a better look when her fingers stopped moving. 'What have we here?' she said, a trace of excitement clear in her voice.

She turned and looked at Holmes. 'Nobody has touched the body since you found it, is that correct?'

'No, ma'am, nobody. I've stood in here since I arrived.'

'Good, I just wanted to be clear, absolutely clear on that.' She slipped her fingers under the blonde hair again and pushed the hair back with her other hand.

The men were on their toes, but said nothing.

'There's your murder weapon,' she said, fingers resting against a pencil. A yellow pencil.

'A pencil,' said O'Neill. 'Are you serious?'

She gently pressed her fingers against the pencil, and pushed back hair so they could get a better look. It stuck out about three inches, so it was possible that the rest of its length, possibly another three to four inches, was buried in Barbara Ryan's neck. Jesus, thought O'Neill, catching O'Connell's eye.

'I've never seen that before,' said the head of the Forensics Unit, 'a pencil in the neck!'

O'Neill winced when he realised the killer's closeness to the victim. This was as intimate as a killing got, and he again thought about its planning and execution. Apart from the upturned vase in the kitchen there was nothing damaged or thrown about the house. It looked very controlled.

Shelly Tobin closed her case and stood up. 'With all the blood around the head, I reckon that her carotid artery was severed. That means that if she wasn't already dead, she would have bled out in less than two minutes. She was a goner as soon as that pencil was stuck into her neck. Very nasty.'

'Time of death?' asked O'Neill.

'Too soon to tell, but certainly six to eight hours ago. I can't be completely accurate until I do a post mortem.'

'And when will that be?' asked O'Neill, itching for her to leave.

'The ambulance boys can bring her directly to Store Street and I'll try and have it done tonight. I'll ring ahead to make sure that there will be someone to assist me. Okay?'

'Thank you,' offered O'Neill, 'that'll be a great help.'

She picked up her case and headed for the door. The two men were looking at the yellow pencil as O'Neill followed her outside.

Shelly put her case into the car boot, opened the front door, got in, and started the engine. She rolled down her driver's window when she heard O'Neill shouting to wait.

'I'm sorry that I haven't called, I really am,' he said, the words thick and difficult to get out. He had been thinking about this moment for almost two months, about what to say, but now that she was here it didn't make it any easier.

Shelly Tobin raised an eyebrow. 'Is that the best you can do, Inspector?' she said loudly as the onlookers giggled. A public, lover's tiff between police officers, and a brutal murder – you couldn't write that.

'Shelly …' he said, looking for some useful words but finding none.

She inched the car forward. 'Call me when you're ready, Danny, and not before. It's been almost three months since we spoke and I don't have that sort of time to wait around – for anyone.' She pressed the accelerator and swept down the road, leaving Inspector Danny O'Neill stranded and embarrassed.

The onlookers looked away, doing their best to keep quiet. They were so caught up with the unfolding drama in front of them that nobody noticed a man on a motorbike, on the far side of the green, slip a small camera into his leather jacket, and head off down the road.

O'Neill went back to speak with Holmes. 'Where's the husband now?' he asked.

'He went to the hospital in our other car. Officers Dooley and O'Hara took him and the neighbour. It wasn't pretty.'

'Fine. Call them and find out how he is, will you? I'd like to have a word with him.'

Holmes took out his mobile and dialled.

While he waited, O'Neill took out a small notebook and made a few notes. First impressions were vital, something that his mentor Joe Dixon had always pointed out. He had solved cases that others couldn't and O'Neill had learned much from him. They had developed a sort of big brother-little brother relationship and since then, O'Neill always felt that Dixon was looking over his shoulder. It was a reminder to do his best, a weight that sat easily.

'Sir, they're keeping him overnight, seems that he banged his head when he fell,' said Holmes.

'Okay, I'll speak to him tomorrow,' O'Neill said, looking around the quiet street and the green where the onlookers were leaving. 'Call the station and arrange for the place to be secured with a guard overnight. The Forensics Unit will be here for some time yet and O'Connell will let you know when they're finished.'

Holmes nodded, paying attention.

'Okay, you know what to do, Holmes, and I'll call the boss.'

O'Neill walked over to his car, leaned on the roof, and made the call. The killing had been so well carried out, in broad daylight, with such precision, that he felt there was more to come. The killer had walked away scot-free and O'Neill suspected that he would want to do it again, need to do it again, to get the rush. It was what drove them and O'Neill cursed his luck. He took off the plastic booties and gloves and tossed into the back seat.

A rumble of thunder made him look at the sky. Dark clouds rolled and tumbled, adding to his growing unease. A flash of lightning, almost overhead, lit the street and he grinned at the drama of it all. Shakespeare could not have written it any better, he thought, and eased his car away from the kerb into the gathering storm.

3

Doyle was reading *The Irish Times* when O'Neill knocked on the open door and entered.

'Morning, Danny. Still running on the strand?'

'Yes, sir, and on a day like today, it was a treat. It would be a sin not to be out there.'

Doyle grinned and looked closely at his detective. 'Well, I must say that you are looking good. The clean living seems to be agreeing with you. Keep it up.'

O'Neill enjoyed the tang of the salty breeze as it drifted in through the open window that had a wonderful uninterrupted view of Dublin Bay. And that really was something. If Doyle could sell the view he would be a very rich man indeed. After all, location was everything.

Doyle folded the newspaper and dropped it on his desk. 'I heard it on the radio on the way in. It was the third item on the news – the *third* item – what's this city coming to?' he shook his head. 'Okay, tell me what we have.'

They discussed the initial findings and who was available to work on the case. 'I'll arrange a meeting for ten o'clock and allocate tasks. Must make a start,' said O'Neill, closing his notebook. 'Can you get some uniforms to carry out house-to-house interviews? We might get lucky,' he added, but his voice lacked any real conviction.

Doyle listened carefully and leaned back in his chair. 'I'll talk with the duty sergeant and arrange for the uniforms to attend the meeting. Anything else?'

'No, nothing, but I'll wait to see what the Forensics Unit and Coroner's report have to say.'

'Good … and how is Shelly?' asked Doyle. He didn't miss a trick. He made it his duty to know his detectives and what made them tick. They were *his* frontline troops, he needed them performing at their best. If they were not up to the job, he wanted to know why.

'She's good … I think.'

Doyle raised an eyebrow. 'You think?'

O'Neill was uncomfortable. 'We had a couple of dates, but I haven't see her for a few months, and that's about it really.'

Doyle took his time before replying. 'It's your business who you see, Danny, but I need you at your best. And with this case, from what you've told me, that's exactly what's needed. So, mind what you're doing, that's all.'

'Will do, sir.'

Back at his desk O'Neill slipped off his Harris Tweed jacket and put it over his chair. He wasn't a 'suit-guy' and preferred a good jacket. Wearing jackets meant that he was able to mix-and-match his shirts and ties, something that his wife Liz had liked him to do. 'You've got more options,' she used to say, straightening a silk tie, and he knew she was right. She was always right.

He checked his emails but there was nothing from Gary O'Connell or Shelly Tobin, so he phoned the Forensics Unit. 'Hi, Gary, any news for me?'

'You must be a mind reader, I was about to call you,' said O'Connell. 'Just a sec.' He put the phone down and O'Neill heard the shuffle of papers.

'Right, first things first. There was no sign of a break-in. We checked all the doors, locks and windows and there's nothing. Nada.'

'So she let the killer in,' said O'Neill. 'No doubt?'

'No doubt, whatsoever. And … there's no sign of any sort of robbery. We don't think the killer went anywhere other than the crime scene. We found plenty of jewellery and almost two grand in cash upstairs in the main bedroom. Nothing was ransacked, the place was untouched. Very surprising, eh?'

O'Neill made notes. 'So we can rule out robbery?'

'Definitely, but we did find a few drops of blood in the hall.'

'In the hall, where?'

'Beside the front door. They might have dropped from the killer when he left the house. We won't be sure until we get a match, but I'll send on the report later.'

'Good, Gary, thanks.'

He looked at his notes, wondering why Barbara Ryan had let her killer in. She must have known him, otherwise why did she do it? And she must have trusted him enough to ask him inside – there was a lot a familiarity there, which cut down the field of suspects. He tried to recreate the scenario, wondering who was so unthreatening to Barbara Ryan that she would invite them inside. A neighbour? A friend? Maybe a work colleague? Who?

An idea came.

The killer must have known that she was alone in the house otherwise it would have been an awful risk. If that was the case, he must have been stalking her. He wrote this down and tapped his pen against his teeth, thinking.

The fan in the corner rotated and tickled the papers on his desk. A large staff roster dominated the wall to his right, opposite the high windows that looked down on the street. He spotted a red dot against his name.

'I'm going for a coffee,' he said to Paul Grant. 'Holmes has pictures of the crime scene on his phone. Make sure to get them from him.'

'Okay,' Grant replied, not taking his eyes off the computer screen.

O'Neill left the room, carefully passed the painter who was decorating the corridor, and went into the toilet. He stopped in front of the mirror, and leaned in close.

'Not pretty,' he said quietly, 'definitely not pretty.' He looked around to make sure he was alone, and looked again in the mirror. He was thirty-seven, but he felt older. How much older? He didn't know, and he realised what a silly idea it was to 'feel older'. You are what you are and that's it. But murder cases had a way of dragging you down and he had seen other men age before his eyes.

The head of fair hair was flatter now, there was less of it, and his eyes looked deeper and more cynical than he liked to admit. Since losing Liz three years ago, he had drunk too much. Anything to ease the pain, but he knew it was only a temporary respite. She was the love of his life, his 'Beautiful Brunette' – something that always made her smile. Life was wonderful with her, as she made him feel like a better person. He laughed more, and before he realised it he had surrendered to her. He didn't mind, he had been a very happy man.

He remembered that night.

He had phoned Liz and asked if she would collect his suit from the cleaners. She, as always, had agreed. He was having a great time at a colleague's leaving bash and didn't want to leave – too much fun. However, Liz was knocked down and killed by a drunk driver, and O'Neill's guilt was overpowering. Standing beside her naked body as it lay on the coroner's metal table was an image that was burnt into his brain. He would never forget it. After nearly three months of 'living in the bottle', Doyle intervened. He was too good an officer to lose, and the confidence the boss showed in him helped O'Neill get back on track. It wasn't always easy; he had fallen off the wagon a few times, but the last eight or nine months had been the best for some time. He was back running regularly on Sandymount Strand and actually looked forward to it. It was a change for the better.

He ran his fingers through his hair and thought about Barbara Ryan lying on the floor of her dining room. She wouldn't be running her fingers through her lovely blonde hair any more, but who was the last person to touch it? Without realising it, he was back into detective mode. He looked at the man in the mirror, his eyes squinting to get the clearest image. The guy seemed to say that he was not alone, understood where he was coming from, and that he should just try to do his best. He could hear Liz's calm voice in his head: 'Do yourself a favour, and start looking outwards again.' She had loved life so much, sitting around feeling sorry for herself was not for her.

The door suddenly swished open as an officer came in and O'Neill stepped out into the freshly painted corridor.

Picking up a coffee and a Danish pastry, he headed back to his desk. He read Gary O'Connell's report. It was exactly as he had expected and he made a few more notes.

The door opened and Pat Brady came in, newspaper folded under his arm. He was the eldest of all the detectives in the station, mid-forties, and dressed conservatively – as always. He liked to wear dark suits, plain shirts, sober ties and was world-wise, if a bit narrow-minded for O'Neill's liking. He often used gel in his thick head of hair – now that was brave. If Pat was anything, he was old school. There was nothing flash about him, but he got the job done. 'Morning, Danny,' he said. 'I see you're the lucky boy again. Anything?'

O'Neill finished his coffee and dropped the paper cup in the trash bin. 'No, nothing yet, but it's early days.'

Brady sat at his desk and swivelled his chair to face O'Neill. 'And the husband?'

'He was kept in hospital overnight. Apparently he banged his head when he fainted. He found her when he came home.'

Brady twisted slowly back and forth in his chair. 'Have you spoken with him yet? Family members are always the first port of call, especially the husband.'

'Not yet, but maybe you'd like to tag along with me when I do.'

Brady sniffed. 'Yeah, and I can use what I learnt on that course I was on yesterday. Strike while the iron is hot.'

'Good. What was it about?'

'It was about Behavioural Science – so I'm the perfect man for the job.'

'And I thought you knew it all.'

Brady waved a finger. 'Now, now, don't be like that. It's beneath you, Danny. We never stop learning, you know that, and when you think you know it all, something jumps up and bites you in the ass.'

O'Neill raised his hands. 'Yep, got it in one. The voice of experience?'

Brady got up. 'Have you set up a murder board yet?'

'No, but feel free to do so.' He slid the file across the desk. 'There's nothing much in it. And I'll print out Gary O'Connell's report for you.'

'Anything from the Coroner?'

'Should be here this morning,' O'Neill replied. 'And I want you,' he said, looking at Grant, 'in on the meeting at ten o'clock. Doyle will arrange for some uniforms, need them for house-to-house work, and we'll see what else needs to be done.'

Brady opened the file. 'I see what you mean about "nothing much," but we must start somewhere.'

A few minutes later he had wiped clean the whiteboard on the back wall and wrote in the few details he had. Where will it end? he thought, and began writing.

Shortly after ten o'clock the meeting began.

O'Neill stood in front of the board and let the officers know the scant details of the crime. Four uniformed officers stood side-by-side, looking a little out of their depth. Doyle sat on the edge of a desk, his arms folded. Paul Grant had turned his chair around and was looking directly at O'Neill, his legs stretched out in front of him.

O'Neill began: 'What I don't get is the killer knocking on the door and being invited in. Firstly, he must have sounded credible for Barbara Ryan to let him in. And,' he paused, 'he must have known that she was alone in the house.'

This was the question he had thought of earlier and he wanted to see if anyone had something to offer.

'Maybe he had been stalking her,' Brady said.

O'Neill nodded. 'I agree, but there's a problem. If she was killed about two o'clock, or thereabouts, then the killer must have been watching the house until the attack. That seems unlikely, as somebody would, more than likely, have seen him hanging around. Bear this point in mind,' he said to the four uniforms, 'when asking questions. Okay?'

They nodded as one.

'So what are you thinking?' Doyle asked, as all the heads turned to look at the boss.

O'Neill shrugged, looked at Barbara Ryan's photo and tapped the marker on his knuckles. 'I think he knew she was alone; so yes, he must have stalked her. And – this is the important point – he must have known that David was not there when he saw his car was gone.'

Brady held up a finger. 'I see where you're going, but he could not be certain that the husband was not in the house just because his car was gone. I mean, Barbara could have taken it. It's possible.'

'Very possible. And here's the rub. He still went ahead and knocked on the door.'

There was quiet in the room with only the sound of car horns intruding.

O'Neill continued. 'I think he must have phoned the house, and when Barbara answered he knew she *had* to be alone. There was one car in the driveway, and whether it was hers or David's it didn't matter, as she was the *only one* in the house. He could have been watching the house from early on and seen David leave. It's possible, especially if this guy is such a planner.'

Doyle liked what he heard. 'So …'.

O'Neill turned to Paul Grant. 'What I want to know is, can we find out if she received a phone call shortly before the attack? More likely to be from a mobile than a landline.'

Everyone knew what he was thinking, and it made perfect sense. The killer phones to make sure that the coast is clear, because he has seen David leave earlier, and as soon as she answers, his plan starts. Brilliant.

Grant sat up in his chair. 'I can do that, but I may need to get permission from the telephone company with something as sensitive as this.'

'Let me know if you need help,' said Doyle. 'I'll make a call to the company or a certain person in The Park.' Doyle was referring to police headquarters in the Phoenix Park, where someone would make sure they had access to whatever was needed for the investigation.

'And don't forget that the telephone cable was cut, probably by the killer.' He stopped, lost in thought. 'And that maybe gives us a better time frame. Because then the telephone company can tell us when it happened, and it was probably cut when the killer was leaving the house.'

Brady was looking at the board. 'That's very good what you just said. And if you're correct, then we are dealing with a very calculating bastard. This could be *very* tricky.'

'Still given to understatement, Pat, and I hope that I'm wrong. I really do. But in the meantime we need to get going.'

Thirty minutes later, after tasks had been assigned, O'Neill and Brady headed off to meet David Ryan at his brother's house. He had been released earlier, as doctors decided there was no reason to keep him in.

'The husband's usually good for it, you know,' Brady offered again, as they got into O'Neill's car.

'Yeah, that would be nice, case closed in no time.' He started the engine. 'But I don't think so, Pat, not with this one. What you get in crimes of passion is overkill, frenzy. They are lacking here. A smack on the head to disable her and one stab wound to the neck. Very efficient, very cold.'

Brady made a face, and nodded. 'I see what you mean, Danny.' He sounded unconvinced. He knew better than to say any more right now, and clunk-clicked his safety belt.

They slipped into traffic and headed for Ballsbridge in silence, the two officers considering the dark implications of O'Neill's words.

★

Shelly Tobin put on her green overalls and headed for the autopsy room. It was a little after ten o'clock and the day outside was warming up nicely. The weatherman on the radio had said that it would be like this for another four or five days. About time, she thought, as did the rest of the country. People did crazy things when the weather was hot, she'd seen the results, but the warm air was something to be embraced.

She pushed through the swing doors and walked along the tiled corridor where the whiff of disinfectant caught her nose.

She fixed her cap, and with a few more steps in the dull artificial light, entered the Body Shop.

'Are we ready, Trevor?' she asked, taking a mask from her pocket and tying it in place. She saw that her assistant had taken the corpse from one of the cold-storage units and wheeled it on a gurney over to the steel examination table where it now waited for her.

'Good to go,' he replied, pulling the sheet from Barbara Ryan's body and taking a step back.

No matter how often she did this it was never easy. She couldn't help but think of what this woman might have planned for the coming weekend: friends around for dinner maybe, a game of golf, shopping, or just sitting at home with her husband sharing a glass of wine. But that was not to be – how sad. How very, very sad indeed. It was a waste, a bloody tragedy.

'Is the microphone on?'

Trevor tapped it lightly and heard the live buzz. 'Yes.'

Shelly examined the body for marks, scratches, and other signs from the attack, and called them out clearly as she proceeded. She saw the bruising around the neck and pointed to where she wanted Trevor to wash with the jet spray. The water hissed and blood flowed along tiny grooves into the drain below. The puncture mark in the neck was black and blue, and gaping.

She continued and felt a large indentation at the back of the head. That must have been where she was hit with the vase, she thought, and called it out. There were other bumps on the top left side of the head and she knew that the killer had bashed it repeatedly against the floor. 'Help me turn her over, please,' she said, and the two of them flipped the body with practiced ease. More observations were noted before she decided to start cutting.

Although this appeared the most difficult part to the uninitiated, she thought otherwise. Going inside had a real purpose, and that made it easy. On the outside there was the person, the individual that people knew and cared for, the recognisable face that had lived and loved and been someone. It was who they were. Inside, they were all the same. Well, almost.

A heart is a heart, and once you've seen and handled one, they're all pretty much the same.

She flipped the switch on the small electric saw and steadied herself. The blade whizzed, its high-pitched screech bouncing off the walls, making Trevor suck in his breath.

'Right,' she said, and carefully brought the blade down. A fine mist of blood covered her rubber gloves as she expertly made the first incision. Trevor watched, his eyes focused in deep concentration on the blade as it cut with such ease, and went deeper. Minutes later, she put the saw down and slowly, expertly peeled the skin back. It was gruesome, bloody work, but she never blinked. Not once.

4

The room was warm and dank, the windows closed and curtains pulled. A layer of stale cigarette smoke hung in the fetid air, a dirty-blue presence barely disturbed by his breathing. Every time he blew a stream of smoke, he watched as it climbed, then crashed, into the silent unmoving barrier. The rushing smoke mingled with the hanging cloud, before it weakened and was slowly subsumed into a greater swirling mass. It was a lesson in cosmic physics, he thought, his very own universe that he could observe and control.

He had learned from life thus far the absolute importance of control. That's what it was all about.

He leaned back on the sofa, his head on a soft cushion and tilted at a slight angle. An ashtray rested on his chest and moved with the easy rhythm coming from below. He was relaxed in his nakedness and ran his fingers through his greasy hair. He stretched his toes and took a long drag before blowing another plume of smoke into the universe above his head.

'There's been a murder in Booterstown,' said the presenter on the news, grabbing his attention. He reached to the floor, picked up the remote and increased the volume. He listened intently as the scene changed to the one outside the victim's home and continued for another forty or fifty seconds. 'And now for the sports news,' said the voice. He hit the mute button.

He sat up a little and put the ashtray on the table, which was covered with newspapers, unopened envelopes, and a selection of empty beer bottles. A camera with a zoom lens, its straps hanging over the edge, was fully charged and ready for action.

Directly across from him the fireplace stood empty, the old wire guard dusty and unused. There were various small statues of elephants and frogs on the mantle piece, none of which he'd bought. Granny, God bless her, collected them, and there they would stay. A wind-up clock, silent, was in the centre with a candlestick on either side. Above all the clutter was a small collection of photographs of girls and women, all blonde and all taken from a distance.

A black X was drawn across the image of Barbara Ryan. He picked up a knife and stuck it into it – the final act. The blade shook for a few seconds and he was excited. He still hadn't washed and he could almost smell her on him – her fear, her struggle, and finally her submission. He closed his eyes at the memory and felt his chest rise and fall. He exhaled loudly.

It had been good, really good. After all the planning and anticipation, the moment had been everything he wanted it to be. It had been so easy. What had he been worrying about? He grinned and wiped his lips with the back of his hand. He had smiled, disarming her, controlling his urge to look around when a neighbour passing them said hello. Yeah, that was impressive. He liked that – he was in control.

He was surprised when she put up such a struggle; she was stronger that he had anticipated. Must remember that next time, he thought, nodding his head. She had nearly slipped from his grasp and they had crashed through the kitchen doors before he tripped her up and she fell onto the cream-coloured carpet. He remembered the bright carpet and the first specks of blood that flew and splashed across the patio window. He knelt on her back, and with her long blonde hair wrapped around his fingers, he slammed her face into the carpet as she screamed. 'No, please, no … for God's sake, stop,' she pleaded as he leaned down and spat into her ear. 'You're all the same, all the fucking same.' He smashed her head again and again into the carpet until he felt the fight slip from her. He reached into his pocket, took out a pencil and rammed it viciously into her neck. The blood exploded like a geyser and he was both stunned and excited at the same time,. 'Fuck me!' he shouted, and stood up, looking at the body lying at his feet. He was buzzing, his mind and body alive like never before. Yeah, it had been really good, better than anything. Better than any fucking thing. The best.

5

They drove along the Rock Road and O'Neill looked out at Dublin Bay and the tall towers of the Poolbeg Power Station in Irishtown. Smoke leaked from the stacks and drifted high as the on shore breeze carried them along. The DART raced towards the city, its sleek carriages a moving emerald streak against the blue waters of the bay.

'What's on the radio?' O'Neill said, and pushed a button. Some economist was talking about 'things getting worse', so he pressed another button and heard classical music. 'That's better; had enough bad news,' he said, and leaned back.

They passed Booterstown Station, and the Punch Bowl pub on the left, when something hit the car.

'Jesus!' screamed O'Neill, standing on the brakes and sliding to a halt in the bicycle lane.

'What the fuck!' shouted Brady, opening the door and looking at the smiling face of a local councillor. His campaign poster had fallen from a nearby lamp post and now lay across the car's windscreen.

O'Neill was out of the car at once, and extremely agitated. He reached over and pulled the election poster from beneath one of the windscreen wipers where it was snagged, and threw it on the ground. 'And who the fuck are you anyway?' he shouted, kicking it away.

'Ray Lowry, he was in the recent local election,' said Brady, picking the poster up. 'We should report this. These posters are meant to have been taken down within a week of the election, and that's nearly three weeks ago.'

'Okay … put it in the boot and you can give them a bollicking later. And I mean a real bollicking. They fucking deserve it. *That* could have killed somebody!'

'Death by poster,' Brady quipped.

O'Neill grinned, finally. 'That's enough weirdness for one day, Pat.' He opened the boot and the smiling politician found a dark, uninviting home.

'That's the right place for you, mate,' said Brady as he closed the boot and got back into the car.

The Merrion Gates were closed at the level crossing as a train passed and cars backed up, waiting. On the left, St.Vincent's Hospital was bright and busy, the new extensions sitting comfortably with the older structure; they were easy on the eye. They got caught at the traffic lights at the bottom of Ailesbury Road or Embassy Road as the locals often called it, due to the number of countries that had their embassy there. It was one of the most expensive roads on the Monopoly Board and the fabulous red-bricked houses were testament to that. Through Ballsbridge they turned left and drove along Pembroke Road, slowing down before turning into Wellington Road.

Christopher Ryan had done well, very well indeed, by the look of things. His house, set well back from the road, had a Mercedes and a Porsche parked in the pebbled drive. It was like an image from some flash advertisement in a glossy car magazine. The three-storey house, where a steep granite staircase led to a yellow door, was pretty, and the red-leafed creeper around the sash-windows completed the look. Yes, there was money in boy bands, mused O'Neill, as he pushed the old gate open.

It didn't creak.

Christopher Ryan opened the door almost immediately. His eyes were red, from crying, no doubt, and his face couldn't hide the tiredness. His dark hair, with traces of grey above his ears, was uncombed, adding to his sad demeanour. Murder had reached out and touched him. It was as if a big stone had been thrown into a pool of water and the ripples kept on going. Nobody ever knew where it ended. That was the real tragedy.

'I'm Inspector O'Neill and this is my colleague Detective Pat Brady.' They shook hands and Ryan took a deep breath, letting out a low whistle.

'My brother,' he said, 'is in a bad way, Inspector. A really bad way. Never seen anything like it.' He shook his head at the thought of what the last twenty-four hours had brought, his eyes showing his disbelief. 'I don't think he slept, comfortably I mean, so please be easy on him. He's my younger brother and I know him inside out.' He paused. 'He's not hard, never has been. He's an accountant for Christ's sake. Nothing nasty going on there, or maybe you know something?'

O'Neill shook his head.

'In here, if you don't mind,' he instructed, bringing them into the front room. 'David's in the kitchen. I'm trying to get him to drink a cup of coffee but … I'll go get him.' He took a few steps, stopped and turned. 'I collected him earlier. The doctor said he would better be off with family, you see. I wasn't trying to hide him away.'

O'Neill shrugged. 'These are strange times, Mr Ryan, and nobody knows for certain what to do. Don't worry about it.'

'Thanks.'

O'Neill walked over to the marble fireplace, above which hung a gold-framed mirror. He ran his fingers through his hair and adjusted his tie as Brady took in the paintings and beautiful furniture. A long glass table displayed magazines on cars, photography and classical music. The high sash-windows were pristine, but he noted a slight flaw in the glass that made the cars outside look fatter. It was not unusual, especially with such old glass – it added to its quaintness. A deep red rug lay in front of the fireplace that was protected by a brass fire surround. Above, a chandelier sparkled, casting small prisms of light onto the cream walls.

'You'll be alright, come on,' said Christopher, bringing his brother into the room, an arm around his shoulder, protecting him. Like he'd done since they were kids, O'Neill imagined. Big brothers protecting little brothers – it was the way of the world.

David Ryan looked very much like his brother; the same shaped mouth and nose and a full head of hair. He was thinner than Christopher, but not skinny. He didn't carry much weight, and O'Neill reckoned that he must work out or do some sort of sport.

But it was the face that got him. He'd seen many people whose lives had been knocked sideways by murder, and they were never the same after it. Something snapped, and the past, that place where things were familiar, was gone forever. It was now poisoned, a place to be avoided. It was soul destroying, and many people never resurfaced after they fell into the pool of despair that sudden, violent death brought about.

Yeah, he knew all about that.

'David, this is Inspector O'Neill and his colleague. They have to ask you some questions. You understand?' Christopher Ryan said, holding his brother's shoulder.

David, head on his chest, nodded and raised a hankie to his nose.

Christopher sat down and took his hand away.

O'Neill cleared his throat. 'David, I'm very sorry for what happened. Really I am, but I have to ask you some questions. Alright?'

David's head shook and his shoulders sagged.

Brady took out his notebook and stood near the window, out of the way.

David Ryan lifted his face and his eyes were raw from crying. They seemed to have fallen into his skull, just stopping before they completely disappeared. His skin was pale, and the spiky stubble on his cheeks and upper lip added an unhealthy greyness. He was lost in his own world, a world turned upside down and damaged beyond repair. He was a sad sight.

'David, can you please tell me what happened? Please take your time, there's no rush,' O'Neill said, his voice even and clear. He had read the notes in the file but he wanted to hear it from David himself, and he knew that it was not going to be easy.

It wasn't.

'Have you any ideas why it happened, David? Is there anybody who wanted to hurt Barbara, or you?' he asked, his tone quiet and friendly. Over the next thirty minutes, David relived, painfully and without tears, the previous afternoon.

O'Neill ran his tongue across his lips, moistening them, but he didn't take his eyes off David Ryan. First impressions were important and he watched the broken man closely, his senses tuned in, and waited.

Christopher patted David on the knee. 'You're fine, you're doing fine.' He glanced at O'Neill who smiled a 'Thanks'.

Then the words came, with no rhythm or stress – just words. 'I've no idea, none whatsoever. I'm lost, absolutely lost.' He waved his hands. 'Why me, I've done nothing? Harmed nobody. And then this … Jesus.' He started crying, and Christopher put his arm around his brother's shoulder.

O'Neill decided that the man had been through enough. 'We'll leave it at that for the moment,' he said, 'but I'll be back tomorrow.'

'Thank you, Inspector,' said Christopher Ryan.

O'Neill raised his hand. 'It's okay; we'll let ourselves out. Stay where you are.'

In the car, Brady read through his notes. 'What do you think?'

O'Neill tapped the steering wheel as a bumblebee buzzed against the windscreen.

'Do you mean is he guilty?' he said.

Brady nodded. 'Yeah.'

O'Neill thought about David Ryan's face, his eyes with the thousand yard stare and his body as limp as a broken doll. His voice, low and unsteady, was fearful and barely under control. He was a mess.

'Don't think so, Pat, unless he's one helluva actor. An Oscar winner.'

Brady sniffed doubtfully, a sneer creeping from the edge of his mouth.

The reply was too quick, thought O'Neill, as he tapped the steering wheel again.

'No, he was too distressed, Pat. Really broken up.' O'Neill loosened his tie. 'I don't think he did it, and neither does his big brother. He would have to go to some effort to fool him first, you know. He's known him all his life, looked after him, protected him, and I've no doubt that he could spot if David was lying.'

'But I'd like to know a bit more. I mean, if he is covering for David, then big brother is not going to say anything.'

O'Neill listened, his eyes closed. 'Hey, anything is possible; you know that. But here's the thing.' He turned to Brady. 'Do you really think that David Ryan, a man I think never said boo to a goose, killed his wife? And … and got his big brother to cover for him?'

Silence.

O'Neill shook his head. 'Sorry, Pat, I don't see it. David Ryan is weak and we would break his story in no time, and what would that do for big brother?' He closed his eyes again. 'No, there is absolutely nothing in this for Christopher, but feel free to check him out.'

Brady nodded. 'Fair enough, but I'll do some digging.' He looked at O'Neill. 'I've worked plenty of cases like this; the husband is never far from the action. Know what I mean?'

O'Neill nodded. 'Yeah, I know what you mean, Pat, but …'.

Brady closed his notebook. 'But it's always better to eliminate him *properly* …'.

'Exactly, and dig as deep as you have to.' O'Neill turned to Brady. 'I may not be as cynical as you, Pat, but check his story, inside *and* out.'

Brady slipped the notebook into his pocket, feeling better now that he had won a little battle. O'Neill was a good cop, but sometimes he could be a bit airy-fairy and could not see the obvious. He had noticed indecision creeping into O'Neill's work since he failed to catch the killer of that young girl in Killiney. Everyone felt bad about that one, but O'Neill took it personally. And now he was a little too loose in his approach for Brady's liking, but he kept that thought to himself.

O'Neill started the engine and checked that there were no more posters about to drop from the sky.

It was safe.

He swung the car out onto the road and took a final look across to the house where two brothers, grown men, were crying like babies. It was not good.

6

After Sergeant O'Connor had put an officer on guard in front of the house, he arranged for the other three officers to conduct house-to-house interviews, and then headed back to the station. He would have to check and re-jig the work schedule and he needed authority from Doyle for that. And, of course, the inevitable overtime. Murder cost money – always.

McEvoy would go to the left, O'Brien to the right and Keaveney would take the houses behind. 'And don't leave anybody out,' O'Connor had said firmly. 'You can go back later, but I don't want gaps. Understood?'

They understood.

They also understood that this sort of work could be as boring as hell, so the sooner they started the sooner they would be finished. They had done this sort of thing before and didn't expect to find out anything useful. 'Best of luck,' said O'Brien as he turned and walked into the adjoining garden. Keaveney was already walking to the corner, tapping his notebook against his thigh.

'Yeah, you too,' replied McEvoy.

On the green, a dog was barking and chasing a football that two small boys were kicking.

The sun was beating down as Garda McEvoy opened another gate and stepped into a well-kept, tidy garden. A tall hedge, recently clipped, surrounded the garden and gave a quiet air of privacy. The lawn was mown and the borders around it had been cleared. It was reflected in the window that looked out onto it and McEvoy liked what he saw. Someone was very garden-proud, he thought, and pressed the doorbell.

The door opened and Harry McEvoy knew he was in trouble. He swallowed hard and tried to hide the sound with a cough.

'Ma'am,' he said 'we're investigating the death of Barbara Ryan, your neighbour, and I wonder if you wouldn't mind answering a few questions?' The last few words tumbled out and he felt a bead of sweat slide off his shoulders and run down his spine.

The woman in the doorway was holding a small spade in a gloved hand and had clay on her knees. She was wearing tennis shorts and her blouse was tied in a knot above her naval. Her red hair was tied up in a bun, silver clips holding everything in place, while a few strands escaped behind her ear. And her eyes, blue like the water on a tropical beach, looked right into him.

'And who are you?' she asked, her voice soft and warm.

'My name is McEvoy, Officer Harry McEvoy, ma'am.' More beads of sweat ran down his back and he felt even more uncomfortable.

She moved back from the door. 'Well, Officer McEvoy, please come in.'

McEvoy stepped into the cool of the hall and had to almost rub against the woman who didn't move an inch. His heart was going a hundred miles an hour and he began to understand what it might be like to be caught in a spider's web.

She closed the door and walked into the kitchen, waving for him to follow. 'This way.' She put the spade down on a chair, took off her gloves and washed her hands. 'I'm Jilly Lynch, and I'm as thirsty as hell. Been working the garden all morning. So, I'm going to have something to drink. What would you like?'

McEvoy tugged at his tie. 'Orange juice would be fine, thank you, Mrs Lynch.'

The room was dark, north facing, and well appointed. Glass-fronted cupboards and matching counter tops filled the far wall. Beside it was a walk-in fridge and sink where plates and cups were drying. An oven topped with a silver extractor unit waited for work. A vase with a mix of flowers – from the garden, he guessed – stood on the windowsill beside a pair of sunglasses, and the fresh smell of lavender filled the room. The place definitely had a woman's touch – it was spotless.

Jilly Lynch took two glasses from a cupboard and placed them on the counter, opened the fridge and poured orange juice from a carton. She put a glass in front of McEvoy and sat across the table. She took a long sip and moaned at the relief. 'God that's great,' she said, and wiped the sheen of perspiration from her forehead. 'And just so we get off to a proper start, its Miss Jilly Lynch, okay?'

McEvoy was confused. 'Sorry, ma'am, but I thought you were married.' He held his hands up.

She smiled; a beautiful, perfect smile that made him feel weak at the knees. Or maybe was it the sun shining on the top of his head all day. He didn't know. He took a long sip of the ice-cold orange juice.

'Kicked him out two years ago, useless bum. I knew he played around but there's only so much a woman can take. Know what I mean?'

McEvoy had no idea but smiled a response.

'So I'm back to being single again, and you know something, Officer McEvoy … it's great. He was such a waste of space.' She took another sip and leaned forward. 'So, what are you going to ask me then?

McEvoy blew through his lips and watched as Jilly Lynch, single, enjoyed his discomfort. 'Did you see anything out of the ordinary yesterday, say between one and three o'clock?'

Jilly turned and looked out the window and slowly drew fingers along her neck and wrapped a chain around a finger. She didn't reply for some time and McEvoy didn't mind taking in her beautiful profile. She was gorgeous, but well out of his reach.

'The first thing I must say is that I am, although it may not appear so, deeply upset at what happened to Barbara. I've known her for almost ten years, and she was always friendly.' She took a deep breath. 'I did not see her socially, but we she was a good neighbour. I'm shocked … I mean nothing like this has ever happened around here before. It's crazy.'

She sat back and took a long sip. 'I was coming back from the newsagents and I waved over to Barbara. She waved back and then went on talking.' She looked at McEvoy.

'Who was she talking to? Do you know?'

She shook her head slowly, thinking. 'No, I've never seen him before. So….'

McEvoy made a note. 'And what time was that?'

Jilly Lynch made a face. 'Don't know exactly, probably after two o'clock. Yes … definitely after two o'clock because I called a friend when I came in and it was nearer to two thirty.'

McEvoy made more notes. 'And what was this person like? Age, hair colour, height?'

'Not sure about his age as I never saw his face.' She paused and rubbed her eyes. 'It's odd, now that I think of it.'

'Why's that?'

She looked at McEvoy. 'Even when Barbara waved over to me he didn't turn around … to see who it was,' said Jilly.

'I see what you mean,' said McEvoy 'like he didn't want to be seen?'

'Exactly, that's exactly right.'

'And what about his appearance – hair colour, length?'

She closed her eyes and leaned her head back, thinking. 'It was dark and it was on his shoulders. I remember that. Don't see too much of that nowadays, do you?'

'No, ma'am, you don't.' He made a note. 'Height, any idea?' He took another sip of his cold drink and felt as though it almost hissed as it slipped down his hot throat.

She was staring at McEvoy and he was feeling even more nervous now. 'He was a little shorter than you, Officer McEvoy … I think,' she stood, and picked up her glass. 'We could check … just to be sure.'

'Err, check, ma'am?' was the best he could manage, the words slipping clumsily from his drying mouth.

She stood up and came around the table, smiling. 'Stand up, please. In the door frame there, that should give me a good approximation of the man I saw.' She raised her brow. 'Let's do it.' There was no argument.

McEvoy stood up carefully, took two steps and stood in the doorframe, feeling as though he was on fire. He thought about the fights that he'd broken up outside pubs late at night, and the thugs who swore at him threatening to tear his head off. That stuff was easy, real easy, but standing here in front of a very sexy, older woman was something different. And very unnerving.

Jilly Lynch stood close to McEvoy, really close, and he could smell her perfume and sweat. He closed his eyes for a moment as his pulse rocketed.

She looked up at him and smiled. 'Yes, I'd say that he was a little shorter than you, Officer McEvoy. Maybe three or four inches, at the most. About five-ten, would that be right?' she said and sat back down.

'I'm six-one and five-ten sounds spot on. Thank you.' He sat down and made another note. 'Anything else?'

She blinked; a thought crossed her mind. 'Yes, there was something else.'

McEvoy waited and wondered if she was going to tease him some more. He couldn't wait to get out of the house and back into the blazing sunshine. It was a better alternative.

'He was carrying something.'

McEvoy's look was quizzical. 'Like what … a newspaper, a briefcase?'

She tapped a finger against her lip. 'No, no, no … more like what people carry when they're doing surveys. You know the sort of thing?'

'Like a clipboard,' said McEvoy, the word coming of its own accord.

'Yes,' she cried, 'that's it exactly! A clipboard.'

McEvoy jotted this down. 'Anything else?' he asked, hoping perversely that Jilly Lynch had nothing further to add.

She relaxed and leaned into her chair and ran a finger around the rim of her glass, a low hum rolling across the table. 'That's all I can think of, Officer. I hope that I've been helpful?'

McEvoy closed his notebook. 'Yes, ma'am, you've been most helpful, thank you.'

'If you have any more questions don't hesitate to call *anytime.* You know where to find me.'

McEvoy stood up awkwardly and almost knocked his chair over. He forgot to say goodbye and left Jilly Lynch's house in a hurry. In the hall he stumbled on the rug, and closed the door as she started to laugh out loud, his discomfort now complete.

★

Back at the station, Brady added a few notes to the board, but they meant nothing really. So what did they have then? The perfect murder, that's what. No clues, no motive, no witnesses … no nothing. This was going to be a bastard.

A knock on the door turned his head, and in walked one of the young officers who had been assigned to carry out house-to-house interviews. 'What is it?' Brady asked.

Officer McEvoy walked in slowly, looking for O'Neill. 'Can I have a word, sir?'

O'Neill looked up from his desk. 'What is it, got something for me?' He raised an inquiring eyebrow. 'Come over here, pull up a pew.'

McEvoy came over and sat down. 'It's about the house-to-house interviews, sir. The ones down in Booterstown.'

O'Neill's eyebrows rose a little higher. 'You got something then?'

McEvoy shifted in his chair. 'It's like this, sir,' and he told him about his interview with Jilly Lynch. Brady listened, perched on the edge of his desk.

'Sounds like some woman, doesn't she, Pat?' said O'Neill, rubbing his hands and grinning across the table.

'Sure does. Too much for Officer McEvoy, eh?'

McEvoy blushed and bit his lip.

O'Neill leaned forward and put his hands on his desk. 'Good work. Well done.'

McEvoy smiled.

'Now do me a favour and write it up just like you told us. And then give it to Detective Brady. Okay?'

'Will do, sir. I'll do it straight away.' He stood up.

'And that's it all? Nothing from anyone else?'

'No, sir, nothing. Between O'Brien, Keaveney and me, that's it. Nobody saw or heard anything. In broad daylight, it's hard to believe, sir.'

'It is hard to believe, but it happens like that sometimes.' He opened his hands up to heaven.

McEvoy understood and went off to write his report.

O'Neill looked at Brady. 'What do you think?'

'Don't know. Might be something, then again it might be nothing. Might just be some sexy bird playing a naïve Officer McEvoy. Who knows?'

O'Neill tapped his desk. 'Agreed, but we'd better look into it.' He paused. 'Who carries clipboards around anyway? Check it out and let me know. Get Paul to lend a hand, he can do some fancy stuff on that computer and see what that shows up.' He stood up. 'Going to have a word with Doyle.'

O'Neill told Doyle about Clipboard Man as he had decided to call the unidentified man who had been seen with Barbara Ryan.

'A start,' said the boss.

'Yes, sir, and we'll follow it up. And I might need some more bodies to carry out more interviews. Can you spare any, sir?'

Doyle steepled his hands and the tips of his fingers brushed against his mouth. 'I'll check and let you know, okay?'

'Fine.'

'One other thing, Danny. I've been talking with a friend of mine in The Park, Commander Eamonn Farrell ...'.

'I know him, sir. We all played golf last year in Powerscourt; he's a big hitter.' He remembered the big man with an even bigger swing. He was a fine golfer with a single figure handicap.

Doyle sniggered. 'In more ways than one, Danny.'

'I can believe it.'

'He wants to send in a profiler, to help us with this case.'

O'Neill was surprised. 'A profiler? Do you think we need a profiler, sir? It's not a serial killer we're after. They live in America, not South Dublin.'

Doyle shrugged. 'It's not my call, Danny. It's from HQ and we've got to go with it. That's it.'

O'Neill moved closer. 'And why may I ask do they think we need a profiler, sir?'

'Somebody up there is very interested in the pencil. It's different, so they're interested. Now you know as much as I do. The detective will be here tomorrow morning, so look sharp.' He grinned and took the top off his fountain pen. 'Letters, Danny, the curse of management. See you later.'

O'Neill left and walked back to his desk and checked his emails. There was one from Shelly Tobin. He phoned her.

'Hello, Danny,' she said, 'you got my report?'

O'Neill was looking at the report on his computer screen. 'Yes, thanks.' He paused and ran his finger along a line of the report. 'So the killer bashed her head on the floor before stabbing her with a pencil.'

'That's right, not a pen – a coloured pencil.'

'Wow.'

'And the smack from the glass probably only dazed her, so he had more work to do ... and that's what he did. Bashing her head only rendered her defenceless, not dead. The stabbing killed her, no doubt about it.'

'You said it was a coloured pencil – is that the outside colour or the core?' asked O'Neill.

'Hmmm, very perceptive, Inspector.' She told him that the core was a soft yellow, a style of pencil usually used by artists.

'So you think that I might be looking for someone who likes to draw, eh? That could be anybody!'

'I know, Danny, but that's what the evidence tells me.'

'Christ, that's all I need.'

Shelly continued. 'It's more likely an artist than an architect or engineer. They tend to use hard core pencils; you know, the style from 9HB to H.'

'HB?' he said quietly, and uncertainly.

'It means Hard Black, Danny. This is 5B, a softer core, and more suited to work by artists. That's it.'

'Okay, thanks for that.' He paused and made a note. 'And what about time of death?' He could hear papers being flicked back and forth as Shelly searched a file.

'Sometime between one o'clock and four. That's the best I can do. Is it helpful?'

'Yeah, it's helpful, thanks. A witness saw someone talking to Barbara Ryan a little after two o'clock – so that fits.'

'Good.'

O'Neill knew he had to say something but right now was not the time. And anyway, he didn't know what to say. For as sure as night follows day he would screw things up and regret it. He was good at that, too good, and knew he had to have a script ready before even *talking* to Shelly. 'And now The Park are imposing a profiler on us,' he said, not knowing where the words came from.

'A profiler,' Shelly said automatically. She sounded surprised.

'Somebody is interested in the use of a pencil as a murder weapon. They must have nothing much to do, if you ask me.'

'Well, it is different, I'll agree with that. And having a profiler can only be a help.'

'I certainly hope so,' offered O'Neill, wanting to finish the call.

'Danny, everyone needs some help, from time to time,' she said, 'everyone.' The phone clicked dead and O'Neill was left listening to the sound of silence.

He walked over to the board and looked at – nothing. That's all they had, except, of course, the clipboard. It wasn't much. Of all the cases he had worked, he felt he had never had so little to go on. Had the killer been lucky in leaving so little evidence or was he a clever bastard who made no mistakes? They all make mistakes at some time, he thought, and wondered what was to come. It was not a good feeling, but then looking back wasn't much help. Joe Dixon used to say, especially in difficult cases, that it was not so much like looking for a needle in a haystack; it was trying to find the correct haystack first.

It was a sobering thought and one that he took with him later to Sandymount Strand. Soon he was lost in a steady rhythm and even the cawing gulls kept their distance as he ran along the water's edge. Two words came to mind – pencils and clipboards. What would Joe Dixon have to say about that? He kept running, as out to sea, the sun was an orange ball silently sinking into a shimmering Dublin Bay.

7

The ladders and sheets had been removed from the hall of the police station as the painters began work on the other side of the building. The smell of fresh paint still hung in the air and the heat seemed to intensify it. Creamy coloured and smooth, it was a far cry from the heavy green that had been there before. It was meant to be friendlier, made for a better working environment, at least that was what some psychologist was meant to have said, but then he or she probably never set foot in a busy police station.

Paul Grant tapped away at his keyboard, his phone wedged between his ear and shoulder. It was a position he was familiar with. 'Okay, okay,' he said, 'that's fine. Thanks, I really appreciate that.' He made some notes, checked the details on the screen again, and pushed back his chair.

He had his hands behind his head when O'Neill came into the office and caught his eye. 'Any news for me, Paul?'

Grant sat up. 'Did anyone ever tell you that you've got great timing?'

'I can think of a few girls. Why?'

Grant smiled and beckoned him over. He tapped his computer screen. 'I've just been talking with the telephone manager.'

'And ...?'

'And guess what? A call was made to the Ryan house just after two o'clock – 14:05:24 to be precise. It lasted only eight seconds and was made from a mobile phone that we cannot trace. It's odd because, as you can see, all the other callers are identified except one made at 12:34:53 that lasted seven seconds. It looks like your hunch might be correct.'

O'Neill looked closely at the screen, satisfied at what he saw. 'Thanks, Paul, this could be important. He turned and walked to his desk.

Dave Conroy was back in the office. 'You expecting someone, sir?' he asked, noting O'Neill's dark suit, ironed shirt, silk tie, and trousers with a sharp crease down the middle. 'Hope she's worth it after all the effort.' Conroy winked at Brady who quickly looked away and returned to his desk.

O'Neill straightened his tie. 'We've got a profiler coming this morning, and I don't know if it's a he or a she, but there's no harm in scrubbing up. Cleanliness is next to godliness, or something like that,' he replied, grinning. 'What about the robbery?'

'We caught the bastard – a gobshite really. He tried to drive a van like it was a sports car and he eventually crashed, driving onto the roundabout in Killiney, and that was the end of it. He's in a cell downstairs licking his wounds.' Conroy looked pleased and his smiling eyes confirmed it. They were brown and set in a face that preferred to smile rather than frown. Standing at six feet three inches, most people who met him preferred if he smiled. An expert in some form of oriental hand-to-hand combat, he could take care of himself, and belied the boyish face crowned with black hair that was longer than any of the other detectives.

'What wounds?' asked O'Neill.

Conroy sniggered. 'Well I told you he was a gobshite, and this one didn't put on a seat belt. So, he smashed into the steering wheel and damaged his already damaged bad looks. Broken nose, teeth knocked out and a pair of black eyes that only a Panda would love.'

O'Neill and Brady laughed. 'I hope all that's in your report. You couldn't make that stuff up,' Brady said, shaking his head.

'And I believe that you've got yourself a beauty,' said Conroy, walking up to the board.

O'Neill brought him up to date – it was easy.

He printed off Shelly Tobin's report and was looking for a staple when Brady walked over.

'I spoke to David Ryan's partners yesterday and they said he was with them in a meeting with their bankers until lunchtime when he left the office.'

O'Neill sat back and looked at Brady. 'And what time was that?' It couldn't be that easy slipping out and killing his wife, could it? he thought.

Brady grinned. 'He left the office at about 1:30p.m., and was back later – just before 2:30p.m....'

'So, what are you saying then? That he might have killed his wife?'

Brady pulled up a chair and leaned on O'Neill's desk. 'On my way home last night I took the same drive that Ryan would have taken, and I did it in less than fifteen minutes.'

O'Neill nodded. 'Good stuff, Pat, but....'

'But?'

'But you drove at a later time of the day when it was quicker, less traffic. So does your theory really help?'

Brady wasn't giving in. 'Don't forget the time of the murder is a guesstimate, Danny. It's not definitive.'

'Okay, I'll give you that.' O'Neill sat back, joined his hands, and twirled his thumbs as he thought. 'I suppose he could have driven home, killed Barbara, and then gone back to the office. And the timing fits.'

'Oh, it fits alright,' said Brady clearly.

'But at the same time he might have a very innocent explanation for his whereabouts.'

Whose side are you on? Brady thought. We're trying to catch a killer, and you, the cop in charge, is doing your best to let this guy go. He hated this shit. 'Innocent *until* proven guilty,' Brady countered.

O'Neill nodded. 'I'll keep that in mind, Pat.'

'And, by the way, I spoke to someone about that poster.' It was now standing against the wall beside the electric fan. 'He was very apologetic and will be collecting it tomorrow.'

'Good, at least we cleared something up.' O'Neill smiled. 'A good start to the day, well done.'

His phone rang. It was Doyle. 'A word.'

The corridor was clear now, no painters to dodge past as O'Neill straightened his tie and knocked on Doyle's door. The room was bright and Doyle was standing at the window, talking. He turned. 'Good morning, Danny, this is Detective Christine Connolly, our profiler.'

The woman who reached out and shook his hand was not what he had expected. In fact, if he was being honest, he hadn't known what to expect.

He was pleasantly surprised with Christine Connolly. She was dressed in a dark trouser suit and a white shirt, beneath which he could see a silver neck chain. Her dark hair was cut stylishly short and her bright eyes told him that she was observant and smart. They shook hands and he could see and feel her assessing him from head to toe. No doubt Doyle had already marked her card about him; it was to be expected. It was the nature of her job, and he felt as if he was going through an X-ray machine that missed nothing. Her firm handshake was a good sign. He liked that.

'Christine is here to help us with the Barbara Ryan case. I've given her a brief low-down on what's happened, so maybe you'll bring her up to speed as soon as possible,' Doyle said, looking at them.

'Will do, sir.'

'Thank you, Inspector,' said Connolly.

'I'm going to hold a meeting in the main room shortly to review the case and assign tasks. I'll call when I'm ready, sir. You might want to sit in,' he continued, turning his gaze to Connolly.

'Sure thing, Danny. Call me.'

Christine Connolly got plenty of admiring looks when she followed O'Neill into the Detectives' Room, with heads turning at the attractive new addition. She noticed the momentary silence.

'Gentlemen, this is Detective Christine Connolly, and she'll be working with us for a while.' He turned to her for a moment. 'HQ have sent her here and she's to be told everything about the Ryan case, just as if you were talking to me. Okay?'

Heads nodded.

'Good, we'll have a meeting in thirty minutes and see where we are. Don't anybody go missing. I need you all here. Right.'

'Right,' said Nolan, speaking for the team.

O'Neill turned to Connolly. 'Fancy a coffee?'

'Sure,' she replied, tucking her thumb under the strap of the bag that hung on her shoulder.

A few officers sitting at a table eyed Christine Connolly as she went to the counter. O'Neill saw McEvoy elbow another officer who made some comment to those at the table. A look from O'Neill told them to behave and they kept their chat quiet.

He led the way to a table by the window that overlooked the harbour where early morning sailors were making their way to rocking boats. The breeze stirred the flags in the yacht club, and walkers enjoyed the brisk conditions on the pier.

'Nice view,' she said, sitting down and taking a sip of her coffee. 'Better than the one I have in the Phoenix Park. My window looks down on a grey courtyard – doesn't come close to this. This is terrific.'

'It's nice alright, but I suppose you get used to it. You get used to everything, in time.'

Connolly smiled. 'Very profound, Inspector. And so early in the morning.'

He didn't reply but drank his coffee and took a bite of the Danish pastry. He brushed away the crumbs and licked his lips. 'So what *exactly* has you here, Detective? Is the pencil thing really that interesting?'

She looked directly at him. 'The pencil is mightier than the sword, isn't that what they say?'

O'Neill sniffed. 'The pen, I believe, is the word used. But, I hadn't thought of that. Very good.'

Connolly drank some more and put her cup down. 'When my boss heard about the pen, sorry, pencil, he told me about it and, I have to say, I was intrigued. Hey, it may be nothing, but then again you never know. But if it is something, then it will be interesting being involved … from the start. Well, almost the start.'

'And what do you know about *interesting* cases? I'm not sure it's the right question, but I hope you know what I mean.'

She turned and looked out at the harbour and said nothing for a long time. He studied her profile; nice nose and full cheeks that showed little make-up, and an elegant neck where the sun glinted off her necklace. The sunlight danced playfully on a few loose hairs that stuck out from behind her ear. For a moment he thought he was looking at Liz and closed his eyes. His heart missed a beat, and when he opened his eyes he saw, thankfully, that she was still admiring the view.

She faced him, holding her cup in both hands. 'I spent eighteen months in Quantico, studying with the FBI. It was very informative. Maybe not what you would expect someone like me to be doing, but I was sent there by HQ. I have a law degree from Trinity College. I studied psychology at Edinburgh and I have been with the force for almost nine years.'

'Fast tracked?'

She made a face that said it was not her fault – just the way things were. 'I studied Behavioural Science for three years and when the opportunity came to go to Quantico, well, it was too good to miss. America is the "land of serial killers." They have made a science from studying them, their make-up, and what makes them tick. It's an ongoing process.'

'I've never worked with a profiler before, so how do you think you can help?'

She put her cup down. 'It's good that you haven't, otherwise the country would be in a right mess.'

'Agreed.'

'Profiling looks at the evidence and tries to find patterns, unique patterns, that indicate certain crimes were carried out by one person. They might be the type of weapon used; place of attack; and how the bodies are left. It could be anything, that's why it is so important to learn as much as we can from each crime scene.' She paused. 'It may not be totally accurate, but we are getting better.'

O'Neill nodded. 'That's fine by me. I need all the help I can get, so welcome aboard.'

'Thank you, Inspector.'

'And did you get involved in any cases when you were there?'

She nodded her head. 'Yes, but only on the fringes of an operation. It was useful though.' She wiped a crumb from the edge of her mouth. 'The killer looked so normal. That's the thing with most of these guys, they don't look like the monsters we expect them to be. That's why it's so hard to catch them.'

'Well, I hope that we'll be able to use your knowledge to catch Clipboard Man or whoever the bastard is.' His voice left no doubt about his hatred for the killer and his determination to catch him.

She looked across the table and liked what she saw. Doyle had told her about O'Neill and his record of success. It was the best record of any of the detectives in the station and she knew that the man across the table was the right man for the job. When he spoke about the case his eyes showed the steeliness that she recognised from her FBI colleagues, the quality that was necessary to conclude a difficult case. He was no quitter.

He changed tack. 'I suppose you're going to tell me you met Patricia Cornwell when you were in Quantico? I've read a few of her books and she always mentions the place.'

She leaned closer and her voice dropped. 'Inspector, you don't *really* expect me to tell you that, do you?'

He laughed and the officers at the other table looked over and then just as quickly turned away. 'Enough,' he said, 'we should get back up and see what we have. Okay?'

She drained her cup. 'Fine with me, Inspector.'

★

O'Neill stood in front of the board and didn't see much there. A few names and times, but apart from the Clipboard Man, there were no leads. He turned and looked at the faces watching him. Pat sat on his desk next to Dave Conroy who was fiddling with the knot on his tie. Paul Grant, looking more scrubbed up than anybody could remember, was sitting beside Christine Connolly, his smile barely suppressed. Doyle was last to arrive and settled near the door.

'From what the Forensics team tell me, Barbara Ryan must have let her killer in as they have no signs of unlawful entry. That's one,' he said sticking out his index finger. 'There was no sign of theft even though there was plenty of money and jewellery in the house, that's two. Forensics did find some traces of blood not belonging to the victim. That's three. Someone telephoned the house shortly before the murder. At least the timing suggests that, but we'll know more when we get the final report from the pathologist later on. That's four.' He turned to the board. 'A neighbour saw a man talking to the victim around the time of the murder and he was carrying a folder or clipboard, that's the best she can remember.' He turned back. 'That's five, and that's where we are now. It's not much.'

Connolly put a hand up. 'If Clipboard Man is our target, what do you think he was doing?'

O'Neill looked at the faces for an answer. 'I don't know. What do people with clipboards usually do?'

'Surveys,' offered Conroy. 'Asking stuff about what you eat or what TV programmes you watch. One of them came to my door last week and wanted to know what I liked to drink. She was there for a long time,' he said. The laughter broke the tension.

O'Neill looked at the board again. 'Okay, if that's the case, we need to know if he went to other houses. We'll need to carry out more house-to-house interviews and see if anybody remembers anything like that. Might be luckier second time around asking a definite question.'

'Makes sense,' said Doyle, nodding. McEvoy rolled his eyes to heaven when O'Brien gave him a little nudge.

'Right, Christine, I want you to check the notes from the initial house-to-house interviews and see if Clipboard Man was mentioned. He should be if he was carrying out a survey. Otherwise ...'.

'He's our man,' said Brady, winking 'Nice One' to O'Neill.

'And the pencil?' asked Connolly.

'Yes, the pencil.' O'Neill took a few steps in front of the board, and turned. 'Nobody knows about the pencil apart from us. It stays with us. Do not say anything about it to anyone, and I mean anyone. Clear?'

It was loud and clear.

'It's very strange – I've never heard of one being used to kill before. Was it an opportunistic weapon or did he plan to use it to murder Barbara Ryan?' O'Neill was thinking out loud and nobody interrupted. 'If, and this is stretching it a bit, if Clipboard Man is our man, then he must have stalked the house and got to know the family routine. He knew that David would be at work and phoned Barbara to make sure that she was at home, *alone*,' he stressed. 'So, that level of planning suggests nothing was random.' Everyone was paying attention, with the only sound being the whirring fan competing with O'Neill's carefully spoken words. 'He might even carry a favourite weapon with him. If this guy is such a meticulous planner, then why shouldn't he plan to bring along his own murder weapon?' He looked down. 'It's just a thought, but I do believe that our guy is a planner, he likes to control.'

He rolled his neck, relieving a stiffness that was as much imagined as real. 'Paul, you can search, or whatever, on that computer of yours and see what you can find. You'll have to identify companies who carried out surveys in the area, or whether it was someone from the local council. Who knows?'

'Will do.'

Dave Conroy raised a hand. 'Why don't I check back for previous attacks? Not murder files, but attacks that might be similar. This bastard had to start somewhere, didn't he?'

'Go for it. It'll keep you out of the sun, you know it's bad for you anyway,' said O'Neill, looking at the most sun-tanned face in the room. 'You can catch up on some reading, too.' A ripple of laughter filled the room.

Doyle looked at Christine Connolly and she smiled, indicating that she was fine.

'Right, that's it everyone, so let's go,' said O'Neill. He went to his desk and checked his emails. There was a reminder to visit his dentist later and he rolled his tongue across his teeth and noted the time. 'You can work at my desk,' he said to Connolly, 'I'm off to see the husband with Brady.'

The traffic on Seapoint Avenue was heavy, with cars heading into town and as many going in the opposite direction to check out the regatta in Dun Laoghaire harbour. He turned on the radio and heard U2, singing 'I Still Haven't Found What I'm Looking For.' Brady angrily flicked it off. 'What the fuck do you know anyway?' he spat.

O'Neill didn't say a word.

8

The electronic notice board changed to show 10:15a.m., indicating that the train for Dublin was due in three minutes. The sun was high in the sky, bathing the city in a clear hot glow that had an effect on what the passengers were wearing. T-shirts and shorts were everywhere – yes, the summer was here to stay. Many showed signs of sunburn and sunglasses were a must for those talking and joking on the platform. It was going to be another hot day with just a whiff of a sea breeze tickling the skin. Booterstown station was a mix of old and young, most of them looking forward to a day in the city. Some, no doubt, would be hitting the summer sales that shops were putting on to encourage the crowds.

Nobody paid attention to the man leaning against the wall in the last piece of shaded area on the platform. He was wearing a short-sleeved shirt, chinos, and on his feet he had a pair of NIKE trainers. A baseball cap with NY above the peak covered his dark hair; a pair of mirrored sunglasses covered most of his face. They not only kept out the sun but allowed his eyes to wander and not be followed. He loved sunglasses – they made him feel invisible and he loved that. Money couldn't buy that shit.

The train slowed and people moved forward, ready to get on. He waited until a blonde-haired woman moved and he casually stepped aboard behind her. The doors hissed closed and he stood in the corner, shielded by a group of Spanish students where he had a clear line of sight to the blonde woman. It was the way he liked it. The train headed into the city, racing along the bay where yachts with brightly coloured sails tacked their way across the blue waters.

The train pulled into Pearse Street station and passengers hustled to get off, talking and laughing as they went. The man in the baseball cap waited until the blonde woman joined the crowd on the platform, before stepping down onto the black and white tiles. It was like walking on a giant chessboard, he thought, and it's my move. He liked that, liked it a lot.

Outside, some people hung around talking, others turned left along Westland Row towards Nassau Street, and a few turned right towards Pearse Street, which was bathed in bright sunlight. The blonde turned left and he followed at a discreet distance, the lively Spanish students and others still between them. He wasn't panicked, he knew her routine, and from previous trips he had a good idea where she was headed. Planning was everything, he knew that. It's what he had done with Barbara Ryan and look how that turned out: like clockwork, like a fucking Swiss clock. Perfect, in and out like a flash, and not a word. Neither the radio nor television had anything to offer – they had nothing. That rag, The Local, had a piece in it, but it was less than useless. What did any of them know? Nothing, and that's how it was going to stay. He was in control and walked a little taller, his confidence growing with every step he took along the pavement.

The crowd in front of him thinned out as the Spanish students turned into Trinity College, past Sweny's Chemist on Lincoln Place. The tour buses parked on Nassau Street disgorged their travellers into the sunlight but the blonde stepped around them, crossing the road in front of the Kilkenny Design store. Was she going in there for lunch? Panic rippled through him for a few moments and he slowed to check his watch. The place was nice but small and not what he had expected. Not from her. She'd never gone in there before. Fuck, I don't like that, he thought.

She checked her hair in the reflection of the tall glass windows, brushed it with her hand, and kept walking towards Grafton Street.

He breathed a sigh of relief and soon fell into step behind her, confident that he knew where she was going.

The girl continued up Grafton Street past Brown Thomas, making a right turn into the cool shade of Johnson's Court. The church was emptying after Mass and he had to push his way through the crowd to keep up. He now knew where she was going and was less than ten feet away from her when she walked across Clarendon Street and up the steps into the Powerscourt Townhouse Centre.

People jostled in the narrow passage that opened out into the large atrium that was bathed in diffused sunlight from the glass roof. Above, balconies with shops looked down on the hustle and bustle of the main restaurant where a queue was growing. The blonde waved and a friend called out, 'Over here!'

Two men in casual summer wear turned and liked what they saw. She slipped in front of them and hugged her friend, an attractive young woman with long brown hair and sunglasses strategically placed on her head. They all did that, he thought, as he passed them moving on towards the far end of the busy shopping centre.

He climbed the stairs and spent some time looking at paintings in a trendy art shop before making his way to the balcony. He leaned on the smooth rail to take in all the life below as it went about its bustling business.

He took a camera from his backpack and casually snapped a few shots. He was like any other tourist enjoying the sunshine and the buzz in one of the city's favourite shopping arcades. Slowly he panned around and through his lens watched the blonde and her friend talking, hands going back and forth, animating the conversation. He slowly zoomed in on the blonde's face and snapped. He took another one and whispered, 'You're mine, all mine.'

Suddenly, something poked him in the ribs, and he froze.

'Mister, you take picture, pleeze?' said the girl when he turned his head. She offered him her camera and smiled.

He looked at her and her taller boyfriend and reckoned they were Polish, and if not, then definitely two of the many Eastern Europeans who had come to Ireland in search of work. They were in their early twenties and both seemed happy to be enjoying the day. She had short mousy-fair hair with greyish eyes in a round face; her partner looked to be in the military, with a closely shaved head and colder blue eyes set in dark sockets. Probably from too much work, he thought, and took their picture. 'Another one, for luck,' he said quietly, and snapped again.

He handed the camera back to the smiling girl.

'Thank you. I hope you have good time,' she said in a thick accent, and her partner beamed.

He gave them his best smile. 'Thank you, I'm having a great time,' and turned back to the scene below.

She was sitting down now and he whispered the words again. 'You're mine.' He looked around the noisy centre but heard only his own words. He slung the camera around his shoulder, went down the stairs, and was soon lost in the teeming crowd.

9

The pain behind John O'Toole's eyes was blinding and showing no signs of getting any better. The stuffy office, with the smell of stale smoke hanging around like an uninvited guest, was stifling. He felt like throwing up but knew there was nothing left in his stomach. The taste of puke hadn't gone, even after a large mug of strong coffee. He was feeling really rough and made sure the door was closed – he didn't want to talk to anybody, he couldn't handle it right now.

The office was small and stuffed with old newspapers. Stacks of them stood at odd angles, dominating the room, covered in dust, unwanted. His desk was crammed with more of them and his correspondence trays overflowed. There was just enough space for his keyboard, monitor, notebook and another mug of coffee that was now cold and growing a dirty skin.

He checked his diary to see what he was supposed to be doing: he had to check out the local girls' school to do a piece on their winning hockey team. What a drag! That's what it had come to. After showing early promise in the business, he had stalled and couldn't get going again. He saw others progress, younger reporters with a hunger to succeed. They passed him by and his resentment grew. So did his drinking and before he realised it, or wanted to, he was an old alcoholic hack going through the motions. Those far-off dreams of making it onto one of the big national dailies were a fuzzy memory now, too painful to think about. He had gone as far as he could go, and working for *The Local* was no more than punching in a card each day. His dreams were gone, just like last night's banter in the pub. Booze was his best friend and had been for far too long.

He was sliding – going nowhere.

The pain spiked again. 'Fuck,' he said, and a tear fell from his eye. He was suffering.

Outside, the young and energetic employees went about their business, getting the next edition of *The Local* ready. Deadlines were still deadlines regardless of your hangover.

The ringing phone demanded his attention, and he opened his eyes.

'Johnny boy, how are ya?' Marty Murphy's squeaky voice grated on O'Toole's sensitive condition.

'Fine, boss. Couldn't be better,' he lied and closed his eyes again.

'Drop in, I want to have a word,' said Murphy, and hung up.

What now? thought O'Toole, slowly standing and shaking himself awake. It didn't make much difference. He straightened his tie and dragged fingers through his hair. Murphy wouldn't notice and wouldn't care either.

The main office was busy with plenty of telephone chat in progress. The lights from the computer screens danced on the ceiling, giving the room an eerie feel. All around, desks were stacked with papers, behind which young boys and girls sold advertising space and took instructions. Most of them were paid on commission and they worked hard to make a living. It was a noisy room and O'Toole made his way through it as quickly as he could.

Passing a darkened window, he caught a reflection of himself and stopped. He took a closer look and realised the shape he was in. He felt bad inside and now looked just as bad on the outside. He had to stop drinking or *it* would stop him, and soon.

Murphy's office was open and he entered a room that was even more cluttered and dirty than his own. Stacks of newspapers and magazines lined the shelves and hadn't been disturbed in years. A few media awards from long ago hung on the wall behind the large desk that Murphy seemed to fill. He was overweight, nearly twenty stone, and his red face made him a certainty for a heart attack. Despite only being in his mid-forties, he looked much older, and a thinning hairline gave his round face a comic look. He was a picture of ill health if ever there was one. Looking at him wedged behind the crammed desk, O'Toole suddenly didn't feel too bad. How sad was that?

He looked up from making corrections, pen in hand. 'Good morning, John, how goes it?'

'It goes, Marty.'

Murphy looked at him but didn't comment on the condition of his ace reporter. He saw the bags under O'Toole's eyes and the crumpled shirt that hadn't seen an iron in a long time. The unkempt hair and the five o'clock shadow finished the dishevelled look that had taken O'Toole years to perfect. He was on the slide, but at the salary *The Local* paid him, he was the best Murphy could get. His physical condition was less the editor's concern than O'Toole's journalistic output. 'What have you got on your plate now?' he asked.

'The hockey story.'

Murphy tried to push his chair back but there was hardly any room. O'Toole knew that Murphy drank too much, and in the three years that he had worked there, Murphy had ballooned. He sat up noisily, the leather squeaking in weak resistance, his shirt revealing dirty underarm stains. 'That murder the other day – I want you to sniff around. Call that cop friend of yours and see what you can find out.'

'What's the big deal, Marty? The radio crowd have already got it covered. What chance have we got?'

'Johnny boy, how often does a woman get murdered in her own house in broad daylight? Tell me that.' He shrugged. 'It's local. It's on our own doorstep so we should cover it – know what I mean? Nothing ventured and all that.' His eyes narrowed.

O'Toole didn't argue, he couldn't afford to.

'People die all the time. Some are killed accidentally and some get themselves murdered. Most deserve it, sure, but this woman …'. He stopped and cleared his throat. 'It just seems wrong to me. I mean, it could be anyone's mother, daughter or wife. It's crazy I know … it's just a feeling. That's all.'

'Okay, Marty, I'll call him and see what I can find out. Don't expect much though.'

Murphy shrugged and went back to his corrections.

10

They drove along the coast road, past the big houses at Seapoint that had a clear view of Dublin Bay all the way to Howth. The sea was calm and in the distance a cruise liner was making its way into Dublin port.

'So, what's with the profiler?'

O'Neill shrugged and turned to Brady for a moment. 'From what Doyle has been told, she's very good at her job … and anyway, another pair of hands is what we need right now.'

'That's it?' Brady was surprised.

O'Neill slowed for the traffic lights. 'Doyle didn't ask for her, and neither did I, if that's what's bugging you.' Another shrug. 'No secrets.'

'Well, if she's as good a profiler as she is a pretty girl, then we'll catch this bastard in no time.' Two women wheeled prams on the pavement, chatting in the sunshine.

O'Neill chuckled. 'That's it, Pat, nothing like a bit of sexism to start the morning, eh?'

Brady laughed. 'I wouldn't have it any other way.'

The lights changed and he moved off.

Without realising it, O'Neill was lost in thought: he was uncertain about the case and where it might be headed. It was a feeling that he was not used to, at least not since the Helen Murray case four years ago. She had been attacked late one night coming home after work, and had been stabbed to death. Her body was found the next morning lying in the winter's first snow by a boy on his way to school. It had been an intensive investigation but nobody was ever charged. A former boyfriend with a less than perfect alibi had looked good for it, but that was all. No evidence, nothing. Helen Murray never did get the justice she deserved. It hurt the investigation team badly, but O'Neill took it personally. It was the first time that he'd failed and the feeling stayed. He went over the case from time to time but nothing new ever showed up. 'Can't win them all,' a voice inside his head said. 'You can only do your best.' It was something that Joe Dixon would have said, and that's what he had done – his best. He was under the spotlight like never before, especially with the profiler involved, and he needed to focus. Getting some answers from David Ryan would be a pretty good start to the morning.

He got out of the car and it felt as though the rising heat was trapped between the trees and tall houses. He noted the dust on his shoes when he walked across the road, and the leaves above that lay dead still. Nothing stirred in the hot summer air that had been late in coming and was now making up for lost time. He felt his shirt sticking to him and tugged it away. But it was only a momentary relief.

A pleasant smell drifted from the roses in Christopher Ryan's garden. There were red and yellow bushes, neatly trimmed and tied up along one side of the garden, fronted by a small strip of grass. It, too, was neatly cut and the border was leaf-free. Probably had a gardener in every week, he thought, as he and Brady climbed the granite steps and rang the doorbell.

When the door opened, Christopher Ryan's red eyes had softened and he appeared calmer than on the previous day. His short-sleeved shirt, pressed dark trousers and polished slip-on shoes attested to it. It was an attempt at normality and it was good to see, thought O'Neill, as Ryan invited them inside and closed the door. 'Good morning, Inspector, any news?'

'No, nothing yet. It's very early in the investigation but we are doing our best. We have a team in place, Mr Ryan, but I still need to talk to your brother. How is he today?' asked O'Neill, noticing the years that seemed to have been added to Ryan's face overnight. Although he'd obviously showered and shaved, the darkness inside couldn't be hidden.

'Much better, he's much better, considering ...' said Ryan.

The two policemen nodded, this was good.

'A doctor came after you left yesterday and gave him something. Helped him sleep. He's the better for it. He needed it.'

'That's good to hear. Plenty of sleep is always good,' said O'Neill. 'Can we speak to him? I do need to ask him some questions and sooner would be better. I'm sure you understand.'

Christopher Ryan understood and went to get his brother. He pointed to the front room. 'Please, I'll be back in a moment.'

Pat Brady again looked up at the paintings on the high walls and smiled. He pointed to a large oil painting of girls on a sunny beach, the figures mere brushstrokes, but they rendered a beautiful impression. 'That one,' he said, 'is by Louise Mansfield and must have cost thousands. She's wonderful, her stuff is very popular.'

'And expensive too,' said O'Neill, having a closer look.

Pat Brady pointed at the painting on the other wall. 'And that one is by Graham Knuttel, and his stuff sells for even more. Mr Ryan is quite a collector.'

O'Neill looked at both paintings and preferred the girls on the beach. 'I didn't know that you were such a connoisseur, Pat. Kept that one quiet.'

Brady grinned. 'Did art in school, liked it but I was never that good. I go to exhibitions in the National Gallery, and sometimes walk along Merrion Square on Sunday mornings, when the artists are there. Some lovely stuff on view ... and some very ropey stuff, too. Anyway, it's all in the eye of the beholder.'

'Couldn't agree more,' said O'Neill, hearing footsteps outside the door.

David Ryan looked better than he did yesterday, but then that wouldn't have been hard. His eyes were not as red and he'd shaved. His face was pale, but he walked a little straighter. Good for him, thought O'Neill, nodding his hello.

The two brothers sat down on the long white sofa and Brady eased his way out of David's eyeline and took out his notebook.

O'Neill sat opposite Ryan, not wishing to be looking down on him. He didn't want to appear superior and wanted to observe David's body language. A slight twitch of a facial muscle or the quick dart of an eye could tell so much – and, right now, he needed all the help he could get.

'Good morning, David, and I hope that you are feeling a little better.'

David Ryan nodded once. 'Yes, thank you.'

'That's good, I'm glad to hear it.'

Christopher Ryan squeezed his brother's shoulder.

'Now, David, I know that this will be difficult for you, but I need to ask you some questions. I need to get whatever information you have so that I can find the person who killed Barbara. You understand?'

Another nod. 'Yes.'

'Excellent, and please tell me if you want to have a break. Take your time, that's all I ask.'

David Ryan wiped his nose with a hankie, and looked at O'Neill. 'I'm ready.'

O'Neill glanced at Brady. 'David, have you any idea why this happened to Barbara? Is there anybody who she or you had difficulty with?' O'Neill asked, his voice quiet and controlled.

David shook his head and looked up. 'No, none whatsoever. Barbara was such a loving person, she wouldn't hurt a fly. I've absolutely no ideas, none.'

'Any problems with neighbours or at work? I mean, someone could be trying to get back at you for something. It may sound unlikely, but people do strange things.'

David bit his lip. 'Nothing, Inspector.' He shook his head. 'I've been thinking exactly the same thing, over and over, but nothing. I can't think of anybody who would want to hurt Barbara. Or me. Nothing. I'm sorry.'

'You don't have to be sorry, David, not at all.' O'Neill paused, gathering his thoughts. 'Friends, what about her friends, David? I wonder if they can help. You know how it is. Women talking with women, stuff they don't discuss with us men. Who was she close to?'

Ryan answered immediately. 'Jenny Collins is her best friend, has been since junior school.' He looked at O'Neill. 'They were supposed to be playing golf together yesterday. That's what was strange when I got home.'

'What was strange?'

Brady stopped writing and looked up.

'Barbara's car was in the driveway. She would normally make her way to the club and then be home for tea. So when I saw it there I thought that Jenny must have collected her.' He sniffed. 'She just got herself a new open-top sports car and loved driving around in it. Top down, of course.'

O'Neill smiled at the image. 'And where can I find Jenny?'

Ryan reached into his pocket, took out his phone and read out Jenny's number. Brady put it in his notebook.

'And tell me, David, was Barbara a member of any other clubs or groups? Like a reading group, a tennis club or something?'

Ryan rubbed his face and held his hand to his mouth, thinking. 'She used to go to the library, from time to time. She did not play tennis, and no, I never saw her paint or anything like that. She cooked, cooked very well. She liked trying new recipes and dishes, and loved all things Italian. And we liked to take walks.'

And that was it. A quiet life summed up in a few minutes. It was one of the things that O'Neill felt bad about and couldn't really understand why. A life, be it seven years or seventy, could be summed up in a few sentences. All those dreams and emotions cut short, never to be fully realised; never seeing her husband again or any of her friends. Life could be cruel and he saw it written on David Ryan's face. He was going to have a tough time ahead and O'Neill silently wished him well.

O'Neill rubbed a finger against his mouth. 'David, we found a message on the answering machine. You said "sorry about last night". Can you tell me what you meant?'

David Ryan exhaled. 'I let Barbara down, Inspector. She had tickets to a Mozart concert in the National Concert Hall, but I forgot about it. I was working on a report for the meeting with the bankers, and it slipped my mind. Barbara was very upset.'

O'Neill glanced at Brady who shrugged. Next question.

O'Neill continued. 'We are trying to establish an exact time for the crime, or at least as accurate as science allows, and we need to know where you were around 1:30p.m. After the meeting with your company's bankers.' O'Neill's words were casually delivered, nothing sneaky or underhand, and he knew Brady was holding his breath.

Ryan looked at the carpet and coughed into his hand. 'I was … at lunch.'

O'Neill leaned forward. 'So, you didn't go home?'

'No, I did not go home, Inspector.'

O'Neill nodded. 'Good. And where did you go for lunch?'

David Ryan shivered uncomfortably. His brother sensed something and stiffened. 'I had coffee with a friend who lives on Strand Road.'

'The one in Sandymount?' queried Brady.

Ryan nodded, but kept his eyes on the carpet.

'With …?' asked O'Neill, suddenly aware of the change of atmosphere.

Ryan coughed into his hand and cleared his throat. 'I was with Ann Lawlor.'

Christopher Ryan squinted, wincing slightly, wondering what was going on. David off having lunch with some woman that he had never heard off? That was a surprise. What next? What was he up to?

'And I expect that this … Ann Lawlor can corroborate your story?'

Ryan nodded and his response was almost inaudible.

O'Neill had a quick glace over to Brady who remained stoney-faced, giving nothing away.

O'Neill glanced at Christopher Ryan who sat wide-eyed beside his brother. 'And how well do you know Ann Lawlor?'

Ryan composed himself, exhaled loudly, and looked at O'Neill. 'She used to work in the office, left last year. I, we, had a very short relationship, but that's over.'

Maybe Brady was right after all, O'Neill thought. 'When did this relationship start and end, Mr Ryan? This is very important.'

Ryan ran his fingers through his hair and sat upright. 'It started after the office Christmas Party two years ago … and lasted until about Easter. Three months or thereabouts.' His voice was stronger now, the benefit of 'confession being good for the soul' kicking in.

O'Neill had not expected what Ryan had just said, and knew it might be a game changer. 'I appreciate what you've said and I will talk with Ann Lawlor as soon as I can.' His tone was very serious. 'I need to rule you *in* or *out* of this investigation, and right now Ann Lawlor is your best alibi.' He stood up and buttoned his jacket. 'I need her phone number and address, and do not try to contact her until after I speak with her. Is that clear?' It wasn't a question; it was an order.

'I understand,' said Ryan, and put his head in his hands. Christopher put his arm around his shoulder.

O'Neill stepped close to David Ryan. 'What you've just told me puts a different complexion on things. So, before I leave, is there anything else I should know?'

Ryan shook his head back and forth. 'No … nothing.' He wiped his mouth. 'I know I've been a fool, but I didn't kill my wife, Inspector. You must believe me.'

O'Neill buttoned his jacket. 'I don't have to believe you or anybody else, David, at least until I have a word with your *friend*.' He turned and headed for the door.

'We'll go and see her now,' he said to Brady, opening the car door. 'I want this cleared up immediately.' He took his jacket off and tossed it angrily into the back seat.

Brady nodded, but said nothing. He was right after all; the husband did it. The quiet man had been tempted by some young thing and finally snapped. It was the oldest story in the world, and David Ryan was only the latest fool.

Less than ten minutes later they were outside Ann Lawlor's house.

'Right,' said O'Neill, 'this should be straightforward. I'm not concerned, right now, about their relationship, I just need her to confirm.'

'Or deny,' chipped Brady.

'Or deny, his story.'

Don Cameron

O'Neill rang the bell and got no reply. He tried a few more times while Brady looked in the front window. 'Take a look around the back, Pat,' O'Neill said, just as the next-door neighbour opened her front door.

'She's not in,' she said, looking at both men. She was probably in her sixties, O'Neill reckoned, and her eyes never left them. Her dark hair, laced with silver streaks, was tied up in a bun and she wore little or no makeup. She didn't need it – she was a very good-looking woman. Her hands rested on her hips and O'Neill felt that she had been working. Gardening, maybe.

O'Neill showed her his ID. 'I'm Inspector O'Neill and I'm looking for Ann Lawlor. She lives here?'

The neighbour nodded.

'And you are?'

'Tara Feeney. I've known Ann since she moved in … about nine years ago. She's a good neighbour.'

O'Neill listened and made a note. 'That's good to hear. These days, it seems as if the concept of being a good neighbour is almost gone.'

Tara Feeney smiled.

'When did you last see her?' O'Neill asked as Brady got up on the wall and dropped down into the side passage.

Tara Feeney looked O'Neill over, from bottom to top. 'Yesterday. She put a small travel bag into the backseat and drove off. She often goes away, it's not unusual. She has a summer chalet in west Cork. She's probably down there. She's an artist, you know, and has a studio there.'

'Have you been there?'

'Oh, yes. It's lovely down there, in Baltimore. You really feel away from it all when you've spent a few days there. Life is very *slow*, you know.'

O'Neill grinned. 'There's nothing wrong with that, from time to time.' He closed his notebook as Brady jumped down, shaking his head – nothing. 'Nice talking with you,' O'Neill said, and closed the gate behind him. There was nothing more to do here, so they headed to the station as the neighbour watched them go before heading back indoors.

11

Back at the station, Brady updated the board and drew a line from David Ryan to Ann Lawlor. It meant nothing, but it did show that something was happening.

O'Neill took off his jacket. 'Right, Pat, try and contact Ann Lawlor and get her to call us immediately.'

Brady nodded. O'Neill was finally seeing this murder for what it was: a crime of passion – and that the husband did it. He knew it all along, so why couldn't O'Neill see it too? He didn't care – he was right, and that's all that mattered. 'Sure thing, Danny, I'll call her in a mo.'

O'Neill got a coffee from the restaurant and headed back upstairs where the heat was palpable, even with two fans on the go. He got the number from Brady and dialled Jenny Collins, Barbara's best friend. His correspondence tray was filling up but it would have to wait. He took a quick look. Memos and more memos. And a schedule of dates from the Police Golf Society that he checked and approved.

'Hello,' said the female voice.

O'Neill introduced himself.

'Oh,' she said, the surprise obvious. 'How can I help?'

He told her about his meeting with David Ryan, and that he now wished to speak to her. She was Barbara's best friend, wasn't she?

'Yes, we were friends forever. Since we were in junior school.' She sounded nervous. 'Longer than I care to remember. Friends for life.'

He could hear the anguish in her voice; it was unmistakable. 'I'm very sorry that you have lost such a good friend, but I would like to talk to you. The sooner the better.'

'I'm at the golf club now and will be here for another little bit. I ... just had to get out of the house, Inspector. Be among friends, you know.' She sniffled. 'I loved Barbara, and I'll do anything to help.'

'I hear what you're saying. I'll be along as soon as I can. How's that?'

'Fine, that's fine. By the way, I'm at Foxrock Golf Club. Do you know it?'

'I know it very well, played it many times. See you later.'

He checked his emails and read the report from Gary O'Connell. It was what he had expected, nothing new in it. Next, a joke from one of his golfing buddies brought a smile. And then a message from John O'Toole of *The Local*. Sniffing around, no doubt. He could wait, but Jenny Collins couldn't.

★

Foxrock Golf Club was looking good in the late afternoon sunshine, its red-tiled roof adding to the warm glow. The car park was busy and O'Neill got a spot near the back and walked past the putting green where a few players were getting in some last minute practice. The smell of freshly cut grass was in the air when he walked to the back of the building and into the Secretary's Office. Scorecards covered a table and various clubs stood against a wall waiting for their owners to return.

'Can I help you?' asked the man at the desk; his silver hair short and spectacles perched on the end of his nose.

'Yes, I'm here to see Jenny Collins. She's expecting me,' O'Neill said, and showed his warrant card.

The man looked shocked. 'Is there something wrong?' he queried nervously, pushing his chair away.

'Nothing that you should be worried about.' He said no more and waited as the man passed him and went upstairs, shooting a quizzical look at O'Neill as he went. All around was the organised clutter that kept the club running – timesheets, handicap details, competition schedules and results. All very time consuming and important, but made easier these days by the computer that was purring away on the crammed teak desk.

'This way,' said the man. 'She's in the bar. Do you know where it is?'

O'Neill nodded. 'Yes, I've been here before. Thanks,' he said, and made his way up the red-carpeted stairs.

Jenny Collins waved him over, stood up and offered an elegant hand. 'Hello, Inspector. Can I get you something to drink?'

'A coffee will be fine.'

Coffees were ordered and they sat in a corner of the room far away from any eavesdroppers. Club gossip was one thing, but murder was something else altogether.

'So how can I help, Inspector?' asked Jenny Collins, eyeing him over the rim of her cup.

The woman across the table had been crying, her eyes red raw. She probably hadn't slept last night and the makeup couldn't hide the haggard look. She was distraught, tense and by the way she was tightly gripping her cup, angry. He knew the effect that a sudden and vicious murder had on family and friends – Jenny Collins was another casualty.

O'Neill put his cup down. 'Firstly, may I say how sorry I am for the loss of your best friend. It's not something that has happened to me, and I hope that it never does.'

Jenny Collins put her cup down and sniffled into a hankie. She let out a long sigh, and looked at O'Neill. 'I'm sorry, you must think I'm an awful fool.'

O'Neill shook his head. 'Nobody should be in your position, never.'

Jenny wiped her eyes with the back of hand. 'God, I must look absolutely dreadful.' She looked around but nobody was talking any notice.

O'Neill took a sip and put his cup down. 'David says that you and Barbara were the best of friends, that you go way back.'

She nodded.

'If you know her, sorry, knew her, so well, do you think that there was something in her life that might have caused this?'

She took her time before answering. A stray hair fell across her eyes and she brushed it away easily. She had a full figure in a white polo shirt that told him she was someone who kept herself fit. She was a walking advertisement for all those keep fit gurus, proof positive that you can look good if you want to. For a woman in her mid-forties, she would put many women twenty years younger to shame. But it was the green eyes above high cheekbones that were most striking. She must have broken quite a few hearts along the way, he thought, and will do so for a while longer. And seeing those eyes with their distant, uncertain stare was something he would not forget.

He waited, aware only of the woman across the table who was slowly gathering her thoughts.

'What are you suggesting, Inspector?'

'I'm suggesting nothing; I'm trying to find out why a woman – an innocent woman by all accounts – is murdered in her own home. Whatever you can tell me will be appreciated.' He didn't mention Ann Lawlor. He picked up his cup, took a sip, and held it between his hands.

Jenny Collins leaned forward. 'If you're thinking that she was involved in any funny stuff, you know, hanky-panky, then you're barking up the wrong tree,' she said slowly and with some venom. 'That was not Barbara, never was. She …' Jenny Collins banged her fist on the arm of the chair. 'Never, do you hear me, Inspector? Never.' She sighed and shook her head.

O'Neill held up a hand. 'I'm not barking up any tree at the moment. In fact I wish I was, as there is very little to go on. Nobody knows anything.' He put his cup down. 'Apart from a neighbour's vague memory of somebody talking to Barbara shortly before she was killed, we have nothing. Nada. So, is there anything you can tell me about your best friend? Anything at all?' He stayed sitting on the edge of the chair, not retreating until he got an answer.

She twirled her cup in its saucer, uncertain how to say whatever it was she wanted to say. How do you sum up nearly forty years of friendship and get it to mean something useful? Something that would give a stranger an idea of the person concerned? It wasn't going to be anything in-depth, just a thumbnail picture of the woman who had meant so much to those close to her, and whose death had turned their world upside down.

'You're right; she was my best friend. I was very, very lucky to know her. She was always there for me and played it very straight. No messing around. Passed her exams each year in school and college. No repeating for Barbara. No siree.' She laughed at the memory. 'She would go off to America or Australia and spend the summer working and making money so that she would have enough for the following winter, and for clothes. She loved nice clothes. She was very independent, Inspector. Always had some money if I was stuck, and God only knows how often that happened.' She smiled at the memory. She looked around the bar, but at no one in particular. 'She qualified as a solicitor but never practiced much,' she added. 'She worked part-time in a solicitor's office, but it was nothing serious. She was on the committee here, and she liked to write short stories.'

'Short stories?'

'Yes, and they were very good. She had a number of them published. She was very proud of that.'

'And when did she meet David?'

Jenny Collins looked into the distance, back to more carefree days. 'In her last year in college. They met at some faculty party and she was smitten.' She paused. 'It does happen, Inspector.'

O'Neill made a face and drank some coffee.

Jenny Collins continued. 'They got on really well and were married within eighteen months.' She looked directly at O'Neill. 'Sadly there were no children. She would have loved to have one, but it wasn't to be, and she got on with her life. She was devoted to David. They were very close, Inspector. To be brutally honest with you, I envied her.'

He didn't say anything.

'It was the happy life that I and so many women seek, but few of us find.' Her eyes glazed over, and she rubbed them with a hankie. She exhaled a deep sigh.

'Did you never marry?'

Jenny Collins leaned back, the tension in her body easing a little. 'Too busy, Inspector. I opened a boutique in the city and after many years of hard work, travelling and what not, I built quite a good business for myself. It took time and I had to be, well, selfish, if I wanted to succeed. That's my story, Inspector.' She smiled, anticipating his question. 'And yes, I've known men but,' she shrugged her shoulders, 'never found the right one for me. You understand?'

'I understand perfectly, and thank you for being so open. I didn't mean to pry.'

She put a hand up. 'I know you didn't, but there it is. Still single and …'.

'And driving your sports car, that can't be bad,' he joked, trying to sound as friendly as possible.

She shrugged. 'Haven't grown up yet, I guess. Maybe never will.'

The television was showing a golf competition and a loud shout went up when a player made a long putt. Outside, the sun was sinking, bathing the room in its orange and gold light.

'So I take it you have no idea why Barbara was killed, other than being in the wrong place at the wrong time?'

Jenny Collins shook her head slowly. 'Nothing, Inspector. She was such a good person and with her it was a case of what you see is what you get. No secrets, no funny stuff. It wasn't in her nature, Inspector. Not in a million years.'

'And David, what about him?'

She frowned, surprised. 'You don't think that David did it, do you, Inspector?'

O'Neill pinched his nose. 'I don't think anything at the minute, but in cases like these the husband is always a suspect. It happens.'

Jenny Collins shook her head like a disappointed teacher asking a question and finding out that nobody was listening. 'I'm sorry, Inspector, but David couldn't do it, couldn't have killed Barbara. He can hardly raise his voice.' She leaned closer. 'In fact, I'd say that he's really a bit of a wimp. Nice, intelligent, yes, but a bit too soft.' She took a sip of coffee and looked at O'Neill. 'Did I really say that?' she asked, and sat back in her chair.

'Yes, you did, and thank you.'

They looked at each other for a long moment.

'Finally,' said O'Neill, 'David said he thought Barbara was meant to be playing with you yesterday.'

Jenny Collins sat up, alert. 'Yes, she was, and I wondered what was keeping her. She's usually a good timekeeper.'

'And did you try and contact her?'

'I did. I phoned a few times, but the line seemed dead.' She put her hand to her mouth shocked at her words. 'Oh, I didn't mean that.'

O'Neill ignored the comment. 'And tell me, what time was this?'

Jenny Collins still had a hand to her mouth. 'It must have been around 2:30, or so. We were meant to play at four o'clock and I wanted to check that everything was okay.' She reached into her bag and took out her mobile phone. She tapped buttons and said, 'I called her mobile at 2:35 and again at 2:46. And I also dialled the landline at 2:49, but got nothing.' She was thinking about what she had said, and realised that Barbara might have been struggling for her life when she was on the phone. It was an uncomfortable thought.

After that there was nothing more to say.

O'Neill stood and said goodbye to Jenny Collins. She had lost her best friend and he knew that she was still in shock, although she was doing well to hide it. She was a strong-willed woman and she was going to need all her reserves of inner strength to help her face the future. It was not something that he wished upon anyone, especially someone on their own, but if anyone could handle it, Jenny Collins could.

Security lights were on in the car park when he left and headed back home to Sandymount. It had been a busy day, but even so he hadn't made much progress. The profiler might have found something, or at least have some ideas, but that could wait. He decided to go for a run in an effort to clear his head.

An hour later, he jogged slowly to a stop just past the old swimming baths, his mind a whirl of thoughts.

What if David Ryan was the 'wimp that turned'? It was hard to believe, but it wasn't looking too good for the accountant. And if he was the killer, then O'Neill really had to reassess his approach. And if that's what he had to do, so be it. Was he losing his edge? He didn't think so, but others would make the assessment. And Brady's insufferable righteousness was definitely beginning to get under his skin, much as he hated to admit it. 'Bastard,' he heard himself say, and glanced around to make sure he was on his own. He took a few long, deep breaths, straightened up and started running again. Nothing was any clearer, so he ran on, hoping that the jumbled ideas floating around in his head would find a natural place in the unfolding scheme of things. It was all he could do, and besides, he needed the exercise.

12

He had been cruising on his motorbike from Blackrock to Killiney before stopping in Dalkey. The crowd outside The Queen's pub was colourful and noisy, with everyone straining to look cool. That was vital, and as he cast his eyes about the jostling group he saw her. He pulled deep on his Galois and never blinked as the smoke drifted in front of his eyes. She was so like her ... so like the woman who caused so much pain....

She finished her cigarette and blew a stream of smoke into his face. 'Like that, you little brat?' she spat and laughed, running her fingers through her bleach-blonde hair. He just managed to duck as her swinging hand caught the top of his head a glancing blow. He ran from the table to his room and slammed the door shut. 'That's it, run away like your useless father!' she shouted, 'that good-for-nothing bastard ran away when I needed him most. He left us, he never wanted you ...'. She stopped and he heard her bang the table hard. 'The waster, the prick, he ruined my life!' She was screaming now and he started to shake because he knew what was coming. 'And you, you little ungrateful shit, are just like him. What the hell did I do to deserve this life? Je-sus! I was going to go to college, but look at me now. It wasn't what I wanted, do you hear me?' He pressed against the door and closed his eyes, not wanting to cry. He heard her push her chair back on the wooden floor and then suddenly the doorbell rang. There was a momentary silence and he heard her talking to a man. Her latest admirer, who like the other men only ever came around once or twice, and were never seen again. They all had a sly look in their eyes and showed no interest in him. But she didn't *mind. She laughed and pushed his door open. 'I'm going out now, so behave.' He didn't say a word and waited for the front door to close. He was on his own now. He spent the evening drawing and sketching in his favourite art books until he fell asleep on his bed.*

The next day after the man had left she started screaming again and burst into his room. He jumped up, trying to stop her from destroying his books. 'No, no, please don't!' he pleaded, but she was stronger and pushed him away. 'Men, they're all the same, all the fucking same,' she shouted, as she picked up his colouring pens, breaking them into small pieces. He was crying and shaking when she finished and walked out slamming the door behind her. All around the room the pictures that he had spent hours working on lay like confetti. His pens were smashed and he crawled about collecting the bits, hoping that he might be able to use some of them again. She had acted badly before, but never like this. He went about his business as quietly as possible, all the while vowing that one day he would get even. The tears stopped and he felt that something inside him had changed. He wasn't sure what it was but he could feel it and didn't fight it. The future would be his, and when the time was right, he would let her know it.

13

Christine Connolly closed the last folder. 'Nothing, absolutely nothing,' she said, and leaned back in the chair.

'What's that?' asked Grant, looking up from his terminal.

Connolly composed herself and took a deep breath. 'There's not a mention of Clipboard Man in any of the interviews.'

'None?'

'Nothing at all, except what the neighbour saw. So, it looks like he might be our man after all.' She stood up and walked over to the window. 'It had to be part of his plan, had to be. Otherwise it makes no sense.'

Grant was listening carefully and enjoying the view. Christine Connolly was wearing a cream shirt and slim-fitting pants that help show off her eye-catching figure. Her perfume, subtle and intense at the same time, drifted in a room more used to strong, blunt aftershave. It was a pleasant change and much appreciated.

'The phone call to the house minutes before he's seen by the neighbour … it makes sense.'

Grant nodded, and sniffed deeply.

'He knew that she was alone, *definitely*, and so he could carry out his plan.' Connolly grinned. 'He's very good, this guy, and loves being in control. It's all about control.'

Grant's brow lifted.

Connolly stood in front of his desk. 'This is no random act. No way. This guy has planned it, and planned it well. It's what drives him. The need to control the situation is everything. He's in charge. He *needs* to be in charge.'

Grant sat up. 'And if he needs it, as you say, does that mean he'll *need* to do it again?'

Connolly turned and looked down on the busy sunlit street where shoppers and skateboarders moved. 'The murder was not about robbery, rape or any of the normal types of attack. It's deeper than that. Our man will feel stronger now, and yes, I think he'll do it again.'

'Shit,' said Grant, putting his hands behind his head. 'Are you saying we might be looking for a serial killer?'

Although only one person had been killed, the manner of the attack suggested more were to come. The case had barely started and it was already clear that things were going to get worse. Connolly turned, looked at Grant, and without saying a word, went off to the restaurant.

★

Downstairs in the cool of the basement, Dave Conroy was sitting at a computer and feeding it questions. He started with attacks in which pens or pencils were used and, after getting no hits, moved onto skewers and other pointed objects. He refined his search for attacks in households and on women that bore any likeness to Barbara Ryan's fatal one. He sat back, lit a cigarette, and waited while the electric brain did its thing.

It was a thankless task. He took a long drag, exhaling through his nose. A line of green dots ran along the screen as the search continued in silence and Conroy leaned back in his chair, thinking. Thinking about the information that might have been input about a crime and wondering if he was using the right words to get a hit. Shit in, shit out. He grinned at the phrase used by the techies to stress the importance of inputting information correctly. It was that simple. You put shit information in, you get shit information out. He took another drag and hoped that someone had their shit together when they were inputting. He crossed his fingers and watched the dots.

Smoke hung in the room and he put out his cigarette. He stood up, stretching his legs. Around him, metal cabinets stretched almost to the ceiling and wrapped themselves around the walls of the room that was kept at a constant temperature to preserve the documentation. He was happy to be out of the stuffy room upstairs where Grant was sitting close to Christine Connolly. Lucky bastard, he thought. He was about to light another cigarette when the computer screen changed and displayed a message, 'Match Found', listing five file numbers.

'Fuck me,' he said, and wrote down the information. He looked at the numbers and wondered, and hoped. No, it can't be that easy, he thought. He pushed his chair back, stood up, and ran his fingers along the list of file numbers, willing a connection. Carefully working his way around the room, one by one, he pulled the case files out. He recorded the case file numbers in a ledger that rested on a shelf by the door, secured by a chain to the wall. Sensitive information like this had to be accounted for at all times, and everyone knew that Doyle was a stickler for this. Only last year an officer had been in serious trouble for not recording his removal of such a file and Doyle had made an example of him. A reminder in large black letters hung above the ledger – Sign Out or Get Out.

Conroy closed the door and, with the files under his arm, went to the restaurant for a coffee. And a think.

★

O'Neill was at his desk when Connolly came back into the office.

'Any luck with the interviews?' he asked.

She shook her head. 'Nothing,' she replied, and told him what she had already told Grant.

'Jesus, that's all we need,' he said, and exhaled loudly. 'A fucking serial killer, are you serious?'

'As serious as I can be, sir. I'm thinking as a profiler, looking at the evidence and making assumptions.'

'Assumptions,' shot O'Neill. 'I need more than assumptions. Assumptions never caught a killer, did they?'

Paul Grant watched the exchange and said nothing.

Connolly wasn't fazed not in the least, and gently brushed a loose hair behind her ear. 'Sir, from what we know, and you agree it isn't much, I've suggested a scenario, that's all. It may be true, or it may not. I don't know, and nor does anyone else, except the killer. But we must have a plan, just like the killer has. And if we follow it, and change it when necessary, then we have a chance to catch the killer. Otherwise we're flying blind.'

O'Neill regretted his outburst and knew Connolly was doing her best. She was sticking to her guns and he liked that. 'Sorry about that,' he said. 'What else have you got?'

Dave Conroy came in and left the files down. 'Got a minute?' he said to O'Neill.

O'Neill waved him over. 'Go on,' he said to Connolly.

'As nobody else has reported seeing Clipboard Man, he looks good for this. He is a planner, we know that from him making the phone call before the attack, and a very plausible actor, because he *got* inside the house.' She looked at Conroy and back to O'Neill. 'A woman might open the door to anyone, but bringing them inside is much more interesting indeed.' She paused. 'I think that she knew her killer, and that's why she let him in.'

Conroy spoke. 'You think she knew him, and knew that he wasn't a threat?'

'Yes. She must have known him well and felt safe in letting him in. Now that raises a question.'

This time O'Neill spoke. 'And what's that?'

'How did she know him? From where?'

There was silence in the room at the weight of her words.

O'Neill stood and paced up and down. 'So we need to find a connection, right?'

'Yes, sir,' replied Connolly, watching him closely.

He nodded. 'Clubs, groups, classes or whatever she belonged to; someone must know something. But, of course, we might be completely wrong. We don't know.'

'No, sir, we don't.'

Conroy pointed to the files on his desk. 'I've checked files for the past three years for stabbings and found five cases that might help. A pen, pencil, or something similarly pointed was used, and I'm going to contact the victims to see what they remember.'

O'Neill held his hands up. 'Go for it, Dave, we need something. And, Christine, thanks for your thoughts.'

She nodded. 'It's not much to go on …'.

'I know,' he said, 'but we must consider all the options, whatever they are. I'll tell Doyle, thanks.'

When O'Neill left the office, Paul Grant handed Connolly a list of businesses in the area that carried out surveys, including the local council. 'That's all I have,' he said.

She looked at the long list, then back at Grant, and made a face. 'No time like the present,' she said, and picked up her phone.

After more than an hour of repeating herself to no avail, she got a business that might just be able to help. 'The owner, Gerry O'Reilly, is on his way in. He's stuck in traffic, an accident or something, but he's the one to ask,' said the receptionist, a young girl by the sound of it, thought Connolly, writing the address on her pad.

'That's great, I'll be there in half an hour.'

'A result?' asked Grant.

'Could be. Some company called DropIt Deliveries in Ringsend, and they have carried out surveys, but the receptionist couldn't say when. So I'm going to see her boss.'

'You never know,' said Grant. 'You just never know.'

O'Neill came into the office and picked up his jacket. 'I just got a call from a barrister. I have to be in court this morning to give evidence about that robbery in Stillorgan last year.'

'The Post Office?' asked Brady.

'Yeah, the very one. The scumbag is banged to rights but you know how these things go. Especially when the barristers start all that flowery stuff. They can make these scumbags seem like altar boys.'

'Best of luck,' said Connolly.

'Thanks, and I'll see you all in the morning, or earlier if we get this thing finished.'

'Busy boy,' said Connolly, after O'Neill had closed the door.

Grant lifted his cup. 'The best, not one for sitting around is our Inspector. He's a doer.'

Connolly pushed her chair back. 'We need more like him. He's an interesting man.' She didn't try to hide her admiration.

'Can't stop the profiling, can you?' Brady smirked.

She pursed her lips. 'Force of habit, Detective.'

He knew there and then that she had 'profiled' all the officers on the case, and decided to leave it at that. 'In that case, we should *force* our way down to Ringsend, and drop in on DropIt Deliveries.'

Connolly shook her head. 'I don't think you're going to make it as a comedian, Detective. In fact, I know you're not, so just leave it and drive. Deal?'

'Deal it is, but I'll have to get a pool car.'

They collected the car from the car pool manager and headed for Ringsend. A flotilla of yachts, their sails rippling in the breeze, made their way across Dublin Bay. It was a postcard image with a few puffy clouds to complete the scene.

The traffic on Strand Road was light. 'This is where our Inspector runs every morning,' said Brady, tapping the window in the direction of the beach where the tide was on the way out.

'Looks like a great place to do it. Lucky man. And what do you do in the morning?' she asked, looking over at the twin towers of Poolbeg Power Station.

'I,' he started and wondered if this was some sort of loaded question. She was a profiler after all and, by her own admission, was always at work. 'I jog in Marlay Park – up in Rathfarnham most mornings. Good for my leg. At least that's what the physiotherapist says.' He ran his hand over his left thigh. 'It's beginning to feel stronger recently, so maybe in another month or so I'll be fit to play tennis in the club again.' He felt hot under the collar and decided he had said enough.

'Accident?'

Brady glanced at her and then back to the road. 'Trying to stop a scumbag escaping with a load of money stolen from a betting office. Myself and another officer gave chase in our car and when the scumbag's car crashed I got out and chased him.'

'Go on, what happened next?'

'Well, I rugby tackled him, and in doing so I smashed my leg against a lamppost. Didn't break it, but …'.

'And the thief?'

'He banged his head on the pavement and was knocked out. Hope it knocked some sense into him, but I doubt it.'

'I'm impressed, Detective. What a busy and brave bunch you are. No wonder Chief Doyle is so highly thought of in HQ with such a good team around him.'

Brady grinned. 'Thanks, and yes, we are a good team.'

They drove through Irishtown, around the sharp curve where the local library was, and turned into Thorncastle Street. He parked near the old church and the smell from the Liffey was both pungent and unpleasant. A cargo ship heading down the river blew its horn and the seagulls took to the air, screeching an angry response.

Christine Connolly pressed the bell and spoke into the intercom. She pushed the door and they stepped into a narrow hall where motes of dust floated in the streaky sunlight. Stacks of pamphlets of many different sizes lay against the wall, ready for distribution. 'Must be busy,' she said, and took the first step on a creaky staircase.

At the top of the stairs, a young girl sat on a chair polishing her nails. As Connolly thought earlier, she was probably only twenty years old, but like so many young girls, she was trying to look older. She wore a black T-shirt, tight black jeans with boots and too much black mascara that did a good job of hiding her attractive brown eyes. What a waste, she thought, and smiled at the girl.

A radio was tuned to a rock station that blasted out the Thin Lizzy favourite 'Jailbreak'. The girl reached over and killed the sound when she saw the two police officers.

'You must be the police,' she said, and glanced from Connolly to Brady, and back again.

'Yes, we spoke earlier. Is Mr O'Reilly in yet?'

'Yeah, he got here a few minutes ago. I told him you were coming.' She got out from behind her desk. 'I'll tell him you're here. Just a mo.'

Connolly and Brady could see into the room behind the receptionist's desk, stacked with more leaflets and bibs, stencilled with 'DropIt'. In the corridor leading to O'Reilly's office, piles of leaflets waited their turn to be put through an unsuspecting letterbox.

'Recession proof,' he said, raising an eyebrow.

'I wouldn't have believed it, but appearances can be deceiving,' Connolly replied, looking at the impressive work in progress.

'I didn't think that I'd ever hear you saying that,' he said, poking his head into the room with all the leaflets.

'Live and learn, that's what I say,' she replied. They could hear a man's voice on the phone at the end of the corridor. 'Gotta go,' it said. 'I've got visitors,' and he hung up.

Gerry O'Reilly waved them into his room and pointed to a pair of chairs. 'Please take a seat. Now, how I can help you?'

Surprisingly, his room was almost paper free. There was a filing cabinet and television set in one corner and a coat stand in another with a cream jacket hanging on it. O'Reilly sat behind a mahogany desk and checked out his visitors, his eyes flicking anxiously between them. His hair, dark and greying at the temples, was short, and his pink cheeks and forehead said that he'd been in the sun recently.

Connolly spoke. 'I am investigating a case and have reason to believe that the person I am interested in might have carried out a survey recently. You know, the house-to-house type of thing. And I want to know if you've done any work like that lately?'

O'Reilly was surprised and he couldn't hide it. He blew out a stream of air. 'Crikey, what a question! I thought you might be calling about something else!' He looked quickly from one to the other.

Connolly leaned forward in her chair. 'Believe me, Mr O'Reilly, I have no interest in your business other than what I've just asked. Rest assured.'

O'Reilly's shoulders relaxed. 'We don't do much survey work nowadays. Clients say it's too expensive, especially with the internet and everything. Things are very tight out there, you know.'

'You seem to be doing okay with all those leaflets and papers stacked about the place,' Brady said, instantly regretting butting in. This was Connolly's call and he told himself to shut the fuck up. So, he shut the fuck up.

'We've been lucky, I guess,' said O'Reilly, 'but it's still not easy. I need everything I can to keep the ship afloat. These days, if you don't advertise then you die. People think you're out of business and before long, that's exactly where you are. It's the old phrase of "speculate to accumulate." '

'Surveys?' said Connolly, reminding him.

'Sorry. Surveys, yes. Let me check.' He pulled over his keyboard and started to type. He made faces as he looked at the information until he found something. 'Did a survey in Kilmacud and another one in Stillorgan last year, that's all I've got. Any use?'

'Nothing in Booterstown or Blackrock?'

He shook his head. 'Not that I know of, but ...'.

His visitors were looking intently at him. 'But what?' asked Connolly.

'But ... sometimes small jobs don't always make it onto the system. Know what I mean?' he said, and his face reddened.

'As I said, Mr O'Reilly, I don't care about your off-the-books work. I take it that's what you're referring to?'

O'Reilly reached up and loosened his shirt button – he suddenly needed air to breathe. He nodded.

'Like I said, I really don't care and nothing you say will leave this room. So, what can you tell me?' Connolly was firm but fair as O'Reilly tossed a coin in his head and saw the way it fell. It was heads.

He spoke quickly, wanting this interrogation to be over. 'You'll have to speak to Dano; he's the best man to answer your questions. Kathy will give you his number. It's the best I can do.' He opened his hands, indicating that that was all he could tell her.

Brady wrote down the name. 'And who is, Dano?' asked Connolly, happy now that she had a thread to follow.

'He's my distribution manager. Well, that's what I call him anyway. Been here for four, maybe five years, and knows his way around. Most people come for a few months and disappear. And if I don't pay cash in hand then I don't have a business. You understand?'

'I understand very well.'

'Good, that's good. I can't help you any more, so I'll have Kathy get Dano's number for you.' He was a relieved man and couldn't wait for them to be off the premises. Outside, Kathy gave them the number and Connolly asked if Dano was working today.

Kathy ran a finger along a chart on the wall behind her desk. 'He's working in Sandymount today. Around the Green, Gilford Road and Park Avenue. They're doing a drop for an insurance company and a new health spa. You can't miss him,' she added.

'And why would that be?' asked Connolly.

'He's six feet tall and has long fair hair. Sometimes he wears it in a ponytail. You'll see what I mean.' A nervous giggle escaped and she stopped it with her hand.

'Thank you, Kathy, you've been a great help. Bye now.'

Back in the sunshine, Brady looked at Connolly but said nothing.

'Alright,' she said 'seeing as we are so close we might as well check him out.'

'So, off we go and see lover boy.'

Connolly laughed. 'Yes, that was obvious!'

They drove back past the library but took the right onto Tritonville Road, a sweeping left onto Sandymount Road and finally into the Green. Five roads met around the small green park that was surrounded by high railings, and where children played in the sun. A statue of W. B. Yeats, who was born only a few hundred yards away, kept silent guard on the fun and games.

The sun was high in the sky and the small houses afforded no shade as they drove.

They passed Sandymount Avenue but didn't see anybody wearing a DropIt day-glow yellow bib. Gilford Park was on the right but Brady kept on straight, eyes searching for the bright bibs. He eased around to the left and at the corner of Durham Road, Connolly shouted, 'Stop, I see something!'

Brady parked the car and they got out. There were two men with satchels, each wearing the distinctive bib, working the street on one side each.

'Let's have a word,' said Connolly.

They walked towards them past tidy gardens in front of much sought-after houses with the desired Dublin 4 address. Location, location, location, Brady thought.

Connolly recognised Dano from the description, his fair hair hanging loose, hiding the wire from his music player. He spotted her as he closed a gate and took the earphones out, dropping them into his satchel. He stopped.

'Have you been expecting me?' asked Connolly.

He smiled. 'Sure have, wondered what was keeping you.' He ran his fingers through his hair and Connolly understood why Kathy had said, 'You can't miss him.' Dano was over six feet tall, with fair hair that fell to his shoulders, and a charmer's grin. Kathy would be putty in his hand, as would a lot of other girls. She knew he was checking her out as his eyes casually looked her up and down. She was used to it by now. She offered no encouragement, certainly not while on duty. It was just part of the game.

Connolly displayed her ID and explained why they were there. 'Any surveys recently?'

He looked down and ran a hand across his mouth. 'Naw, nothing like that for ages. Not since last year at least. It's all drops now. It's cheaper.'

Connolly decided to open up a little. 'I'm looking for someone who is shorter than you with dark hair. Maybe not as long; to his collar. Mean anything?'

Dano shrugged. 'God, that could be any of a number of dudes who've worked with me. It's not much to go on, is it?'

'No, I'm afraid it's not.'

Brady leaned over to Christine. 'Clipboard.'

'Right,' she said, 'nearly forgot. When you carried out the surveys last year, did you each have a clipboard?'

'Of course,' he replied. 'I still have mine back in the office. It's in the store room.'

'Good. But what about the others, did they hand in their clipboards?'

Across the road the other man with the yellow bib stopped. 'Alright, Dano, need a hand?'

Dano turned. 'No problem, Macker, we're just talking. Go on, I'll catch you up. Okay?'

Macker took a long look before he opened the next gate and went in.

'Off the top of my head I can't tell you, it's over a year ago. In this business there's such a huge turnaround of faces. Here one day, gone the next, that's the way it goes.' He picked up his satchel and rested it on his shoulder.

'Tell me, Dano,' she said, her voice quieter, friendlier, 'why do you do it?'

He smiled genuinely. 'It pays okay and Mr O'Reilly allows me organise the work schedule. I can suit myself, pick the best routes, and then keep an eye on the others. It works. And …'.

The two police officers waited.

'… it gives me time to write.'

'You're a writer,' said Connolly, 'how interesting. What kind of stuff do you write?'

He drew his fingers through his hair and shook it loose. 'Mostly short stories, I've had a few published.'

'Wow,' she said. 'Who would have thought?'

He grinned. 'Now I'm writing a novel. Science fiction, sci-fi, you know the type? Should be finished by the end of the summer. That's the plan anyway, so wish me luck.'

'Best of luck,' said Connolly. 'I hope it works out for you.' She opened her bag, took out a business card and handed it to him. 'If you think of anything, anything at all, please contact me.'

Dano looked at the card. 'I'm playing football with a few of the guys who used to work for DropIt in Herbert Park later and

I'll ask around. It's the best I can do.' He slipped the card into his shirt pocket. 'You'll be the first to know, Detective Connolly.' He popped his earphones back in and continued on his round.

'What does the profiler think?' asked Brady, barely hiding his contempt.

'He's a handsome boy, don't you think?'

'Hmm,' he said, begrudgingly. 'His type lives on the edge of legality, always will. It's genetic.'

Connolly watched Dano as he sauntered along the path, bag hanging casually from his shoulder, lost in music. 'He's not looking for trouble, he's … just being a bit of a smartass. He's a confident sod, I'll give you that, but I don't think he's a bad sort. So I guess we'll just have to wait and see if he finds out anything.'

He started the engine. 'Fair enough, but if we hear from him, I'll buy you lunch.'

She thought about that for a moment and decided that he was probably correct. 'You're such a non-believer, aren't you?' she said, facing him. 'And I'd like a big pizza from Bits & Pizzas the day Dano calls.' She smiled at the idea as they drove past the strand, where joggers and strollers were enjoying the sunshine.

Brady wasn't sure what to say; he didn't want to get drawn into anything with this clever woman, so thought it best to keep quiet for now.

14

D ave Conroy made the short drive to Eaton Square. He parked beside the small green around which terraces of Edwardian red brick huddled close. The park was busy with adults and children enjoying the sunshine. Trees moved easily in the breeze, their leaves and sunbeams dappling the path in small abstract shapes. The salty sea-air drifted warm and cool over the school building at the bottom of the square, where a weathervane on a chimney turned slowly.

After hours spent on the telephone, Conroy had established that one of the five victims he was interested in was dead. Killed in a car accident almost two years ago. Two of the women had left Ireland and a fourth was living in Castlebar, County Mayo. She had nothing to add and started crying hysterically before slamming the phone down. So, he was left with one name, a woman just back from holiday, and who was probably not in the best mood to answer painful questions. Shit happens, he thought, and hoped that he could get something, anything, to help the case. What he was doing was a longshot, but it was a shot, nonetheless.

Conroy opened the gate and saw a curtain upstairs twitch. He wasn't surprised, and walked past a small plot of grass that was in need of cutting. A rose bush, its pink flowers open in full bloom, stood beside the porch and he sniffed a beautiful bouquet. He pressed the doorbell.

The door opened a few inches and a woman looked out. 'Yes?' she asked.

Conroy passed over his ID, which she examined closely.

'I called earlier,' he said calmly.

The woman looked closely at Dave Conroy and then at his card. A moment passed until the door opened fully and Margaret Power handed back the ID and invited him in.

The hall was narrow with a white rug on a polished wooden floor. A grandfather clock that stood beside the stairs chimed and Conroy saw his reflection in the glass front. Two travel bags lay unopened on the floor. They would have to wait; police business and old nightmares took precedent. It wasn't the way it was meant to be, but that was the way it was.

They moved to the kitchen and she pointed to a chair. Conroy sat down, placing his notebook on the farmhouse-style table.

'Like a drink?' she asked. 'I'm having one.' It sounded as though she needed it.

Conroy held his hands up, protesting. 'No, thank you, a coffee would be fine.'

'I'll put the kettle on then.' She filled it, plugged it in, and poured herself a glass of red wine. A large glass.

She opened a cupboard and took down a cup, coffee and milk from the fridge. As she did this, Conroy looked around a room that was tidy but fitted with all the necessities. Fridge, cooker, glass-fronted cupboards and the old pine farmhouse table where he was sitting. Five more matching chairs made a stylish, rustic set. A wine rack held a dozen full bottles and Conroy wondered how long they would last. Not too long if I was living here, he thought, and checked himself.

Margaret Power put his coffee on the table and sat down opposite him. She took a long sip of her wine and folded her arms. 'So what do you want to know?' Her tone was friendly, but wary.

'I'm not sure.'

Her eyes narrowed, confused.

'I'm involved in a case that I think has some similarities to yours. A woman called Barbara Ryan was murdered a few days ago, in Booterstown. Did you know that?'

'No, no I didn't. As you can see I've just come home – how could I?'

'Of course, but I had to ask.' He paused and looked at his notes. 'Her case and yours may not be connected, of course, but I have to check this out. You understand?'

She nodded.

'So, your attacker, is there anything that you can remember about him? I'm sorry to reopen an old wound, but it might be important.'

The face that looked back at him couldn't hide the pain that was lurking just behind her eyes. The Spanish holiday had left its mark with a healthy suntan on her face and arms, and her blonde hair was bleached almost white. She was a picture of health, but her eyes couldn't hide her nervousness.

She closed her eyes and took a deep breath, composing herself. 'It was horrible, really horrible, and I try not to think about it. He nearly killed me, you know. I was very lucky, Detective.'

Conroy nodded. 'I know, I've read the file.' There was nothing to add.

'A file, what does that say about the horror of it all? You can't quantify that, can you?' She spat the words out and shivered at the ugly memory.

Conroy said nothing, but he watched her closely.

'Nothing, that's what it says. Absolutely nothing.' She held up a hand. 'Sorry, sorry, it's not your fault, Detective, but it can still be very raw. Alright?'

'I'm sure it's difficult … please take your time.'

Margaret Power put her chin on her chest and closed her eyes again. Thinking about that night, the night things changed, was painful, and Conroy saw her wince. He'd interviewed victims before and every time it was different. Some of them, who had put it behind them and moved on with their lives, spoke in the third person; distancing themselves from the event, as if somehow it hadn't happened to them. It was their way of coping and who was he to judge them? They had survived and that was what mattered.

For others it was an every day thing.

In the garden beyond, Conroy saw the trees sway to a gentle rhythm, their leaves bathed in the sunshine, as Margaret Power relived her horror. The fear lived deep, a cancer of the mind that only time and love could hope to cure. The ripples of that night just kept on rolling, a sick, perverted tide that brought only pain and tears.

She looked up, her eyes glazed, close to more tears. 'He called me a slut.' She sighed.

'A slut,' echoed Conroy, and wrote the word.

'Yeah, I remember that bit. "A slut, you're all the same," he kept shouting. It was insane.' She buried her face in her hands.

The room was silent.

Conroy took a sip of coffee and wrote slowly, thinking. 'And his voice, what was that like?' he asked.

'Normal, I guess. From Dublin definitely, but …'.

Conroy tapped the pen against his lip watching her all the time. She was a beautiful woman and he was at a loss, a complete and utter loss, to understand *why* someone attacked her. *Why*: such a small word that asked such big questions.

'Do you remember anything else about him, anything at all? Do you think that he was taller than you?'

She took a sip of wine and swirled the glass slowly. 'Yes, a little, and I also remember thinking that he smelled like an old boyfriend.'

Conroy raised an eyebrow, not daring to probe.

Margaret Power saw the look on his face and sniffed. 'What I mean is that he used to smoke those strong-smelling French cigarettes. That's the smell I remember.' She drank some more wine and put the glass on the table. 'That's it, Detective, that's all I can tell you.' She pulled back the collar of her blouse and rested a finger on a small scar. 'That's what the bastard left me, Detective. Another inch and I might not be talking to you.'

Conroy made another note and then looked across the table. 'You've been very helpful.' He paused. 'I am very sorry that you had to go through it all again.'

Margaret Power rose. 'If it helps put the bastard away then I'd do this every day, Detective. Believe me.'

He believed her and now saw the fight in her eyes. 'Fool me once, but not any more,' they seemed to say, and that was good.

He said goodbye and walked down the path. He stopped and turned. 'Thanks again, and I'll let you know what happens.'

Margaret Power was watching him closely. 'Nobody did the last time.'

'Last time?'

'Yes, last time,' she said firmly. 'Nobody bothered to get back to me then.' The door closed before he could reply, and Margaret Power was alone again with bags to unpack and painful memories to overcome.

Connolly was updating the board when Conroy arrived back. He told her about his meeting with Margaret Power and his observations. More names and words, but there was still no connections. Nothing. No change. It was as if Barbara Ryan's murder was just another random act of violence, and her killer was in the wind. Gone.

15

He was ready.

He knew it, could feel it ... he could almost taste it. He felt a shiver of excitement tingle down his spine. He opened his eyes and looked in the mirror.

Taste blood. Wow, he hadn't thought of that before. That would be different ... really different.

He allowed the curl on his lip to grow and he knew what he was going to do. It had been a week since he had done Barbara Ryan and the urge to act again had grown steadily. He could not deny it. He did not want to deny it. Things had changed. He had changed. He was different now ... stronger. Stronger like he'd never known. Since he'd crossed that murderous line he walked taller. Now he was the keeper of the most secret of secrets. As he went about and passed people in the street, he knew that none of them had the slightest idea that he was — and had become — a killer. He had risen above them all, and now he looked down upon the little people as they scampered and jostled, going nowhere. He had grown and tonight he would grow even stronger. There was no stopping him, and he felt his lip curl a little more.

She looked at him, smiling, unaware of what was to come. He touched her picture and felt a delicious tingle in his groin. Mmm, yeah, this was going to be nice, real nice.

He thought about her now and the anger increased. His breathing quickened but he took a few deep breaths to slow everything down.

'Control, stay in control – it's everything. You can do it, you must do it, you will do it – you were meant to do it.

★

He zipped up his black leather jacket, pulled on his helmet and closed the door. The roads were quiet as he cruised through Blackrock and turned left onto Mount Merrion Avenue, cranked the accelerator and zoomed up the long hill. He swung right on to Stillorgan Road and soon turned into the college campus at Belfield. He had made this trip many times and knew the layout intimately. He drove past the empty security gate, put out the headlight and moved quietly up the small rise past the trees and car park on his left. He was watching all the time but nobody was about. He parked the motorbike against a tall bush where it was almost invisible, and listened. He heard nothing.

He slipped his helmet off and laid it on the motorbike's seat. The only sound he heard was the traffic on the main road that was now bathed in an orange-coloured, tungsten glow.

He scanned the glass buildings above him and saw only a few lights on. It was summer time and most of the college staff were away on holidays, except for a few academics putting in some hard-earned research. She would be coming from the Science Block on the other side of the lake, soon. He felt the excitement rise. He checked his watch and slowly, carefully, made his way past the research centre, and stopped. He saw her car, parked where he expected it to be, and slipped a small hammer from his jacket. He tapped the ground with it. He was ready.

He was crouching behind a small copse of bushes when he heard her footsteps climbing the incline to the car park. He stood up slowly, looked around, and saw that she was alone. It was time.

He let her walk past before he swung the hammer, hitting her on the top of the head. He was drawing the hammer back again when she buckled and fell heavily to her knees, her whimper almost unheard. He hit her again and felt her blood splatter on his face. He could taste her. He was wild, feral, as he swung and hit her again. She moaned her last desperate breath. 'You're all the fucking same,' he hissed into her ear and savagely jabbed a pencil into her neck. He was kneeling on her when she let out a final bloody wheeze and went limp.

He stayed there for a few seconds, tore the chain from her neck, and wiped his lip with the back of his hand. He could still taste her blood. He wanted to scream in exultation but stopped himself just in time. He was breathing hard, but he was in control. It felt great, better than before. He got even, just like he said, and she would never forget. He was a man who kept his word and soon they would all understand.

He rolled her body behind the copse, all the time listening intently. He heard nothing. Minutes later he put on his helmet, let the motorbike coast down the incline, slipped it into gear at the roundabout, and headed into the night.

16

He poured the last drop of wine into his glass and sat back. He had been thinking about the case for hours and he had a pain in his head. Across the room, Tiger, Liz's cat, watched him. She had loved the cat and after she was gone it was a little reminder of her. 'So, what do you think, Tiger? Any ideas? Because I've none.'

The cat moved its head sideways and then headed to the kitchen.

'I know, I know. You want some food.' He followed, finishing his wine and put some food down for the cat. 'Right, I'm off to bed. See you in the morning … maybe.'

In his bedroom he stripped off and got into bed. His mind was still alive with ideas and they wouldn't stop. 'Please, let me sleep, please …'.

★

The sand squeezed between his toes, its heat ticklish and pleasurable. His sandals swung in his hand and the warm breeze filled his shirt. His other hand was around Liz's waist and strands of her long dark hair flew, brushing against his face. He was smiling as they walked along the beach at Biarritz, the heavy rolling surf a noisy soundtrack.

He started humming.

'What did you say?' Liz asked.

' "On the Beach," ' he said. 'It's a song by Chris Rea.'

'*I know it. It's a favourite of mine.*'

He stopped and pulled her close, their noses almost touching. Her eyes were wide and smiling and the corners of her mouth turned up in a slow smile. 'And you're my favourite. Always will be.' They kissed and Danny hoped that this moment would never end. He was happier than he had ever been, and held her tight.

Liz broke the kiss. 'Easy tiger,' she said playfully, smiling broadly. She touched his face gently, her fingers moving from his cheek to his lips. 'Later,' she said, and kissed him quickly on his nose.

'*I love you,*' *he said.*

She flicked her hair away from her face. 'I know, and I'm a very lucky girl!'

He squeezed her again and she laughed out loud. 'Later, baby,' she said again. 'Later.'

They walked on, hand-in-hand, their fingers entwined the way their bodies had been earlier that morning, and the way they would be later.

He started humming again and Liz leaned her head on his shoulder. 'I wonder if Chris Rea ever felt this good?' Danny said.

Liz shook her head slowly and squeezed his hand. 'I hope so, I really hope so.'

They continued along the beach; their matching footprints imprinted in the warm yielding sand. He was lost in the rhythm and felt his chest rise and fall in easy response.

The rhythm continued but seemed to be louder. How could that be? he asked himself, opening his eyes. The room was dark, the glow of the clock radio's dial the only light. The time was 1:47a.m.

Liz was gone, in an instant, and he realised that he had been dreaming. It was painful, as he could still smell her scent and feel her touch. He let out a long sigh and the pain of her loss brought a tear to his eye. God, how he missed her.

His mobile phone continued to trill.

He reached over and picked it up. 'Yeah,' he gasped and pushed himself up against a pillow. His mind was buzzing; he closed his eyes, waiting for the bad news. Good news didn't come at this hour.

'Sir, looks like he's done it again,' said Dave Conroy, doing his best to stay calm.

O'Neill closed his eyes. 'Fuck.'

'Sir.'

'Sorry, Dave, talk to me.' He sat up and swung his legs over the side of the bed.

Conroy spoke clearly. 'A security guard doing his rounds in Belfield found the body of a woman. I'm at the scene and it looks as though she has a pencil stuck in her neck.'

O'Neill sat on the edge of his bed and looked down at his bare feet. He scratched his head and let it drop onto his chest. 'Okay. Get a car to pick me up in thirty minutes. I just need to stick my head in the shower. What about O'Connell's men?'

'I've already contacted them, sir. O'Connell's on his way.'

'Good work, see you in a bit.' He looked in the mirror before stepping under the shower and saw dark patches below his eyes. He looked and felt exhausted and realised that he had just swapped one nightmare for another. Is there no escape? he thought, and stood under the steaming-hot water, trying to forget everything, if only for a few minutes.

The bright lights were the first thing that O'Neill noticed as the police car passed the security gate. They cut a hole in the darkness, giving the place an eerie feel. Here we go again, he said to himself, and stepped out.

O'Connell's men had already arrived and set up their bright halogen lights on tall metal stands. They flooded the car park where their Forensics Unit van was parked beside the only car in sight. Two young policemen were unrolling yellow crime scene tape from the branches of surrounding trees, cordoning off the area. As he looked up at the glass buildings beyond, O'Neill saw that they were all in darkness.

The Forensics Unit had already set up a white tent over the scene, and O'Connell and Conroy were standing a few feet away when O'Neill approached.

'Well, what have you got?' he asked.

Conroy glanced at O'Connell and then turned to his boss. 'Angie Murphy, aged thirty-one, was a lecturer in chemistry. She's had her head bashed in and there's a pencil stuck in her neck. Almost the same as Barbara Ryan.'

O'Connell nodded in agreement.

Christ, thought O'Neill, a serial killer in Dublin. It's madness, absolute bloody madness. This sort of thing never happens in Ireland, let alone Dublin. Sure, gangsters shot and killed each other, but at least that was between them: fighting over territory, drugs and whatever, but not killing defenceless women. No, this was different and he suddenly felt out of his depth. It was a scary feeling. Even with all his experience of murders over the last ten years, he knew that this was different. Completely different, but he had to show leadership – that's what he was good at, and what Joe Dixon would expect. 'Show me,' he said, and the three men headed into the tent where O'Connell's men were working the scene. One was taking photographs, another was using a video camera, while two others were on their knees searching for clues. A white marker had been placed on a patch of clay beside the tent. 'What's that?' he asked.

The technician looked up. 'Looks like a footprint, possibly from a boot, so I'm going to take a cast of it.' He looked up to O'Connell, who nodded for him to continue.

O'Connell pulled the tent flap open to reveal the broken and bloodied body. It lay face down, and the left arm was propped against the hedge. Her hair was almost entirely covered with blood that glistened sickly under the strong light.

O'Neill bent down and saw the pencil sticking out from below her chin and knew without doubt that he was after a serial killer. It was hard to take in. Thankfully, the victim's eyes were closed and he wondered just who it was he was after. He thought about Helen Murray and how he had let her down. He told himself that this time he would get the bastard. It wasn't that he wanted to catch the killer; he needed to. Like nothing before, this was his chance at redemption, and in a perverse, fucked-up sort of way, he was grimly satisfied at the thought of being able to prove himself.

He turned to O'Connell. 'Right, Gary, I can leave this in your capable hands. Call me in the morning with your findings. Everyone will want to know about this one, okay?'

O'Connell's eyes had seen the grisliest of murder scenes, but now they looked sad, and O'Neill couldn't blame him. 'He's one sick fucker whoever he is,' he said angrily. 'I hope you get him before my guys do, Danny.'

O'Neill nodded agreement and thanked him with a thin smile. 'I know you'll do your best.'

Dave Conroy spoke. 'The campus administrator is on his way. I'll speak to him when he arrives.' He pointed to the security camera outside the bank. 'We may get something on the CCTV camera, so I've also contacted the bank manager.'

O'Neill looked around the car park and the darkness beyond. 'Any idea of time of death, Gary?'

'No, but we will when Shelly Tobin gets here.'

The mention of her name made O'Neill turn to face O'Connell. 'Good, and make sure that she contacts me first thing.' He looked around again, taking in the silence. 'Looks like our man knew what he was doing.'

Conroy and O'Connell looked at him, and waited.

He drew his hand across his face. 'He attacks late at night when it's dark, and in a very quiet place. Apart from the traffic down on the main road this place is completely secluded. It's perfect for an attack.' He looked about the car park and the tall bushes that surrounded it. 'This is not a random killing. No, this took some planning. Our guy knew about her movements, right down to her working late tonight.' He rubbed his chin, deep in thought. 'It wasn't about getting lucky, he must have stalked this woman.' He looked at the two men who were following his every word. 'Now that's worrying.'

'Very fucking worrying,' added Conroy, the words falling involuntarily from his lips.

All three men were silent, the hissing of the camera flashes disturbing their thoughts.

'I'll call Doyle now and I'll see you in the morning, Dave. You can take care of things here, okay.' It wasn't a question.

'Will do, sir.'

'I know, Dave.' He turned to Gary O'Connell. 'And we'll speak early, okay?

'As soon as ...' he replied, and went back into the tent.

O'Neill phoned Doyle to give him the bad news, and his first thoughts on who might be responsible. He had never heard Doyle swear before and was surprised when he did. 'Thanks for the call, Danny. I'm going to inform HQ. I'll see you and the team first thing in the morning. Goodnight.'

O'Neill then realised that he had another call to make, and dialled.

A sleepy, surprised voice answered. 'Yes …'.

'Mr Ryan, this is Inspector O'Neill, and I need to know where your brother is.'

'What? Do you know what time it is?'

'Where is David, is he at your house? I need to know now, so please tell me if he's there.'

Christopher Ryan exhaled loudly and O'Neill knew he was on the move, heading to check on David.

Moments later he spoke. 'He's in bed, Inspector. He's fast asleep.'

O'Neill pursed his lips. 'Okay, that's fine. And he's been there for hours?'

'Yes, of course. I called my doctor and asked him to drop by and give David some sleeping pills. He's been out since around ten o'clock. What is this about, Inspector?'

O'Neill took a deep breath. 'I'll see you in a few minutes, Mr Ryan. I'll tell you then.'

The police car with it's siren blaring headed down Stillorgan Road, as cars moved over and gave way. There was little traffic and O'Neill was running up the granite steps of the house in less than five minutes. A bedraggled Christopher Ryan opened the door and led him to where his brother was sleeping. He shook David and shouted at him but he was unconscious. He managed to groan a few times, and went to sleep again.

'What is this about, Inspector? I demand to know.' Christopher Ryan was standing with his hands in the air, demanding an answer. His eyes, now wide open, were boring into O'Neill.

O'Neill kept looking at David Ryan as his chest fell and rose in steady rhythm. He was definitely asleep, probably nearer to being unconscious, and O'Neill would talk with the doctor later. He turned to Christopher Ryan. 'I have just come from another murder scene, Mr Ryan, and the victim also had a pencil in her neck, like Barbara.' He let Ryan think about that for a few seconds. 'And, although I believe in many things, I don't believe in coincidence. Too flaky, too loose – however you want describe it. I believe in facts, Mr Ryan, it's all there is.' He looked down at David. 'In cases of murder, especially in the home, we always look at the family first.'

Ryan didn't say anything, but he was listening intently.

'So when I find a second victim with a pencil stuck in her neck I want to know where your brother is. Understand?'

Ryan closed his eyes for a moment. 'Yes, Inspector, I understand. And all I can say is that David has been here all night. The doctor gave him a shot of something to make him sleep, and you see it worked.' They both looked at David who hadn't moved a muscle.

O'Neill went downstairs with Ryan close behind. 'I'll want to speak with the doctor, Mr Ryan, so can I have his number, please?'

Ryan gave him the number. 'I am very sorry, Inspector, to hear about the other murder. It's almost impossible to believe. It's …'.

'… not a coincidence, Mr Ryan, but my case just became even more serious, if you can imagine that.'

Ryan didn't answer and O'Neill went down the steps as the door closed behind him.

So much for Brady's line about the husband being the killer. He was back to square one. Shit.

It was almost three in the morning now and there was a chill in the air. Although it was early June, it seemed particularly unseasonable and O'Neill shivered as he got into the waiting police car. He went home, fell into bed and hoped that the demons would leave him alone. They did, but not for long.

17

All the phones in the Detectives' Room were ringing. The media vultures were up early and snapping for information when O'Neill took off his jacket and draped it on the back of his chair, just after eight o'clock. The weather forecaster on the breakfast TV news had said that it was 'going to be a sticky one today'. He couldn't help but grin at the man's ironic words when he looked around the noisy, stressed office.

Dave Conroy had the look of a man who had had too little sleep. His skin was paler now than last week and his hair, although combed, was hanging untidily. He was wearing the same shirt that he had on last night and O'Neill didn't blame him one little bit. It came with the territory and he certainly wasn't going to give his assistant a hard time. He would pull his leg about it later and leave it at that.

At the board, Pat Brady studied the names and details collected so far and wrote something into a notepad. A few more details had been collected and now, sadly, another victim would be added. This really was the last place that you wanted your name to appear. There would be no privacy any more; the intrusion was just another part of the sick drama.

O'Neill waved Brady over. 'For your information, I went from the crime scene directly to Christopher Ryan's house.'

'Oh, yeah?'

'And David was in bed, and had been for most of the evening. The doctor had given him a dose of something that knocked him out. He was unconscious when I went into his room. So he didn't kill the lecturer and he certainly didn't kill his wife, because the same guy has killed both women. The husband did not do it,' O'Neill said, looking Brady straight in the eye.

Brady stuck out his chin and made a face. 'I guess I was wrong. I'm sorry, Danny, you were right.'

O'Neill didn't break his look. 'Thanks, but it doesn't get us any closer to the scumbag who did. We've lots to do, Pat, and your input is always welcome.'

'You got it, Danny, always have.'

'In that case, catch me a killer.'

Brady shook his head. 'Yeah, no problem. And, by the way, I left a message for Ann Lawlor. And I also asked the police in Baltimore to knock on her door – just so she gets the message.'

'Redundant, I think, Pat, but follow it up and then cross it off – it's procedure.'

Brady would do exactly that.

The phones kept ringing and callers were told the same thing – no, there is no connection between the two murders, and yes, a news conference was planned for 4 p.m. Everything would be made clear then, and the press should not be jumping to any *crazy* conclusions. It didn't do the public any good, although that was never a concern of the newspaper editors. A story is a story and that was all that the newspapers wanted. If they jumped to conclusions they were only expressing 'what the people thought' and would worry about consequences later. Much later.

For the police, investigating the families who were living with the horrific, ill-informed and sensational news was the last thing they needed. But the media didn't always *do* responsibility, as O'Neill and anyone above the age of ten knew. He and his team had to keep a lid on things for as long as possible, otherwise the investigation could be damaged. And if this in some way alerted the killer, then it was anyone's guess as to where that might lead.

Christine Connolly replaced her phone and picked it up immediately when the ringing started again. She looked around and saw O'Neill looking over at her. She shrugged her shoulders in a 'this is madness' sort of way, and started to write on her notepad.

Paul Grant, too, was on the phone when O'Neill went to see Doyle. He knocked and received a gruff 'come in' in reply.

The boss looked off. His hair wasn't as neatly parted as usual and his tie hung off-centre. His desk was in disarray, with letters and files scattered untidily over the surface. The mess seemed to explain Doyle's distress.

When he thought about it, he wasn't as surprised by the latest killing as Doyle must be. He was closer to the action, but Doyle still had to run the shop and deal with the PR. An investigation like this was a new experience for everyone, and particularly dangerous for Doyle – especially career-wise. The media were now interested in the case, looking for an angle, and knowledge of the pencil would be sensational. It had to be kept secret for as long as possible, but with a case like this he knew people would be tempted to talk. It would not be the first time it happened and it certainly wouldn't be the last. It would be just another hurdle to overcome.

Doyle put his pen down and indicated for O'Neill to sit. He pulled up a chair and sat down opposite. Neither of them had slept much lately. Welcome to the club, thought O'Neill, straightening his tie.

'Well, the shit really has hit the fan, Danny. The boys in The Park are taking an even closer interest now after another pencil was found.' He shook his head in disbelief.

Through the open window a ship's hooter went off and caught Doyle's attention.

'Just as well Christine Connolly showed up, sir,' said O'Neill. 'She must have known something.'

Doyle managed a wry smile. 'Should be glad for that, I suppose.'

'Yes, sir. Now it doesn't seem like such a bad idea after all. Inspired, maybe,' added O'Neill evenly. He meant it. The profiler who had spent time in the FBI's training centre was a welcome addition. A few days ago he would not have thought that, but things change.

Doyle put his elbows on the desk. 'The bigwigs in The Park are nervous about the pencil detail getting out. So, first thing to do is make sure that this information stays inside the station. Inside the Detectives' Room.'

O'Neill nodded.

'We'll have a press conference at 4p.m. so get your information ready. I'll open the show and you will detail the findings to date, excluding the pencil detail, of course. We can hand out a description of Clipboard Man and maybe a sketch of him if we can get one done. That always throws the media off balance and reduces the number of questions. Are you okay with that?'

'Yes, sir, not a problem. I'm calling a meeting for ten o'clock and we will review everything we have and what we need to do next.' He knew Doyle was studying him and wondering how he was coping. He knew Doyle was thinking about Helen Murray, about Liz, about their effect on him, about whether he was suitable for the job. He also knew that, right now, he was the best man for the job, and hoped Doyle would let him get on with it.

'Good stuff, Danny. I'll drop in, thanks.'

The office was busy with phones constantly ringing. Things were really getting crazy, but he would not allow them to get out of control.

'Right people, listen up.' The talk stopped immediately and Christine Connolly placed her hand over the phone's mouthpiece. 'We all know that what we are dealing with is very serious. It's like nothing we've had to deal with before, so I want, *need*, everybody to know where we're at. We'll have a team meeting in thirty minutes, so if you have something to do, you'd better do it now. Thanks.'

O'Neill checked his emails and then went to the restaurant for a much needed coffee. He had a feeling he would need his wits about him.

★

Brady closed the windows and turned the fans to full speed. O'Neill stood in front of the board, facing a sea of anxious faces. Sergeant O'Connor stood against the wall at the back, alongside the uniformed officers who looked nervous. Last night's murder had lifted the case to a new level and everyone knew that they would be under the spotlight like never before. None of them, except maybe Christine Connolly, had any experience of these matters, and they looked to O'Neill for leadership. 'Grace under pressure,' was what Dixon would have expected, and he was determined to show the troops that he could handle it. 'Firstly, Dave, can you bring us up to date on last night's events, please?'

Dave Conroy's top shirt button was open and his tie hung at an angle. He still looked tired but O'Neill wanted him to give a firsthand account. It was always better that way.

'The woman murdered in Belfield last night was Angie Murphy; single, thirty-one years old and a lecturer in chemistry in the university. Yes, I know someone is going to ask "Why was she there, is the college not closed for holidays?" And the answer is, yes it is closed, but she was working on a technical paper she was planning to present at a scientific conference in Paris next month.' He paused and looked around the room – he had everybody's undivided attention. 'Angie Murphy was a very intelligent young woman with a bright future. She had already been invited to spend next year at a college in California, lecturing and working in her specialist area. Her death is a blow not only to her family and friends, but to a wider audience. It's a sad loss indeed.'

He showed who Angie Murphy was and brought her closer to the team. Although they would never know her beyond the case in hand, she wasn't a mere statistic, but a person who deserved their respect. He turned and pointed at a photo that he had earlier stuck on the board. 'This is Angie Murphy and you can see that she was also, like Barbara Ryan, a very good-looking woman.' The photo showed a smiling blonde woman, her eyes alive in response to something funny that the photographer had just said.

'Here's the really interesting bit,' he continued, and wrote beside the photo. 'She lived on Woodbine Avenue.'

He stopped and looked around, a quizzical frown on his brow.

Brady was the first to speak. 'And where exactly is Woodbine Avenue? That *is* the point you're making, right?'

'Yes, it's the very point I'm making, Pat. Because, surprise, surprise, Angie Murphy lived about 300 yards from Barbara Ryan's house.'

The silence was deafening.

The implication of his words was not lost on his audience. He continued. 'Now, we have a lot to do. One: we have to check out what was happening in Angie Murphy's life before she was murdered. Two: we need to see if there is any place where she and Barbara Ryan may have met. A book club, tennis club, library, I don't know, but somewhere they crossed paths with the killer. And three: the fact that both women were murdered by a pencil, shows that we are most definitely looking for the same attacker. Much as it hurts me to say it, we are looking for a serial killer.' The last two words made everyone look at the board and the two photos. How many more names would be added before the case was over?

O'Neill stepped forward again. 'Thanks, Dave, that was excellent.' He turned to the board and then back to the team. 'So what we need to do, as Dave mentioned, is to find out everything about Angie Murphy and see what, if anything, ties her and Barbara Ryan together. Something must, due to the proximity of their homes; but experience tells me that it will not be that easy to establish a connection. We will need to carry out more house-to-house questioning, so make sure to keep an open mind. Even the smallest thing, the smallest piece of information might be a game changer. Don't rush it – we don't want to go back over the work, but time is precious.'

He turned to Grant. 'I want you to do a similar exercise as you did on Barbara Ryan's mobile phone and landline. And her computer, too.'

'And her phone at work?'

'Of course,' said O'Neill, appreciating Grant's sharpness.

Doyle spoke and all heads turned to him. 'You'll be happy to know that we will be getting some help, Danny. Another six uniformed officers will be arriving this morning and they have been assigned for the duration.'

That was great news; O'Neill was delighted.

Doyle continued. 'Police cars have been instructed to be on the lookout in the area and to carry out random roadblocks. If our man is driving around, stalking or whatever, then this might put the wind up him, knock him off balance – maybe he'll make a mistake. Whatever it takes we'll do it. Carry on, Danny, I'll talk with you later.'

He left the meeting wondering what the following days would bring. It was going to be a difficult time and he needed to be at his best. If he was honest he would have preferred to be at sea, sailing to Wexford, or if the weather was suitable, over to Cornwall where some friends had a house. But it was what it was, and he knew deep down that many of his colleagues would like to be in his position. To lead a case like this, to catch Dublin's first serial killer, was a career defining opportunity and a big boost in future promotion stakes. He would not be forgotten, and a significant move up the ladder was assured if he performed well. He thought about all this but let the idea slip away. His task was stopping a maniac who was out there killing innocent women, that's what mattered most.

O'Neill called Conroy aside. 'How are you today? You look tired.' He had done well with his report to the team but O'Neill could see he was tired. He remembered being in Conroy's position years before and didn't want him to burn out. That was no good to anyone, and certainly not to the team who needed everybody to be present and correct.

There was no point in lying. 'I'm tired. Didn't get to bed until after five o'clock. But hey, I'm only tired, not dead.'

O'Neill nodded. 'Thanks, that was good earlier.' He meant it: Conroy had condensed all the details of the two cases into something short and clear. It was a good sign and he was impressed. 'Right, I'd like you to come with me and we'll check out Murphy's house and see what we can find. After that you can go home early. You look as though you need it.'

Conroy grinned. 'Thanks. A few hours of solid sleep would do the world of good.'

'I'll call O'Connell and Shelly Tobin and then we're off.' O'Neill spoke with Shelly first. She was about to do an autopsy, but her preliminary finding was that Angie Murphy had been beaten about the head, and that the pen stabbing was probably done after death. 'What makes you say that?'

'From the blood splatter we found at the scene and where it landed. If she had been stabbed like Barbara Ryan, the blood would have sprayed high and wide, and neither I nor Forensics found any evidence of that.' She paused and he could imagine her in her green overalls, thinking. 'His attack this time was more ferocious and directed, and the blows to the head were so fierce that they probably killed her almost immediately. It was brutal … he wasn't taking any chances this time.'

Those words sent a chill down the line that O'Neill couldn't escape. The killer had refined his attack method and had allowed for no margin of error. He was getting better, if that was the right word, and Angie Murphy never had a chance.

'And the pencil, what can you tell me about that?'

He heard her shuffling papers.

'Well, it's the same style as was used to kill Barbara Ryan.'

'Wow.'

'And here's the thing,' she said, and paused for a moment. 'I checked out the pencils and you're not going to believe this but …'.

'But what?' O'Neill snapped.

' … this style of pencil has been off the market for years. Nearly thirteen according to the manufacturer.'

O'Neill made notes of what Shelly Tobin told him. 'So what do you think this means?' he said, thinking aloud.

'I don't know, Danny, but the killer has a stash of old pencils. Seems odd, but then people do collect all sorts, don't they?'

'Hmm, they sure do,' he said, and looked into the distance, his mind wandering, looking for a link.

'Danny,' said Shelly, 'are you still there?'

'Yes, Shelly, I'm here,' he replied. 'I'm thinking, wondering … hell, I don't know what I'm thinking.'

'Danny,' she said, concern in her voice.

'Thanks, Shelly, thanks for that. It's just that I've never had to deal with anything quite like this before.'

'None of us have, Danny.'

'I know, but it doesn't make it any easier.'

'I know it doesn't, but if anyone is going to solve this case then it's going to be you.'

He closed his eyes and let the words dance around inside his head. 'Thanks, Shelly, it's very good of you to say so. I needed that and it's nice to know that someone has confidence in me.'

She almost laughed. 'God, if anyone in that station has confidence, it's you. And Doyle certainly knows it, otherwise you wouldn't be leading the investigation.'

He didn't tell her about the other officers who were on leave and how the case dropped into his lap. Or about how he was questioning himself and wondering if could still do it.

'I hear what you're saying and thanks again.' Around him phones were ringing. 'And let me have your final report as soon as possible, won't you?'

'It'll be with you after lunch,' she said clearly. 'Now, allow me do my work. Bye.'

He hung up and called Gary O'Connell. His observations were just as Shelly Tobin had said, and his men were now examining Angie Murphy's car and office. He would send on his report by the end of the day.

'Thanks, Gary, keep in touch.'

The sun was high in the sky as O'Neill and Conroy left the station and drove to see Angie Murphy's father. Another life ruined, thought O'Neill, and he could feel a sickness in the pit of his stomach. Two families had been left utterly devastated. He wondered when it was going to end. Sunbeams bounced playfully on the windscreen and bonnet, oblivious to the dark thoughts that were haunting the driver.

18

The news on the radio was bad; the local station carried Angie Murphy's killing as its lead item. 'And yet another killing in South Dublin,' said the presenter. 'What is the place coming to? It's getting more like Los Angeles everyday. Okay, caller, what did you want to say?'

'I want to know what the police are doing about all this crime. I mean, if it's not safe for a woman to be in her own home or walking from work, then we may as well give up. It's madness, sheer bloody madness,' said the woman angrily.

'I don't know what the police are doing, but you're not the first caller to ask that question, and I'm sure you won't be the last. Our reporter will be at the police press conference later on, so maybe we'll know more. Thank you for ringing in and now …'.

O'Neill turned off the radio and slapped the steering wheel hard. 'What the fuck do they think we are, magicians?' He shook his head. 'Fuck, we might as well be sitting on our arses as far as they are concerned.'

'Not much sympathy out there for us,' said Conroy.

'Hmm, sympathy would be a fine thing.'

'Everyone is spooked, and lashing out. It's to be expected … but not exactly appreciated,' Conroy added calmly.

O'Neill slowed the car. 'You're right, but it just doesn't help, does it? Here we are chasing a killer, a fucking serial killer, can you believe it, and all we're getting is *grief*.' He shook his head again. 'We're not the enemy, Dave, but listening to this shit, you wouldn't be too sure.' The traffic lights changed to green and they drove on in silence.

Joseph Murphy was red-eyed when he opened the door to the two policemen. His hair was uncombed and his shirt was creased. He probably hadn't slept since Conroy brought him the sad news, and it took Murphy a few moments before he recognised him. He left the door open and they followed him into the kitchen.

He sat down and took a sip of tea. 'There's some in the pot,' he said, pointing to the stove.

'We've just had some, thanks,' O'Neill lied and sat down.

Time seemed to have stood still in the kitchen and it reminded him of home, years ago. The gingham tablecloth, gas cooker and the noticeable absence of a wine rack caught his attention straight away. A small fridge was in the corner, piled high with a mountain of old newspapers. He's obviously well informed, thought O'Neill, taking in the tired eyes across the table. Joseph Murphy must have been in his late sixties at least, when he considered Angie's age. Maybe she was the last child. He'd soon find out.

He leaned on the table and watched Murphy, wondering, just for a moment, what the man was going through.

'I'm very sorry for your loss, Mr Murphy, really very sorry indeed. Your daughter was a beautiful woman, and I cannot imagine the pain of your loss. I will not stop in my efforts to catch the killer, but I need you to help me. You understand?'

Murphy's sad eyes met his and he hated looking into those damaged, old eyes. Life wasn't always fair, everybody knew that, but sitting in this kitchen O'Neill knew that the old man had got a real kicking.

Conroy leaned against the sink, out of Murphy's eye-line, pen at the ready. O'Neill said a silent prayer and hoped that Murphy would not start crying. It was understandable, but he needed answers. 'Can you please tell me when you last saw or spoke to Angie?'

Murphy slowly and carefully put his cup down and took a deep breath. He was trying to keep it together and both policemen silently willed him to be strong. He coughed nervously and wiped his mouth with a hankie. 'Yesterday, when she came home for dinner. I made lasagne, her favourite.' He held his hands tightly and moved his fingers back and forth.

'And what time was that?'

'Five o'clock, we always ate at five.'

'Just the two of you?'

Murphy nodded. 'Yes, there's only the two of us, Inspector. My wife died many years ago, and I raised Angie pretty much on my own.'

O'Neill said nothing, letting Murphy find the next words.

'My wife and I were married late in life and Angie was our only child. We doted on her and now ...'. He took another deep breath. 'I'm on my own.' He shook his head and looked up. 'What am I going to do now, Inspector, what am I going to do? Tell me.'

O'Neill let the uncomfortable silence hang there for a few moments. 'I don't know, but, as I said, we are doing everything to catch the person responsible for Angie's death. She deserves it, and God knows you do, too.'

Murphy bit his lip and exhaled loudly. 'Thank you, Inspector.' He took another sip and sat up, his eyes clearing. 'I'm not sure if I can help, Inspector, but please ask whatever questions you must.'

O'Neill smiled gently, acknowledging the man's effort. 'Good, so can you tell me if you have any idea why this happened? Did Angie have any enemies?'

Murphy could hardly believe the question. 'Inspector, my daughter was a lovely girl with not an enemy in the world. And no, she had no steady boyfriend. She did a few years ago, but she's been so absorbed with her work that she has no time for boyfriends. I used to rib her about it, but she would just laugh it off and say that she had time on her side.' He shrugged. 'Time on her side.'

After the questions, the policemen had a look around Angie's bedroom, but didn't find anything useful to the case. The room was tidy, with shelves crammed with books and a laptop plugged in, charging. A small stereo system and a stack of CDs sat on top of a chest-of-drawers. A large watercolour painting of children playing on a sunlit beach hung above her bed; with the beach giving way to blue water that slowly vanished into the sky and the heavens beyond. How appropriate, O'Neill thought, turning away and feeling a pang of guilt. What a waste, what an absolute bloody waste.

They left and O'Neill asked Conroy to arrange for a counsellor to visit Murphy. 'And make sure to have a word with Angie's colleagues, they might have something to add.'

'Will do.'

'Then go home and get some sleep.' He turned to Conroy. 'You look knackered, and I need you in good shape.'

They drove in silence, but O'Neill couldn't help thinking about Joseph Murphy. The old man had done nothing to deserve this, and now his one and only child had been taken from him. Life could be shitty ... no, was shitty. He felt tired and drained. And beaten. 'What would Dixon be thinking?' he thought. He let the idea drift. Outside, the traffic moved easily and people went about their lives, carefree, but for how long? That was the million-dollar question, and nobody had an answer. This case was nothing like anything he had dealt with before. He needed a break. But where was that going to come from? More questions but still no answers.

As he drove, something started to nag at his mind. An idea, maybe Dixon was trying to tell him something. What was it? He squinted a little, trying to focus and see what was there, but just as quickly it slipped away, teasing him. 'Let the idea float up,' he remembered Dixon saying, and sat back. 'It will show itself in its own good time, and be ready to see it then.' It was all he had for now, a fleeting idea.

Outside the police station a van with TV logos was setting up, the technicians making adjustments to broadcasting equipment. A journalist O'Neill recognised glanced at him when the two policemen passed. She took a few steps towards them but O'Neill stopped her with a raised hand.

'I have nothing to say, and you can quote me on that,' he said, and went inside.

'I hope the press conference goes as well,' said Conroy.

'Fat chance,' replied O'Neill, taking the stairs two steps at a time.

The Detectives' Room was noisy as Brady, Grant and Christine Connolly fielded phone calls. It was stuffy, too, and O'Neill opened a window and stood beside it, taking in the gentle breeze and observing the action. On the pavement below a car pulled up and two men got out and looked around. The younger one was carrying a camera bag and the other, balding and carrying far too much weight, a notepad and newspaper. More vultures, he thought, and went to sit at his desk.

There was a yellow Post-It note on his computer screen. He phoned Gary O'Connell, and looking around the room, wondered again just who had caused all this. Where was he now and what was he thinking? Maybe he was planning another attack. But he couldn't do anything about it and would have to wait. He hated that word. The idea wasn't nagging any more and he tried to clear a space for it to let it show itself.

'Danny, how are you?' asked O'Connell.

'Been better, been a lot bloody better, Gary.'

O'Connell shuffled the papers on his desk. 'I haven't found much beyond what you saw yourself. I can tell you that she was not robbed as there was no money taken from her bag. She wasn't raped or sexually assaulted in any way. Her watch, an expensive Longines model, wasn't taken. It wasn't robbery, Danny, that's for sure.'

O'Neill dropped his head. 'Anything else, Gary?' He felt he knew the answer, but had to ask the question.

'We found spit on the victim's face and it matches with the blood from the Ryan house.'

'Spit. You did say spit?'

'Yes. I've seen it before when the attacker is either very excited or a really nasty bastard and he spits on the victim.' He paused. 'It's a gross situation, Danny, and people do gross things.'

O'Neill made a note. 'Yes, Gary, I hear you. Is that it?'

'Almost. We did find a shoe impression. It's definitely from a boot, and the pattern on the sole is similar to the one found on boots worn by motorcyclists. Maybe even couriers. Probably a size eight. So?'

'So what, Gary?'

'So, if the guy that killed Angie Murphy wears size eight boots then he could be the one that killed Barbara Ryan. A size eight boot would more than likely mean that he is not that tall, at least not over six feet. And that is in line with your Clipboard Man. Am I right?'

O'Neill was looking at his keyboard but could hear the cogs in O'Connell's mind whirring away, calculating. 'Sounds good to me, Gary. Now, have you a name for me?'

O'Connell laughed. 'Jaysus, Danny, I'm good but not that good. I wish …'.

'So do I, Gary, so do I.'

O'Connell rang off.

Conroy slammed down his phone, stood up and left the room. It was another useless conversation with somebody who just wanted to 'talk to police' and feel part of the story. It was madness, but it happened. It wasn't easy dealing with a nervous public and the increasing pressure didn't help matters. Tempers frayed and O'Neill knew that he had to keep control of the situation. All around him the vultures were gathering for the feast and O'Neill might just be on the menu.

He sat back and ran his hands through his hair. Time was moving on and he needed to know what Shelly had found. He dialled her number.

'Hello, Danny.'

O'Neill relaxed. Her voice seemed to knock down his guard. He was happy to be diverted. He wanted it, and who better to take his mind off things, if only for a few moments. She was able to do that, effortlessly, like Liz used to. It was a special trait they shared. He couldn't fight it, didn't want to.

'And how are you doing?' she asked.

'Busy, stressed, hassled, chasing a ghost who happens to attack innocent women – yeah, I've got a lot on at the moment,' he said.

'It comes with the territory, Danny, that's the deal. You know that better than anyone … and you can deal with it better than anyone in there.' She paused. 'So don't get too down, it doesn't help.'

O'Neill was leaning on his desk looking at the computer screen but seeing nothing. 'Thanks for the support, that's very kind of you. I ... really appreciate it.' He hoped he was saying the right things and left it at that. He wasn't good with the small talk, especially with women, and didn't what to say next.

Shelly spoke. 'You're welcome, Danny.'

He could hear his voice change and realised that for the first time in ages he was actually relaxing. He couldn't hear the phones ringing any more and the conversations seemed to have stopped. That nagging idea slipped right through his mind and he could almost see it before it disappeared.

'Danny, are you there?' Shelly asked.

'Sorry, Shelly, just trying to make sense of something. Sorry about that.' The tone changed. 'So, what have you got?'

'Angie Murphy was killed with a blow to the top of her head. It cracked her skull, as did another two blows. She was probably dead by the time she hit the ground.'

'The pencil, what about the pencil?'

'That was done post mortem. It would have killed her but the damage was already done. It was a signature gesture, if you like, but not the murder weapon this time.'

'Okay, okay.'

'There was no evidence of any sexual assault either.'

He drummed his fingers on the desk. 'So, this guy does not attack women for sexual gratification or robbery, but attacks women brutally nonetheless.'

'Yes, it's more likely that he's a bit of a novice when it comes to women. You know the type, bad with the females, feels inadequate around them. Needs to control them so that he controls his own insecurity, a bit of a control freak. It's the only way he can operate. And the ultimate form of control is death.'

'I see. So you think that he may be getting revenge for whatever happened in his past that made him feel inadequate around them? And he needs to kill them to prove to himself that he is better than they are?'

'Or she was,' Shelly added.

He let her words sink in. 'You think he's working out his aggression towards one woman?'

'He sees them as substitutes. I've read about that sort of thing, but I'm sure the profiler will have more to say.'

It was impressive. 'Thanks, Shelly, that's very helpful. And now who has hidden strings to their bow?'

Shelly Tobin sniffed. 'You don't know the half of it. You're not even close!'

There was nothing more to say. 'Thanks again, Shelly, keep in touch.'

She hung up without saying another word, keeping him guessing. It was something that he was doing a lot of.

19

Just after three o'clock, O'Neill and the murder team met to review the state of play. With the press conference less than an hour away, it was vital that everyone was singing from the same hymn sheet and knew what was expected. The tension was palpable and the sticky heat added to the anxious, uncertain air.

'Right, what have we got so far?' He shrugged and turned to the board. 'Not much, except a whole pile of trouble, that's what.'

The blank faces stared back, waiting.

'It looks as though both women were killed by the same person, and that a pencil seems to be his signature. And an old pencil, at that. It's different, like nothing any of us has ever seen before. And,' he stressed, 'it's got to be kept quiet.' He looked around the room and knew they agreed. 'Good. So as far as the press conference is concerned, we have not established any link between the murders, and we need to keep it that way. We are under enough scrutiny already, and the idea of a serial killer on the loose would make this investigation almost impossible.'

Doyle stepped up beside O'Neill. 'I've just spoken to the top brass in The Park and they are right behind us. They know how difficult the case … sorry, cases are, and will deal with whatever flak that comes at us.' He looked at O'Neill and grinned. 'You'll be happy to know that Councillor Whitehead—'

'Shithead, you mean,' snapped Brady quickly.

O'Neill caught his eye, making a face. It wasn't exactly an admonition, more like an acknowledgement of accepted fact. 'Pat, please …'.

Doyle continued. 'He had a right go at me yesterday over the lack of progress in the case. Said he was speaking on behalf of the local traders who were beginning to lose business. "Protecting their interests" – I think was what he said. What rubbish! He never did anything for anybody unless there was something in it for him – even the dogs in the street know that. If he wants "to help" the investigation, then he should be supporting us and not trying to score cheap points. Anyway, he will be getting a call from the Department of Finance later today – about a possible audit of his finances, I believe. That should soften his cough and give us more breathing space. Carry on, Danny, and I'll see you before we go downstairs.' He then left the room and O'Neill continued.

'Christine, make sure that we have photos of both women for distribution.'

'Will do,' she answered.

'And make sure one of them is a black and white picture. That should reduce the immediate likelihood of someone making a connection. With a bit of luck it will put them off the scent.'

'Very good, sir,' she said. 'It will be fun watching the vultures in their confusion.'

Others nodded and knew just why Inspector Danny O'Neill was such a clever bugger.

'Pat, you help Christine and then keep an eye on proceedings from the back of the room. A different perspective and all that.'

'Should be interesting,' he replied, anticipating the exciting scene downstairs.

O'Neill tapped the board. 'And the rest of you keep doing what you're doing. Don't waste a minute. Time is murder.'

Paul Grant looked at the others. 'I've never heard that before, but I like it, in a dark sort of way.'

O'Neill raised his hands. 'Thanks … and keep at it, we'll soon get a break-through.' He wasn't sure that he really believed it, but he had to let the team know that he did. If they didn't believe, well, there was no point carrying on. He needed it for Liz, for Helen Murray and for the two recent victims. But most importantly, he needed it for himself.

★

Christine Connolly checked the room once more before the journalists were allowed in. A dozen chairs were laid out in three lines, leaving plenty of space against the walls for TV cameras and photographers. She placed photos of Barbara Ryan and Angie Murphy on a flip chart beside the desk that Doyle and O'Neill would use. As O'Neill had instructed her to do earlier, she closed the windows and removed the tall electric fan that stood in the corner. 'No point in letting the bastards get too comfortable,' he had said, and she understood. Getting them out of here as quickly as possible was the plan, and the room was now heating up nicely. It would be almost insufferable with all the bodies and TV cameras whirring – definitely not a place anybody wanted to stay in. She wiped her brow and smiled at what she knew was coming. She closed the door – the fiery dungeon was ready.

Upstairs, Doyle and O'Neill made their final arrangements.

Doyle straightened his tie. 'I'll open proceedings and give a general outline of the cases. Then you can elaborate just enough to keep them interested.'

O'Neill took a deep breath. 'Don't worry, sir, I'll give them as little as possible. Definitely nothing to suggest that the two murders were carried out by the same person.'

'I know you'll be fine, Danny. Don't get rattled, and speak clearly … and slowly. It'll give you time to think – it's vital.'

O'Neill nodded. 'I know, sir. It's just been a while since I've been in front of the cameras …'.

Doyle shook his head. 'Don't worry, you'll be fine.'

'Okay.'

In the room set aside for the press conference, TV technicians were feverishly checking light and audio levels as the journalists fidgeted, feeling the heat. Two young officers stood at the door, admitting only accredited media folk. As Doyle and O'Neill came into the hall there were at least twenty journalists, photographers and TV camera crews stewing uncomfortably inside.

The room had the stuffy feeling of an underground bunker when Doyle spoke. 'Thank you all for coming and we really appreciate you being here.'

Christine Connolly bit her lip and looked down at her shoes.

'This is extremely difficult for all concerned and I would like to make a few points clear. In the past ten days two women have been murdered. My team is working as hard as possible in these circumstances. With that in mind and in consideration of the ongoing investigation, we will *not* be taking questions today.' He heard a strangled 'What the fu ...' from deep in the pack, and then there was silence.

'I'll now ask Inspector Danny O'Neill to bring you up to date on the state of the investigations.' He leaned back in his chair, keeping his eyes trained on the journalists who were now really annoyed, and sweating. He didn't care, and gently eased his shirt from his sweaty back. He noted that most of them, some of whom he recognised, were mopping their faces. As it should be, he thought, and caught Christine Connolly's knowing grin.

O'Neill pushed aside his notes and looked up at the TV cameras, photographers and journalists, and was suddenly aware of the quiet in the room. It was odd, he thought, that all those in front of him made their living by using words – written and spoken. And here they were now, silent. It was as if they had collectively lost the power of speech. Now there was an attractive idea!

'Firstly, my officers will distribute photos of Barbara Ryan and Angie Murphy. These are the two women whose deaths have brought *you* here today.' He made it sound suitably nasty and grubby, leaving little or no room for his thoughts on the fourth estate.

'Hey, one is a black and white shot. What's that all about?' asked one young reporter sitting in the front row. He was red-faced and his brow was covered in a slick sheen of sweat.

O'Neill turned towards the voice. 'And who are you?' he asked evenly.

The young man sat up. 'Charlie Ahern, *The Daily News*.'

O'Neill grinned and nodded a few times. 'Let me tell you this, Charlie Ahern from *The Daily News*, we are investigating two vicious murders, not holding a beauty contest.' He paused and his voice dropped menacingly. 'Do I make myself clear?'

Charlie swallowed hard, his face now redder. 'Perfectly.'

Christine Connolly nudged Brady and her look was as much about surprise as admiration for O'Neill. She knew that he was as sharp as a tack, and didn't fancy being on the wrong end of those piercing eyes.

'Both women, although they happened to have lived quite close to one another, did not, so far as we have established, know each other. There is the obvious age difference of nearly twenty years for starters, which would make a friendship unlikely.'

'So you're saying that there is no connection between them?' It was John O'Toole from *The Local,* looking decidedly uncomfortable in the surroundings. This *was* big league stuff, and a million miles away from the local hockey games that he reported. His was sweating profusely and his face was like a ripe tomato. O'Neill almost felt sorry for him. Almost.

O'Neill had expected this question and had thought long and hard about a reply. This was the only reason the vultures were in front of him. They wanted him to say that a serial killer was on the loose in South Dublin so that they could race back to their offices and write up sensational eye-catching headlines. Not this time, boys, he thought, and flicked a stray hair from his brow.

'Of course there's a connection,' he said, and there was a dramatic intake of breath. It was sensational and caught everyone by total surprise. 'Both women have been brutally murdered, that's the connection. What more can I say?'

Journalists gawped at him and at each other before O'Toole managed, 'But …' and was drowned out by the shouts and screams from the sweaty journalists.

'You're taking the piss!' cried one standing against the wall.

'What do you mean?' shouted another, his eyes staring at O'Neill.

'Quiet!' roared Doyle. 'This is no way to behave. We are involved in a most serious matter and I expect you to behave appropriately.' He shook his head. 'You must appreciate the seriousness of this situation and forget the point-scoring that you have in mind. If you'll all quieten down, Inspector O'Neill can continue. Thank you.'

There was a rustling of notepads and mumbles of disquiet for a few moments, but they soon stopped. The atmosphere in the room was now very uncomfortable. About right, thought O'Neill, before continuing.

'Now that I've answered that question, I have to appeal to you, your viewers, listeners and readers to give the police any knowledge they may have about these matters. You may not think that what you know is important, but you should let us be the judge of that.'

He pointed to the flip chart and the two photos. 'Look at these photos, and think. Think hard. When did you last see either of these women and where was it? I know that it's not easy, so please take your time before contacting us. Your help is very much appreciated.' He paused again and picked up his papers. 'Whoever is responsible for these crimes needs to be caught as soon as possible, and with the help of the public I'm sure that we can do just that. Thank you,' he said, and stood up.

'You can't leave us hanging …' somebody said angrily.

Doyle, O'Neill and Connolly left the room and headed upstairs as angry voices filled the hall before slowly leaving the building. There was a lot of frustration in the air, but Doyle and O'Neill knew that the TV coverage would show them in a good light. They were officers doing a difficult, dangerous job and here they were being harangued by an unruly pack of newshounds who merely wanted a headline for their own benefit. They had won the sympathy stakes, for now, and that was all that they wanted.

Within minutes, Doyle took a phone call and said very little as he listened. 'Thank you, sir,' he said finally, and put the phone back into the rack. 'That was the Commissioner, Danny, and he was impressed. He's right behind us, so just keep up the good work. We'll soon catch a break – we deserve it.'

'As do the people outside,' replied O'Neill.

'Indeed, Danny, they most certainly do.'

After running hard on Sandymount Strand and feeling less stressed than he had in days, he was sipping a glass of orange juice when someone rang his doorbell.

He opened the door and was surprised to see Shelly Tobin standing there with a large pizza box in one hand and a bottle of red wine in the other. 'I was watching the press conference and I thought you did really well. And so I brought you these.' She raised both the pizza and wine a little higher.

He smiled, loving the moment. 'What a wonderful surprise,' he said. 'I feel as though I've won the lottery.'

Shelly lowered her eyelids. 'Much better than that.'

He felt his Adam's apple jump in his throat. 'Well, what can I say. Come in, come in.'

She stepped closer and he smelt her fragrance. It was intoxicating. She kissed him on the cheek and deftly closed the door with a quick flick from her foot. She was staying and he wasn't about to stop her.

'I'm starving,' she said giddily, 'absolutely ravenous.'

That night was the first night in a long time that the demons didn't come. There was no room for them when there was love in his life. It was what he needed, and he smiled as he listened to Shelly's slow, rhythmic breathing only inches away. He could still feel the smile on his face while drifting off to sleep.

20

lick, stop. Click, play. He held the remote control as the screen came alive and the scene inside the police station began. He was sitting on the edge of the sofa smoking a cigarette, his eyes narrowing as he paid attention. Click, and he raised the volume. He had watched it three times yesterday and now, after a night out cruising around on his motorbike, he was drawn in again.

The room in the police station was crowded and he could feel the nervous tension in the shaky camera work. No doubt the pushing and shoving of the excited journalists made it impossible for the TV cameras to get a steady shot. It added to the craziness, and he grinned at the thought.

'All this for me,' he said quietly, and leaned back.

The scene focused on Inspector Danny O'Neill. He paused the tape so he could examine the man who was leading the investigation. Their eyes met and he felt that this man was dangerous – an opponent to be feared. The piece in The Local *informed readers that O'Neill was the best officer they had and had an unblemished record. Well, almost. He had been in charge of the Helen Murray case that was still unsolved. It was something that 'stuck in my gut', quoted the reporter and something 'that will not happen again.' It was a bold statement and since then O'Neill had delivered on his promise. O'Neill had personally led his team in five different murder cases, all of which had ended in the killers being caught and convicted. He was a tough bastard alright and his line ' ... of course there's a connection' showed that he was a clever one too. He had thrown the media off the scent and kept the unbelievable news of a serial killer* back. Yeah, that was smart, and he gave the policeman a nod of approval. He would have to be careful, very careful, as Inspector Danny O'Neill had a serious agenda. Catching him would no doubt be the feather in his cap, but it would also ease his conscience about the Helen Murray case.

He took another pull and sucked the smoke deep inside his lungs before blowing several smoke rings across the room. In the stale air, the smoke rings slowly unfurled before drifting towards the screen and O'Neill's frozen face. 'You're in my sights just like I am in yours,' he said. 'But I'm invisible. Do you hear me? Invisible, and you'll never catch me.'

He stood up, stretched, and went over to his collection of pictures. Two of them had a big X drawn across them and a knife stuck in the middle, but there were plenty more waiting for him. His girls. He scanned them, and then gently touched each one with the tips of his fingers, but saw only one person – his mother.

He closed his eyes and remembered. Remembered the night when he kept his promise, and everything changed.

She had been out with one of her temporary boyfriends and came home drunk and angry. The boyfriend obviously didn't fancy her enough to 'come inside for a coffee' and she slammed the door in loud frustration. He heard her opening and closing cupboards in the kitchen, shouting all the time about how useless all the men in her life were. She was ranting louder than he had ever heard her before and he prepared himself for the worst. Another beating. And she would probably tear up his drawings and break his pencils – he hated her.

Five minutes later his bedroom door was thrown open and she was standing there with her hands on either side of the doorframe. Her bleach-blonde hair was tousled and her red lipstick smeared all over her chin. She was breathing quickly, gasping almost, and the hall light behind her made her look like an avenging angel.

He jumped out of bed, scared.

'And what the fuck have you been doing, you little bastard?' she spat.

He shivered and took a step away from his bed.

She came into the room waving her arms madly. 'More of them stupid, fucking drawings.' Her voice went higher. 'What a waste,' she spat. 'You're just like your useless father. He was full of shit.' She

130

waved her hands crazily. 'Jesus,' she screamed, 'what did I do to deserve this? FUCK!'

She saw his drawings on the small table by the fireside and picked one up. 'Just look at this, would ya?' She held it up to get a better look and then tossed it at him. 'It's shit, like my life and every man I've ever met.' She turned and stared at him. 'And you, my boy, are just the fucking same. You're all the fucking same.' She kept saying this as she picked up his drawings and threw them around the room.

He was on his knees trying to gather them up when he saw her reach for his satchel. 'Stop, stop, please stop!' he pleaded, but she ignored him and emptied his pencils onto the floor.

In that moment something inside him snapped. After all the years of abuse and neglect, he finally had enough. He dropped the drawings and walked purposefully over to where his mother was stamping on his drawings and breaking his pencils. 'Stop,' he instructed coldly, and grabbed her wrist.

'Wha...' was all she said as she noticed the look in his eyes. They were cold and crystal clear. He felt an icy calm descend over him. He was only twelve, but he was stronger than she was, and she knew she had lost.

'Don't ever do that again,' he said evenly, taking the pencils from her and putting them back in his satchel. He let her go and she put her hand to her mouth to stifle a cry. She was looking at him differently now, and she slowly and quietly made her way out of his room, never taking her eyes off him. As she stood in the hall looking at him he walked to the door and closed it. Not a word was ever said about what had just happened. She had seen the anger in his eyes and felt the strength in his grip, and knew she could no longer inflict her anger and frustration on him. In that moment, he learned the power of fear and control. A bridge had been crossed and she was left on the other side.

The siren from an ambulance or fire brigade brought him back. When he opened his eyes, Inspector Danny O'Neill was looking at him. He was startled momentarily and felt that he had let the police man in on his secret. It was rubbish, of course, but he had a sense of unease that wasn't there before. Pay attention, it said, this guy is dangerous. And now he knew what he was going to do and let the idea float about awhile. He would throw O'Neill off the scent – two could *play at that game. Somebody else was going to die, and he could see the smiling face of the smug bastard whose time was suddenly running out.*

He took another drag, exhaling loudly, but couldn't dismiss the unexpected feeling of being watched.

He looked at the photos and wondered who was going to be next. He knew that the police would eventually make the connection, probably already had, and knew he had to work quickly. He looked at the photographs, from face to face, and selected the next lucky girl. 'You're all mine, darling,' he said quietly before blowing a smoke ring at her.

He was in charge and that was how it was going to stay. Fuck Danny O'Neill and the rest of them. He was going to show them, show them big time. It would be his proudest moment. He turned the television off and watched Danny O'Neill disappearing out of his life. 'Fuck off,' he whispered, 'fuck off, little man.'

21

Two days had passed since the press conference, but the murder team was still answering telephone calls from the public. Most of them proved to be fruitless, but with the extra uniforms now in place they were gathering a lot of evidence.

'Evidence, my arse,' spat Brady, slamming the phone down. 'I never knew there were so many fucking crazies out there. People with wild imaginations and too much bloody time on their hands. Christ.'

Christine Connolly was speaking to another caller and made a 'I know exactly what you mean' face but continued writing. 'What's your name and number, please?' she asked and then the caller rung off. She too slammed down the phone. 'What a waste! This is getting us nowhere.' She pushed her chair back, stood up and looked at Brady. 'I'm going to the restaurant; I need a break. Are you coming?'

Brady was already moving to the door. 'Yeah, I could do with one, too.'

'That's exactly what we all need,' chirped Conroy, tapping a pen against his teeth.

A break, yeah, but from where? The case was proving impossible. It was frustrating, but they all knew that they had to stay at it. It was old-fashioned police work they were doing and not some slick CSI stuff that could be solved in one quick go. This was the real world and there were no easy solutions.

Murder was the dirtiest business and didn't give up its secrets easily. Solving the case was all about perseverance and right now, that was all they had.

★

The team sat around once more as O'Neill stood in front of the board. Even with all that had gone on in the last few days, little had been added. He noticed that he had started grinding his teeth, and that was a bad sign; it showed the immense stress and strain he was under.

'Okay, so where are we now?' he asked.

There was silence for a few moments before Christine Connolly spoke. 'We've got nothing useful from the telephone calls. We are still following some of them up, but so far it's a fruitless exercise.'

'Yeah, I've spoken to more crazy people in the last few days than I thought even existed,' added Brady sharply. 'I don't know what it is, maybe it's something in the air, or maybe it's a full moon thing, but some people seem to have it in for their neighbours. And family members.' He held his hands out, palms upwards. 'It's like open season on anybody they don't like. It's mad.' The look on his face told everyone just how annoyed and frustrated he was.

'Is there any good news, anybody?'

'I checked Angie Murphy's mobile phone records and there was nothing unusual there. Nothing like the short call to the Ryan house before the attack,' said Grant. 'I also checked the home telephone and found nothing there either.'

'Does that tell us anything?' said O'Neill, thinking aloud.

The fan hummed one way, then the other, in a sunlit corner of the room.

'Probably means that he knew she would be in the college and there was no need to check up,' said Connolly.

'So he must have been stalking her and knew her routine,' added Conroy.

'Exactly, Dave,' O'Neill said. 'This guy is a planner; there's no doubt about it. But how the hell did he know so much about her? We still have no connection, although there must be one.'

Connolly put her hand up. 'I've been looking into the history of some serial killers to see if there is anything that may help us.'

'And?'

'Well, the big thing about these guys is that they almost always operate to a pattern. One guy, Bobby Joe Long, killed at least ten prostitutes in Florida in the early 1980s.'

'But our victims were not prostitutes,' said Brady.

'I know that, I'm just trying to show a pattern first.'

'Carry on, please,' said O'Neill. 'This may be interesting.'

'There are many other serial killers, but the one that really interests me is Ted Bundy. He is credited with killing over thirty women, although nobody knows exactly how many he killed, but it's probably a lot more. He was a clean-cut guy who studied law.'

She had their attention.

Connolly looked around. 'Bundy did not look like the monster that he was. This was part of the reason why it was so hard to catch him. He was … acceptable.' She paused. 'But the thing about Bundy was that most of his victims actually looked the same. This was unusual. They had long dark hair that was parted in the middle.' She was speaking quickly now. 'Why? Because he had been dumped by a girlfriend who had the same identifying look, and he took his anger out on women who reminded him of her. He wouldn't let it go. Every time he killed a woman he was killing *her* – over and over.'

O'Neill considered it an interesting line of thinking, but what did it do for the investigation?

'So …' he said, encouraging her to elaborate.

She stood up and walked over to the board and tapped the photos of both victims. 'Two women, both were blonde and not unalike. We know that they are roughly the same height and, although not exactly sisters, they do have a lot in common.'

It was true that the women did look alike, even allowing for the age difference. But what else, was there anything else?

'I like what you're saying, Christine, but it doesn't get us any further down the road, does it? How do you think we should use this insight? We can't very well go and tell every blonde woman in the vicinity to watch out. There'd be a riot. So …'.

'I don't know, sir, but I just thought that I should offer it up. At least we should bear it in mind.'

O'Neill nodded in agreement. 'Anything else?'

Conroy sat forward in his chair and caught Christine's eye. 'The woman I interviewed recently, Margaret Power, who was attacked at Sandycove train station, was also a blonde. Coincidence? She remembered that her attacker was taller than her and that he smelt of French cigarettes.'

Nobody said anything and the words floated in the stuffy air.

'It could be that she was an early victim of our killer,' continued Connolly. 'These guys have to learn sometime before they finally cross the line, so to speak. He's moved on and his latest attack was more sinister and better carried out than the first one. His behaviour is escalating, and his technique is improving.'

O'Neill nodded again. 'Okay, but sadly it's not getting us any nearer the bastard. But please keep it in mind. You never know where it might lead.' He paused for a moment and exhaled loudly, unable to hide his frustration. 'Right, carry on with what you're doing. I'm off to Barbara Ryan's funeral.'

The traffic was light as he made his way to Deansgrange Cemetery. Above, the sky was blue and unending; it met Dublin Bay in an azure embrace. The sea was calm with yachts and windsurfers enjoying its salty pleasure. After the recent stormy days, sailors and water lovers were now making up for lost time.

Lost time: how he hated those words. Since Liz's death he often felt that he was living in lost time. Life wasn't the same without her, and burying himself in his work was the only way he knew of dealing with the pain. He had progressed professionally, no doubt, but at what cost to himself? He knew it had hardened him and dulled his senses. That was a good thing for his work, but not much use for a long-term relationship. And now, as he passed Foxrock church and drove down Kill Lane with Dublin Bay a spectacular backdrop, he was beginning to feel he needed someone in his life. Liz had noticed and made sense of so many things that he seemed to miss, and he knew his life had been richer with her. Shelly Tobin wasn't another Liz, never would be, but she stirred feelings that he had bottled up for too long. It wasn't his feminine side or whatever anybody wanted to call it that he was locking away, it was a need not to be hurt again. It had to change. He turned left at the traffic lights and when he stopped near the gates of the cemetery he felt better, a little lighter. Even with all the mayhem and murder about him, he felt as if he were being given a second chance, and was determined to grab it with both hands.

The graveyard was quiet in the sunshine with only the sound of gravediggers at work intruding. Small birds flitted from one headstone to another, chirping happily, unaware of their playground's sorrow.

A small crowd was gathered around the open grave at the far end of the graveyard when O'Neill arrived. He kept his distance and saw Christopher Ryan, looking exhausted. He had his arm around David's shoulder who was visibly shaking and sobbing into a hankie. About fifty people, including Jenny Collins, formed a circle, and in the centre a priest said prayers before the coffin was lowered into the ground. O'Neill slowly turned his head to see if there were any suspicious observers, but he saw nobody. Just a chance, he thought, before leaving and heading back down the narrow gravel path that ran between the lines of ordered graves.

He made his way, as he had many times before, to the corner of the cemetery and stepped into the shade of a giant fir tree. It was cool and he bent down and picked some pine needles from Liz's grave. He put them in a bin a few feet away and then looked down at the bed of small white stones. A few streaks of sunlight danced on the headstone as it cut through the gently moving branches.

'How are you today?' he said, and smiled. 'It's alright for you, you know, here in the sun all day. Me, on the other hand, well, I've been chasing a very dangerous man – a killer – and I haven't a clue about him. He needs to be stopped but … I don't know how. I need a break, so keep your fingers crossed.' A robin landed on the headstone and chirped a few times before flying away. He wasn't one for believing in omens; his job didn't allow it, but he wanted to believe that Liz knew how he was feeling and was telling him that. He smiled sadly and gently touched her headstone. 'I miss you,' he said quietly, and left.

22

The office was uncomfortably warm and stuffy, and pretty much mirrored how John O'Toole felt. Another lost night in the pub talking inconsequential and meaningless nonsense had left him, yet again, with a sore head. Too many pints of beer were bad news, but topping the night off with a large whiskey was a recipe for disaster. He'd known he'd pay it for the next day but he had been beyond caring. He was, as one of his drinking buddies had put it, 'on the crest of a slump.' And how those few words had summed up his position.

He took a mouthful of strong coffee and shivered as the hot liquid ran down his throat, washing away the sins from last night. The sudden thought that he might not live past fifty made him shudder, and he looked away from his reflection on the computer screen. 'Can't keep hiding,' he told himself. 'You can't escape'. He stubbed his cigarette, hating the taste in his mouth. He was about to get up and go to the toilet when his mobile phone rang.

'Yeah,' he said, and drew the back of his hand across his mouth.

'Jaysus, John you sound as rough as a bear's arse,' said the weedy voice, and then it laughed.

O'Toole was not in the mood to be humoured. 'Who the fuck is this?'

'John, it's Donie Driscoll — it's been a while?'

O'Toole scrunched his eyes and tapped his forehead, trying to remember. Too many fucking brain cells gone, he thought, and then he made the synaptic connection. 'Double D, how are you? And to what dubious honour do I owe this call. It's been what, nearly two years?'

'Nearly three years, John, long time.'

'Wow, that long! So what's going on D, staying out of trouble I hope?'

He leaned back and conjured up his image of Double D. The small man, no more than five-five, had features that told of fights and a life lived mostly in the shadows. The grey eyes that moved back and forth like those of a cautious weasel, set in a narrow face that was pale and pasty. Someone who didn't like exposure to the light – someone with something to hide.

He remembered Donie Driscoll alright, and his dull senses perked up. The little hustler might have something, he thought, so pay attention.

'Want to meet, man? Could be worth your while.'

A tease, but Donie had passed him some sweet information in the past, so....

O'Toole's eyes were now wide open. 'Sure thing, D. Where?'

'The usual spot, in an hour.'

'See you,' said O'Toole, and rang off.

The traffic was light, thankfully, as O'Toole drove to his flat in Sallynoggin, showered, changed his clothes and drank some more coffee. When he looked in the mirror he was surprised by the improvement, and wondered yet again what his meeting with Double D would produce.

The warm breeze tugged at O'Toole's hair as he walked along the West Pier in Dun Laoghaire harbour. He bought an ice cream from the local vendor and licked it like he'd done hundreds of times, before walking along the worn granite slabs. The sunshine sparkled off the tiny pieces of quartz, changing with every step he took. To his right the harbour was quiet with lines of boats from the National Yacht Club rocking easily. Overhead, seagulls swooped, cawed and glided in the warm air.

At the end of the pier, O'Toole sat below the lighthouse, its green slanted roof brilliant against the blue background of the bay and sky beyond. He lit a cigarette and watched as some boats readied to sail, while others returning from sea made a steady glide to their berths. Music drifted across the harbour from the bandstand on the East Pier, where a brass band was entertaining a small crowd. He had almost forgotten about Double D when a movement in the corner of his vision made him turn.

It had been nearly three years, but D had hardly changed, not like himself. D was wearing a red polo shirt, jeans and sandals. He was tanned and looked really good.

'Good to see you,' he said, and they shook hands. 'How goes it?'

D nodded. 'I'm good, man. You okay?'

O'Toole smiled. 'As good as can be. No point in complaining.'

They eyed each other for a few moments; it was what they always did, but said nothing. This meeting wasn't about fashion, at least O'Toole didn't think so.

D sat down and lit a cigarette, all the time looking around, his voice high and twitchy, showing his nervousness. He tapped his foot and blew smoke noisily from his nose. He was looking over the harbour and didn't turn his head to O'Toole when he spoke. 'That chick who was killed in Belfield the other night, yeah …'.

O'Toole was listening carefully. 'Yeah.'

Another long, slow drag. 'Well I hear that she was stabbed with a pencil.' He looked directly at O'Toole. 'Can you believe it, a fucking pencil. Never heard of that before.'

O'Toole lit a cigarette, nervous solidarity and all that. 'Didn't know that, D. How … strange. I don't know what to say.'

D. sniffed. 'Jaysus, a reporter lost for words. What is the world coming to?' He tapped O'Toole on the shoulder. 'But here's the kicker. Are you ready for this?'

O'Toole could suddenly feel the blood pulsing in his veins – he was excited. He knew the way D was talking that something big, something that he could get his teeth into, something that might be very important, was only a few breaths away. He watched the smoke from his cigarette float away and disappear in a spiral of grey. His heart thumped in his chest. Sweet Jesus, let this be good.

Their faces were only eight or nine inches apart and O'Toole could see the worry lines around D's eyes. After years of hanging around the edges of criminal activity, D had done time in jail, but was now trying to take a step back. He was less involved, but as is the way with these folk, he still 'heard things'. And it was one of these 'things' that he laid on a nervous and anxious reporter.

'A little bird told me earlier that a pencil was used in the Ryan murder.' D's eyes were steady – there wasn't a flutter, as cigarette smoke drifted between the two men. 'Now is that strange or what, Mr Reporter?'

O'Toole was lost for words, again. 'Fucking strange, and then some. I'd say that it's one helluva coincidence.' He shook his head. 'It's ridiculous.'

D let out a stream of smoke and leaned back against the warm stone. 'Seems like there's a right nutter out there.'

O'Toole was beginning to feel the weight of D's words. Christ, what if they were true? It was the original good news story for a reporter trying to rack a big hit. Fuck, a serial killer on the loose in Dublin. It was crazy stuff, absolute madness. But then again, two innocent women had been brutally killed in a matter of days – so there was a lot of craziness about.

O'Toole took a long drag, the dizziness making him light-headed. He shivered and smelt the strong tangy air. 'And your source is reliable?'

D grinned. 'Good as gold, it's family.'

O'Toole slipped two fifty euro notes into D's shirt pocket, and stood up. 'Nice one D, that's really appreciated. I'd better get going and start drawing something up.'

D. flicked his spent cigarette into the air, where it spiralled its way into the water below. 'Do what you gotta do.'

O'Toole took a few steps and stopped. 'This *is* good? The source, I mean?' He needed reassurance.

D. took the notes from his shirt pocket and put them in his trouser pocket. 'Sweet as a nut,' he said. 'No need to be worrying, Mr Reporter. I have a cousin who works in the coroner's office.' He gave him a thumbs-up, leaned back and closed his eyes. It was still warm and he needed to keep his tan topped up. His image needed it.

★

Smoke drifted from the over-full ashtray as John O'Toole typed and read his words on the screen. He had told Marty Murphy about his meeting with Double D and recalled his open mouth on hearing the news, an almost exact copy of a giant grouper fish ready to eat.

'And the source is good?' was all that the editor asked.

'I'm assured that it's as good as it gets. It's family.'

Murphy slapped his hands and pounded the table with his fists. 'I told you that there was something off about this, John. I knew it, just fucking knew it.' He clapped his hands and rubbed them vigorously. It was a gesture of excitement and nothing to do with any lack of heat. If anything, the temperature had just gone up with O'Toole's news from the pier, or 'the Western Front' as Murphy as called it.

'Write it up, John, you know what I want,' he winked, 'and let me see it. We'll have it ready for the next issue; it'll be a showstopper.'

At his desk he lit a cigarette, took a long pull and contemplated how to start. It was the bane of his life and he silently pleaded for divine assistance, or whatever it was that would help him. God, he needed it like never before. Years of mediocre, dull as ditch-water reporting could all be forgotten with one story. One story and a powerful headline could improve *The Local's* less than certain financial position. It was a godsend – one Murphy was sure to exploit to the full. After all, he was only doing his readership the service they deserved. And like all 'good' editors, he was going to give them what he knew they wanted. To publish and be rich.

Over cups of coffee and an ever-filling ashtray, O'Toole worked to get the right words and rhythm. It's not a Nobel Prize for literature that you're trying to produce, he kept telling himself. Nevertheless, he corrected his work until he was satisfied. He read it twice, then again, each time mouthing the words as he went, and printed it out. He lit another cigarette and rested his head in the palms of his hands, elbows on his desk. He saw no typos or grammatical errors, and took it to Murphy.

A marker in hand, the editor went through the text word by word but found no errors. He read it again, more quickly, but O'Toole's text remained intact.

'Alright?' asked O'Toole.

Murphy nodded and made a face that said he was happy. 'That's a fine piece of writing, John, much better than your usual stuff.'

O'Toole accepted the backhanded compliment, but knew it was true. 'Don't usually write about a possible serial killer on the loose in South Dublin, Marty. That's big news.'

'Sure is, John, so let's tell them about it. He slipped the cover off his marker and held it over the start of O'Toole's piece. 'Must be eye-catching and simple,' he said to himself, waiting for the words to come to him. He moved his head from side to side considering options before dismissing them and starting again. After two or three minutes he had it and wrote it clearly in big letters. He sat back in his chair, satisfied, and turned the page for John O'Toole to see. 'What do you think?'

He frowned. 'But he uses pencils, Marty.'

'Pens, pencils, what's the difference?' said Murphy. 'And besides, this makes a better headline.'

O'Toole looked at the words written at the top of the page and knew that the shit was about to fly, big time. Marty eyed him closely. 'I hope to fuck that your source is good.'

'So do I, Marty,' replied O'Toole, as the genie flew from the bottle.

Marty Murphy, who was never one for understatement, had decided on a short and provocative three-word combination: 'Penman Strikes Again'. This was bound to generate controversy, just what Murphy wanted. More talk meant more sales, and that meant more money. It was a simple business strategy and he didn't care what others thought of him. He was trying to run a business, and if that upset some people then they would have to like it or lump it. 'Fuck the begrudgers,' he thought, and liked his words even more.

O'Toole bit his lip, thinking hard. This was the first time that anything like this had happened in Dublin, and fuck knows where it was going to end. It was a very uncomfortable thought. I might even need a drink later, he thought, wiping his mouth in nervous anticipation. Of course he would need a drink later, a lot of them. And fuck the headache.

23

After following Liam Burke for three days he knew exactly where he would attack the politician. He wasn't stalking like some muppet said on the radio. That was for sick perverts and he wasn't one of them. He was on a mission – and what did they know anyway. Nothing, that's what they knew, absolutely nothing, and he was going to keep it that way.

He had seen Burke up close and personal and resented his smooth manner and easy charm. Smug bastard, he thought, you're the one. He was rich, with all the trappings of success, and he despised him. He hated bastards like him, and sneered when he remembered Burke's line about 'Serving the public'. Well, Mr Burke, it's your time to deliver.

★

The early evening sun was still pleasantly warm as he rounded the playing fields and headed into Mount Merrion woods. He was breathing hard, not that he was under pressure; no, he was just pushing himself hard, like he did with most things in life, he thought, and suddenly felt the cool offered by the shade of the tall trees.

It was quiet in the woods and he raced across a path that was dappled with sunlight and shadow. Most people who jogged around here usually avoided coming through the wood and took the longer route around the football pitches. The wood was old with trees thick on the ground, and after a few strides, silence was his only companion. He wasn't nervous and pushed harder to the highest point, where a break in the tree line afforded a wonderful view of Dublin Bay and the sprawling city below.

He eased to a stop and placed his hands on his hips, smiling at the magnificent view. The bay was blue with the South Wall a long, white finger stretching to the Poolbeg Lighthouse. He saw great swathes of grey and red-roofed houses that occasionally rubbed up against green sports fields. Off to the left, the Liffey wound its way inland from the sea and passed through the city before disappearing into the fading distance.

Squinting, with his hands beside his head like blinkers, he took a few seconds to spot where the government buildings were and felt his chest fill. My new office, he thought, and took a few deep breaths. He nodded to himself and thought about his future as the new politician for South Dublin. He had been elected in the recent general election, on the fourth count, and with his twenty years of experience as a lawyer, he was set for a junior role in the Department of Justice. He would walk away from all those criminal cases and property deals that had brought him the life he had always desired. Now he had more property and more money than he would ever need and a pretty wife whose beauty always drew attention. He had been a lucky bastard, as some of his close friends had said, and he knew better than any of them just how true that was. And that was how it was going to stay.

He wiped the sweat from his brow and rubbed his hands on his shorts. He felt good and the heaving in his chest eased. A newspaper photographer had taken a couple of pictures of him for an article on newly elected members and told him he that was fitter and in better shape than any others he had snapped. He had thanked the man and suppressed a grin. He was proud of his good looks and he knew that keeping fit was essential for both his health and image. He was good at image. So many politicians seemed to become fat and lazy soon after their election and Liam Burke was determined not to be one of them. No, he was going to make a mark. People would remember him. He had been doing that all his life.

A hundred yards or so ahead of him another jogger came over the rise heading in his direction. He was wearing the standard jogger's gear of trainers, long white socks, shorts and a red T-shirt. As he got closer Burke saw that the man was moving slowly, probably in bad shape, he thought, and rested his hands on his hips. He would let the jogger pass first and then continue on his way downhill and back home to Callary Road for a much-needed shower. Twenty minutes and he'd be having a cold drink and then setting up the barbeque. It was June, after all, and the weather had been warming up nicely for the past two weeks. It would be a sin to waste such an opportunity and Liam Burke was not a man for letting things slip through his fingers.

He grinned as he closed the distance between them, and he readied himself. He had checked that there was nobody behind him and had watched Burke as he entered the wood from his vantage point on a large exposed rock. It was not the first time he'd been here and knew that the wood was the perfect place for him to become acquainted with the newly elected politician.

He could see the sweat glow on Burke's face as he smiled at a fellow jogger. It was an unspoken etiquette that he return the smile; a last insidious deceit. He liked that.

From three feet away he drew up his right arm, stretched it out and swung the long knife.

Burke saw the sun glint off the knife just before it slashed across his neck. The sharp blade sliced cleanly, leaving a cut nearly six inches long. It looked as if Burke was wearing a red tie as he frantically reached up to his neck and saw the blood spurt between his fingers. He tried to shout for help but blood shot from his mouth as he staggered, falling to his knees. A ray of sunlight danced on the ground in front of him and he tried to make sense of what had just happened. It couldn't be true but he knew otherwise. The blood covered his fingers and palms and he was beginning to choke as it fell into his throat.

Behind him he heard footsteps fading in the distance. His mind was on fire as he tried to come to terms with his situation, and a tear fell from his eye. He couldn't call out and with one last breath he heard himself gurgle 'Why?' and then fell forward, his face smacking loudly against a small rock.

The other jogger passed the tennis courts where a young boy and girl were playing. They never even looked up as he passed by, and in seconds he disappeared into the warm evening.

24

Gary O'Connell's team were busy when the State Pathologist ducked under the yellow security tape that was flapping in the warm breeze. It was tied in a circle from a number of trees and the team, all dressed in white boiler suits, were examining the area that was bathed in a bright halogen light.

'Evening, John,' said O'Connell. 'I wasn't expecting you. *Someone* must have called?'

John Boyd grinned, his eyes bright behind his silver-rimmed spectacles. He drew a hand across his beard a few times and set his old leather bag down. 'Yeah, the Attorney General himself rang and said that *I* should attend.' He held his hands out. 'He made it very clear that there was going to be no discussion. Certainly not when something like this happens.' He nodded at the white tent a few feet to his left that was lit by another blast from a crime scene photographer's flash. 'Better have a look, Gary, now that I'm here.'

Boyd slipped rubber boots over his shiny brogues and a white coat to cover his three-piece tweed suit. His red dicky bow stood out like a beacon and O'Connell noticed how out of place it seemed with the bloodstained body beside them. Boyd was his 'own man' and scoffed at the newspapers who often ribbed him about his attire. It was, they said, old-fashioned and out of place. The problem for them was that Boyd didn't care what they said. He dealt with corpses of people who had been brutally murdered. And that, sadly, was not old-fashioned or out of place. In the country, where the Celtic Rat roamed, he was busier than ever before. If that was what progress was all about, he certainly wouldn't thank you for it.

O'Connell held a flap open and Boyd stepped past him. The photographer took another photograph but left when he saw O'Connell point to the door.

Boyd stood still and looked at the body that was lying face down. A pool of dark blood circled Burke's head and his hands were crumpled under his chest. His legs were splayed with his right knee twisted at an odd angle. Boyd thought of the letter K and knelt to get a better look.

'He was found by a local man who was walking his dog,' said O'Connell. 'He called the police on his mobile and waited until they arrived. He's still in a state of shock.'

Boyd nodded. 'I'm not surprised, Gary. It's enough to scare the crap out of even the most hardened officers. What a mess!'

O'Connell continued. 'From what we've found out so far, he jogged this way almost every day. It was his routine.'

Boyd was listening, examining the area around the body with his eyes. He saw blood on the stone that Burke's face was resting against and more on the path about two feet away. 'No sign of a struggle?'

'Nothing obvious anyway,' replied O'Connell. 'He seems to have fallen almost straight down.' He pointed to the clay beside Burke's feet. 'A small scuff mark, but nothing else.'

Boyd crouched and rested his elbows on his thighs, thinking. 'If there had been a scuffle the clay and grass would be flattened and disturbed, and there's no sign of anything like that.'

O'Connell shook his head. 'Nothing at all.' There was a slight uncertainty in his voice and Boyd heard it.

'So what do you think? You're the expert.' He stood up, stepping over the body.

O'Connell had been expecting the question. 'I think whoever did this is good. *Really good.*' He wasn't praising the attacker but it was hard not to admit that he had delivered a fatal blow in one, presumably quick, movement. And kept going. 'He's certainly done stuff like this before. It's too … clean.'

'I agree,' said Boyd. He knew O'Connell was good and, right now, his line of reasoning seemed spot on. If that was the case then Burke's death looked very much like it was planned. And if that was true then this was an assassination. Christ, what was the AG going to say? Presidents and senior politicians in far-off, exotic countries were assassinated. But not minor politicians, especially someone who was only recently elected and hadn't had time to annoy anybody yet. No, this sort of thing didn't happen in Ireland, at least not since the Troubles had come to an end nearly twenty years ago. He knew the news was going to be bad, but he couldn't concern himself with that. The facts were the facts, and the new member for South Dublin would not be making any maiden speech. Unless, of course, he had to bargain his way past the Pearly Gates. 'Help me turn him over,' he said, and the two men went about their grisly business as outside, the darkness fell silently.

25

John O'Toole was right; the shit did hit the fan when *The Local* made the news stands. In anticipation of such a reaction, Marty Murphy had printed twice as many copies of the paper than he usually did. 'I'll have to frame the front sheet,' he said confidently when he picked up the first copy as it rolled off the press. He laughed and slapped a high-five with the Production Manager. 'An issue to remember,' he said, his eyes sparkling with excitement.

O'Neill got the news on the radio as he drove to the police station. 'Fuck it!' he shouted. 'Fuck, fuck, fuck!'

The station was buzzing and Doyle was on the phone to HQ when O'Neill went to see him. 'They want to know how this happened, Danny. Any ideas?'

O'Neill had seen the boss upset before, but not like this. He was unsure of what to say next. 'No, sir, I haven't, but the leak's not in here. I can't believe that any of the team would have said anything.' He shook his head. 'But I'll be checking.'

Doyle was looking at the bold headline. 'They've even given the bastard a name. What's that all about? Do they think we're in America? This is not a game. Fuck.' He looked up, his eyes narrowed and seeking an answer.

'I don't know, sir, but I'll be onto O'Toole as soon as I can get hold of him. I want to know where he got his information from. We *have* to know.'

'I suppose you heard about the murder in Mount Merrion last night?'

O'Neill ran a hand over his brow. 'Sure did, it's dreadful news. Did you hear anything about it, sir?'

Doyle pushed his chair back. 'Only that Burke was out for his regular run and … someone killed him. One blow and it was all over.'

Danny frowned. 'One blow?'

'Yes, one blow or slash to the throat and he bled to death. Would have taken only seconds. That's what my opposite number, Joe O'Higgins, in Dundrum told me earlier. The state pathologist was called in, or should I say, told to attend. It's top priority, but it's not our concern.' He didn't need another murder landing on his desk, and a high profile one at that. 'Anyway, you've enough on your plate, Danny, so find out what you can about any leak and let me know. Pronto.'

'Will do, sir.' O'Neill went back to see his team.

Doyle got up, walked to the window and looked down on another wonderful summer scene. The sky was an unbroken blue above the calm waters of Dublin Bay. A windsurfer leaned back, pulling on his sail and skitted over the sea. Across the bay the last of the morning mist was burning off the cliffs in Howth, revealing windows that sparkled like tiny diamonds. It was a lovely day, but was now soiled by another act of mindless violence. Where would it all end?

★

Outside Government Buildings a large crowd of journalists and photographers gathered, talking excitedly about Liam Burke's murder under a cloud of swirling cigarette smoke. One said that, as Burke was known to be a lady's man, a jilted husband might have snapped and decided to carry out his own punishment. It wouldn't be the first time that such a thing happened, and it certainly wouldn't be the last.

'Or maybe it was a partner in one of those dodgy property deals that he was famous for,' added a guy with a cigarette-stained voice and open-necked shirt. He winked knowingly before letting out a loud rough cough.

'There's plenty of them out there,' said someone else as he put his mobile phone to his ear.

'Better form a queue then,' said another, leaning in on the bitchy talk.

They laughed out loud as another black Mercedes slowed and passed by. Inside, the Minister for Justice gave a cursory wave and continued talking with his secretary.

'He looks worried, doesn't he?' said one of the journalists as he and his media mates watched the disappearing state car. Photographers leaned in and took pictures, their flashes bouncing off the windows.

'Yeah, and he's still an ugly bollix,' offered another media man, and the crowd sniggered.

Near the gate two policemen shook their heads when they heard the laughter. 'Jaysus, your man's only been murdered; he's still warm for fuck's sake, and those guys are laughing at him. Scum, that's what they are.'

His younger partner said nothing but grimaced in silent agreement with the noisy reporters.

Inside the elegant building, in a room on the second floor that afforded a wonderful view of Merrion Square, three men sat at a polished oak table. Sunbeams highlighted the golden grains that spread from the centre in twisting, curving spirals. Tiny motes floated in the streaming sunlight, uninvited and uninterested in the grim discussion that was going on.

'So what do we know?' asked Philip Joyce. In office less than a month, he was determined to resolve the issue of Liam Burke's murder as quickly and cleanly as possible. Known for his single-mindedness, especially after ousting the sitting Taoiseach in a stunning coup, he was a formidable performer and never suffered fools – gladly or otherwise. And right now his blue eyes were cold and focused. He was an intimidating sight, and those in the room were on their A-game.

The Attorney General, Christy Law, opened a pink folder and slipped a page from it with the tip of a finger. 'I met John Boyd last night and he said that Burke was killed with a single cut to his neck. Probably done with a long knife that was swung with precision. The wound was six inches across and Burke would have bled to death in no time – a minute maybe. Boyd reckons he might as well have been decapitated.' He paused and cleared his throat. 'There were no marks suggesting a scuffle, and Burke died on the spot. He'll have a full report for me tomorrow, and we'll know if he had anything of interest in his system.'

'Jesus,' said Declan Campbell over his steepled hands. His eyes never moved from Law, who took his glasses off and left them down carefully on the folder.

A silence followed, and was broken when the Minister for Justice, Patrick Cooper, entered and sat down.

'Fill him in, Christy,' Joyce said. He took a sip of coffee and listened to the terrible news and wondered what Burke had got himself into. He knew that he had an eye for the ladies, but he had always been able to handle it and deflect any gossip. Hearsay was one thing, but proving it was an entirely different matter; something that never concerned the media too much. Burke was a legal animal and would have had his bases covered. At least that was what he had told Joyce when they had spoken a few months ago when he was being considered as a candidate. Had he been duped? Joyce hated the thought and how it might reflect on his judgement. He needed answers, and more than that, a killer.

Cooper, a balding man in his mid-fifties and overweight, was stunned. He looked open-mouthed across the table when Law finished. 'Christ almighty, who the fuck did this? Is there anyone in the frame yet? Dissident terrorists, disgruntled drug dealers, who?'

Joyce put his cup down. 'Right now we have absolutely no idea why it happened. Nothing, nada.'

Nobody said anything.

'We need to find out something. The press won't believe that we don't know anything. They just won't, okay?' added Joyce.

'I agree,' added Campbell, who, as the Taoiseach's political advisor, knew he was going to be in the spotlight very soon and needed to have something for the feeding frenzy outside. As the government's spin-doctor he was expected to deflect the bad news, and Burke's murder was going to call on all his experience. Why hadn't he just been caught with his pants down? he thought, and twirled his thumbs, thinking hard.

Joyce sat forward, elbows on the table. 'So are there any skeletons in Burke's cupboard that we should know about?' This was a question for everybody, and although he needed to know any dark secret that Burke might have hidden, he didn't really want to know anything.

'Until some group or other claims responsibility we have to go with the idea of the lone killer,' said Campbell. He leaned forward and looked from face to face. 'I can't believe that it was some irate husband trying to get even over his wife's infidelity with Burke. Seems too extreme. I know he spoke about being tough on drug dealers in his campaign, but it's hardly enough for one of them to kill him. He hadn't done anything to them, yet, and they would pay an awful price if caught. The public would demand that we throw away the key.' He wiped his mouth with the inside of his thumb. 'Let's go with the lone killer line, for now. It's not a lie, and it doesn't give the media anything to focus on.'

'The Penman, could it be him?' asked Cooper nervously.

Campbell was surprised and lost for a quick reply.

'Do you mean that guy who has been terrorising women in Booterstown?' said Law, wiping his glasses.

Joyce turned to his spin doctor, his eyes demanding a response.

Campbell shrugged, slightly. 'From what I know about the Penman, he attacks defenceless women, so there's nothing in common. Is there?' He looked at the others.

The heads nodded in agreement.

'Right, so unless we can find out about some financial shenanigans that Burke was involved in, we're better off saying nothing.' He held his hands out. 'Hey, it's true, and that's worth everything.'

Joyce spoke. 'You're right, Declan, and that's what we'll go with. Shit happens and maybe Burke was just in the wrong place at the wrong time.' He looked around the table. 'I still want the police to give this a high profile, and to continue digging into Burke's background. I want to know why this has happened. Jesus, I still can't believe it!'

Cooper loosened his tie. 'I'll be talking with the Garda Commissioner after I leave here. He'll keep his men in place and I know that they are already digging into Burke's affairs. He's been in contact with the tax authorities and the law society. Let's see what they turn up.'

'Okay, and keep me informed,' Joyce said clearly. 'If it turns out to be a lone killer; then so be it. But if there's a deeper conspiracy then I want it nipped in the bud, immediately. This is not something that I created, and I can tell you gentlemen, that I am in no way going to take any heat for it. No fucking way.'

The meeting ended.

Joyce sat alone in the sunny room wondering what the next few days held. He finished his coffee and left, cursing Burke for bringing this shit down on him. 'Thanks, Liam,' he said under his breath, slamming the heavy oak door behind him.

26

After a brief meeting with the team, O'Neill and Christine Connolly went to see John O'Toole at *The Local*. Nothing new of any significance had come in, so Conroy was back to reviewing more old cases, and Brady was on his way to talk to the neighbours again. They knew from previous cases that people sometimes remembered things days after an event when they felt less stressed.

It was worth a try.

Anything was worth a try, especially when they had nothing to work on. It was as if the Penman, or whoever the killer was, had disappeared into thin air without a trace. It was a weird case and O'Neill was really beginning to wonder if they would ever solve it.

The sky was blue and cloudless and the on shore breeze carried the tangy, salty air. Along the promenade trees swayed gently as boys skateboarded in their moving shadows.

'Do you know O'Toole?' Christine Connolly asked, as she looked out the car window to watch a pair of windsurfers riding the wind.

'Sure do, known him for years,' O'Neill replied, slowing for a set of traffic lights. 'He's a drunk, but he has passed on some useful information from time to time.' He turned and looked at the profiler. 'He was the one at the press conference who asked if there was a connection between Barbara Ryan and Angie Murphy.'

Connolly closed her eyes for a moment and tried to remember the face.

'I want to know *when* he found out that there was a connection. It must have been after the press conference, otherwise he wouldn't have asked the question then.'

'I see what you mean,' she said.

They arrived at a small business estate where a number of the units showed 'FOR RENT' signs. The economic collapse was all around them, and small businesses were hit especially hard. The grass on the sidewalks was long and uncut, and papers floated and scurried along the dusty road.

Connolly looked around, taking it all in. 'A bit run down, isn't it?'

O'Neill sniffed. 'A shithole would be more accurate. The council doesn't bother to clean the roads any more, and you see what it does to the place.' He waved a hand. 'It's everywhere; it's just terrible. And the sad thing is it used to be well maintained – easy on the eye.'

Dublin South Business Park had a grand name but, sadly, it was no longer living up to it. It had opened in the early eighties and a large granite stone at the entrance told that the Minister for Industry had officiated. Those days were long gone, and the few businesses that remained open were struggling, like so many others. The sun may have been shining but few of the companies would say that it was shining on them. Most of them worked under an ominous dark cloud and *The Local* was no different.

Its offices were in an anonymous, two-storey grey building at the end of the estate. Next door, the boarded-up windows showed that 'Gallagher Cement & Stone' had gone the way of so many in the building business. Once the backbone of the Celtic Tiger, the building business had been halved in less than two years.

O'Neill opened the door and asked for John O'Toole.

'And who may I say is looking for him?' asked the receptionist when she put down her copy of *Marie Claire*.

O'Neill produced his warrant card and saw the serious look come over the young girl's face. He smiled as she scuttled off upstairs, and looked around at the bundles of newspapers and magazines that lay in dusty stacks against the walls of the small reception area. A crack in the window, covered with a strip of gaffer tape, seemed to say more about the state of the economy than any of the know-it-all economists who pontificated regularly on radio and TV.

'He's in his office,' said the girl. 'He's waiting for you.'

O'Neill thanked her and headed upstairs.

It had been at least a year, maybe more, since he had been here, and nothing much had changed. Young people, many of them immigrants, were busy on the telephones chasing small ads and drinking lots of coffee. Pay wasn't great, but that was the way of the world in such small businesses. No ads meant no jobs, and the main office was surprisingly busy. It was simple stuff, and he wondered how long the business could keep going. It was just another question that he couldn't answer.

John O'Toole was in his room when O'Neill knocked.

'Come in, Danny,' he said, and turned from his computer. He knew that O'Neill would call and had made sure to clean himself up, and he wore a clean shirt and tie. His hair was washed and combed, and O'Neill thought he had lost a few years since the press conference. He was actually looking half decent – for him anyway.

'Good morning, John, and how are you?'

'Fine, Danny, and you?' replied O'Toole, his eyes moving to take in Christine Connolly.

'This is Detective Christine Connolly; she's part of my team,' said O'Neill. 'Anything I should know, so should she.'

O'Toole nodded. 'That's fine by me. Coffee?'

Both police officers declined.

O'Toole sipped his coffee and looked over his cup with nervous eyes. 'So, what brings you down here, Danny? It's been a while … what, eighteen months?'

O'Neill nodded. 'Yeah, that's about it. Not since that bank robbery in Dundrum. Your information was helpful, you know that, and it was appreciated.'

O'Toole grinned and held his cup with both hands high in front of his face.

'What brings me here today, John, is your new friend – the Penman. I'm very interested in how you found out that our two victims were stabbed. It wasn't information that we released, for *obvious reasons*, and now that it's out there I want to know what you know. I don't like surprises.' His tone was hard and left the journalist in no doubt about how serious the matter was. He would not be leaving the building without a proper explanation, and all of them knew it.

The air, stale and dry, seemed to slip out of the room due to the tension, leaving the place hot and uncomfortable.

O'Toole felt his shirt stick to his back and his pulse quickened. The two faces across the desk stared and waited, and not a single muscle moved. He knew that O'Neill didn't 'do' sympathy and, looking at the woman beside him, he reckoned she was also missing the same gene. Must be a cop thing, he thought, but kept the idea to himself.

He sat up, lit a cigarette, and ran a hand over his hair. He exhaled. 'Sorry, can't help, Danny, confidential source I'm afraid.'

'Confidential my arse,' spat O'Neill, his words loud and angry. He leaned on O'Toole's desk in an intimidating manner. 'Don't fuck around, John. I haven't got the time. Two women are dead and you're sitting there looking all pleased with yourself. Do you think that you are going to win a Pulitzer Prize or something? For fuck's sake.'

Christine Connolly hadn't taken her eyes off O'Toole, and he felt the room getting smaller and more uncomfortable.

'I can't, Danny, honest. If I do then that's the end of my contact.' He raised his voice. 'It's taken me a long time to develop the relationship.'

'What fucking relationship?' snapped O'Neill. 'Don't give me that shit. This is murder I'm dealing with.'

O'Toole was nervous and his eyes darted between Danny and the woman whose name he suddenly couldn't remember. There was no help there. He knew that something like this might happen but had no idea how to play it. His story was a sensation and the emails that he'd received told him that. It was going to be his big moment, but all of a sudden a dark cloud had entered his room. All the years of pain, of dealing with trivial reporting, they could be a thing of the past – he deserved better. But now, with two angry cops in his face, all that promise seemed to be slipping away like last night's hangover. 'Better have a word with Marty,' he said quietly and picked up the phone.

Two minutes later the three of them stood in the editor's room, the stale air stinging like bad breath. Sunbeams struggled through the dust-covered window and cut across the spiral of smoke from Marty's cigarette resting in an overfull ashtray. Christine Connolly felt like she was in a Dickensian novel and now realised why she never liked his books. The smell of stale sweat almost made her gag and she twitched her nose in response. How could someone live like this? she thought, looking at the bulging figure of Marty Murphy. Dark stains under his armpits seemed to be growing as she looked at him, and his hair was flattened and shiny. If someone had told her that Murphy hadn't moved from his chair for a month she would have easily believed it. She would never forget the first time she met the editor, even if it was for all the wrong reasons.

Murphy leaned back in his chair, the leather squeaking a losing resistance. He took a pull on his cigarette and blew a stream of smoke across his desk in the direction of the CD player that sat on an overcrowded cabinet.

O'Toole spoke. 'Danny wants to know the name of my source for the Penman and …'.

'… and you want me to tell him that he can't have it. Is that what this is all about?' snapped Murphy, taking a deeper pull on his cigarette.

O'Toole nodded but didn't look at the cops.

O'Neill nodded slowly as if responding to his own internal debate. Connolly saw that his eyes had narrowed but didn't think it was to do with the cloying smoke. A slight sneer curved his lips and he was not a pretty sight. He meant business and Marty Murphy was about to find that out.

O'Neill took two steps closer to Murphy and leaned on his desk. He looked down at the editor who let out another stream of smoke and seemed pleased with himself. 'Now listen here, and listen well, as I don't have the time to be repeating myself.'

Murphy held his hands up. 'No problem, Detective.'

'It's Inspector, that's the first thing you should know.'

All of a sudden Murphy didn't seem so confident and he nodded, once. The silence in the room added its own pressure and O'Toole wiped his mouth and let out a low sigh.

'I have two dead women and a lot of people scared shitless,' said O'Neill, not taking his eyes off of Murphy. 'And the last thing I need is for them to start worrying about a serial killer.' He paused. 'And believe me, you aren't helping matters. Not one fucking bit.'

Murphy drew a nervous hand across his mouth, but said nothing. He glanced at O'Toole who seemed to have shrunk into the wall, not wanting to be involved. Spineless drunk, he thought, and waited for another earful.

O'Neill straightened up and looked at Murphy and the wisps of smoke that eased past the editor's nervous face. He had split O'Toole away from Murphy, and that left only one. It wasn't that he liked what he was doing, but the newspaper had put sensitive information into print and he couldn't let that happen again. It was bad for the investigation, and that was all that mattered. Finding the Penman, or whoever the fuck it was, was difficult, but *The Local* was making it impossible. It had to stop.

'So, here we are, and I want a name,' O'Neill said, glancing over at O'Toole. 'And let me be very clear, this is not open for discussion. There is no trading.'

Murphy swallowed hard and the noise filled the room.

'I can do you, both of you, for withholding information, and that's just for starters,' said O'Neill, leaning closer.

'You can't do that,' said Murphy, but without any real conviction.

O'Neill sniffed and turned to Christine Connolly who nodded. 'I'm afraid he can, Mr Murphy, and a lot more,' she said.

O'Neill was happy but didn't show it. 'I can have my friends in the tax office in here tomorrow to check up on your situation. They'd love to dig around, and I'm sure they would find something useful. Know what I mean, Marty? All those cash payments and off the book transactions. I know it goes on so don't give me that innocent look.'

'But ...'.

'No buts, Marty, just a name.' He paused. 'And come to think of it, the guys in Health & Safety would have a field day if they *dared* come in. Just look at the place – it's a firetrap.'

Marty Murphy knew that he was in a very tight corner. The game was up. And if there was one thing that he didn't need right now, it was O'Neill threatening him with all sorts. It could be the end – probably would be the end. He looked at O'Toole. 'Tell him, John, just give him the fucking name.'

Three pairs of eyes turned to O'Toole who shivered and ran a hand over his brow. 'It's Donie Driscoll.'

O'Neill thought for a moment and then smiled. 'Donie Driscoll, do you mean Double D?'

O'Toole nodded. 'Yeah, the one and only.'

'And how the hell does he know anything about these murders? It's not his style. He's a small time crook, a little toerag.' O'Neill couldn't hide his surprise and waited for more.

'He told me that he had a family member in the Coroner's Office who ... heard things,' said O'Toole. 'That's all I know.'

'So Donie is, how should I put it, a confidential source? Is that it?'

'Yeah. I've known him for a few years now, and he sometimes passes on bits of information. But nothing as crazy as this.' The journalist had nothing more to say and almost took a step back.

'Good,' said O'Neill. 'I'll have a word with him, and don't call him. That would not be a good career move, as my friends would be here sooner than you could say "Revenue Commissioners." Understand?'

They understood.

O'Neill and Connolly left the small room with a name and a surprise appointment with Double D.

27

John Boyd stepped back from the metal table and lifted the thin white mask from his nose. The bright fluorescent light cast a sharp shadow over the corpse as he moved his hand up to wipe his brow. 'Trevor, can you please go and get Shelly Tobin? There's something I would like her to see. She is the resident knife expert, after all.'

Trevor nodded at the reference, turned, and left the room. Shelly was indeed the resident knife expert, and it was also Boyd's way of complementing his assistant. She was the sharpest tool in the State Pathologist's department, and he often asked her for a second opinion when considering a difficult case. He didn't get his hands dirty much nowadays as life was mostly about politicking and report writing. He had seen enough corpses over the last thirty-or-so years and didn't really miss the blood, guts or smell, if the truth be told.

However, lying in front of him was the cold, stiff body of Liam Burke, its whiteness all the more extreme under the strong unforgiving light. The Minister for Justice was anxiously awaiting this particular report and Boyd knew he had to get it absolutely right. There could be no room for argument or doubt as the little matter of the government's credibility would be in question. And he knew only too well, from his years in committee rooms, that if things didn't go the right way someone would pay a heavy price. In delicate situations like this it was not unknown for lambs to be sacrificed, and he wasn't going to be that public offering. 'What happened, Liam?' he said quietly and then went to the window to look out at another bright morning.

Boyd turned as the door opened and Shelly Tobin and Trevor walked in. 'Good morning, Shelly, and how are you this fine morning?'

'Fine, sir, a lot better than your guest,' she replied, casting a glance at the uncovered corpse. Boyd saw Trevor smirk and raised his brow in agreement.

All three moved over to the corpse and looked down on the politician whose life had been cut short, literally. Trevor had earlier washed away the blood that covered the face and neck area, leaving the fatal gash exposed in all its jagged ugliness.

Boyd spoke. 'Shelly, before I start cutting, I'd like you to have a look at what we have. You know a lot about knife attacks, so I would like your opinion on what we have here.'

Shelly listened but never took her eyes from the gaping wound. She had seen many fatal wounds delivered to different parts of a body and this one seemed, at first glance, to be just another murderous cut. She put on rubber gloves and gently eased the wound open and slid a finger inside and moved it about. The skin was hard and she used a knuckle to keep it open as she probed. Boyd and Trevor watched silently, the only noise in the room coming from the traffic two floors below.

When she was finished Shelly Tobin stood up and slipped off her mask. 'I would say that he was attacked with a long smooth blade.'

'Not serrated?' asked Boyd.

'Definitely not, as there is no sign of skin tearing. The length of the cut would suggest that the blade was probably eight to ten inches long, so we are looking for a big hunting knife. And used by someone who knows how to use it.' She saw the uncertainty on Trevor's face. 'Because whoever did this knew where to strike and got it right first time.'

'So nothing random then?' Boyd queried.

Shelly shook her head. 'Not very likely, sir. I would say that whoever did this knew exactly what he was doing and, sadly, did it very well.'

'Thank you, Shelly, that's been most informative.'

Shelly left and Boyd continued working as the day outside warmed up. Two hours later he peeled off his gloves and left Trevor to apply the appropriate stitching to the corpse and slide it back into its steel cabinet.

Boyd could now confirm that Burke had been killed with a single cut to the neck, and that there was no sign of alcohol or drugs in the victim's body. He had to be grateful for that at least.

★

The office was empty when O'Neill and Connolly arrived back at the police station. A fan was whirring lazily in the corner, lifting papers on Pat Brady's desk. They rose for a moment as if by an invisible hand, before falling back onto the pile.

'I hope that they're all at work,' said O'Neill, slipping his jacket off and putting it on the back of his chair. He spotted the Post-It note on his computer screen and tore it off. 'Boss wants to see you,' it said. He recognised the handwriting – Dave Conroy had written it.

'Anything?' asked Connolly.

He shrugged. 'Don't know, but I'll go right away and find out.' He turned and took a few steps to the door, and stopped. 'Maybe we can get a coffee after?'

'Sure thing,' she said, and turned on her computer.

Doyle, as usual, was signing letters when O'Neill entered. 'Hello, Danny, how are things going?'

'I've been to see O'Toole and Marty Murphy at *The Local* and I got a name.'

Doyle sat back and put the top on his fountain pen. A little smile showed at the corner of his mouth. 'Go on.'

'Apparently O'Toole got a tip from one of his informants, a small time crook called Donie Driscoll. His nickname is Double

D and he fancies himself a bit. He lives in Sallynoggin and I'm going to pay him a visit as soon as I have a coffee.'

Doyle listened carefully, then stood up and walked over to the window. The pier was busy and he could see a crowd gathered around the recently renovated bandstand where a group were playing.

'I had a call from The Park earlier.'

O'Neill could feel bad news coming – it was in Doyle's eyes.

'The murder of Liam Burke is, as you can imagine, making a lot of people in high places very jumpy, and they want, *need*, a result quickly. So, those extra officers we've had are being re-assigned to that case. I'm sorry, but that's the way they want to play it.'

O'Neill was shocked and didn't hide it. 'Shit, do they want us to catch a serial killer or not?'

Doyle walked back to his desk and sat down. 'I know it's tough, Danny, but that's the way it is. At least until they catch *their* bastard.'

O'Neill took a few deep breaths. 'Right, we'll get on with it, sir. Done it before, and no doubt we'll do it again.' The look on his face was anything but happy.

Doyle frowned. 'I know you will, Danny. If anyone is going to catch the Penman it'll be you. Just a matter of time.'

O'Neill made a face. He wasn't looking for a compliment but accepted it. 'Thank you, sir.' he said. 'It's great to know that you're behind us. It's all we need, sir, but this is proving to be a real nightmare.'

Doyle didn't reply; he didn't need to. He took the top off his pen and went back to signing more letters.

O'Neill and Connolly had coffee in the restaurant and he told her about the reassignment of the officers.

'I can understand why the government is so nervous about Burke's murder. They see it as though it could be any one of them, and they want this guy caught.' Christine Connolly put her cup down, and continued. 'Catching the killer does two things for the government. One, it gets him off the streets and the public will be happy.'

'And two?' said O'Neill, as Connolly paused.

'And two, it also sends a message to any political dissidents or drug lords that they will be hunted down if they try anything like this.' She took a sip of coffee.

'Very good, Christine. I think that you are in the wrong place.'

She raised an eyebrow.

'Yes, I think that you should be in government advising these guys.'

She made a face. 'You mean I should be a spin doctor, *sir*?'

'Heaven forbid,' he replied, 'but I do think that you see through the crap very quickly, and that's a skill that is, I believe, more or less intuitive. But hey, you're not going to up sticks and leave this investigation now that we've got a name to follow, are you?'

'No, sir, definitely not. And I can't wait to meet the man whose name sounds like a bra.'

O'Neill almost choked as diners turned to see what the fun was about. He knew they were wondering how he could possibly be laughing while investigating a serial killer. But a funny line was always a funny line.

O'Neill's mobile trilled. 'Hello, Jack, what's going on?' he said, making a face.

Connolly watched him as she drank her coffee and then looked out at the bay and the yachts bobbing about in the blue water.

O'Neill nodded. 'Send it to my email, Jack. The address is doneill146@gmail.com, and I'll print it off. I hope that my swing is okay, I haven't had much practise lately.'

He moved his fingers, indicating that the voice on the other end was a talker and Connolly grinned. He rang off and put the phone in his pocket. 'Golf match on Saturday,' he said, picking up his cup.

Connolly put her cup down. 'I wouldn't have believed that there were 145 others out there with your name. I'm surprised.'

O'Neill wiped his lip. 'Do you play snooker?'

She was surprised. 'No, but I used to watch it on television with my father. He played it in his golf club.'

'Well, the highest score a player can get is 147.'

'A maximum,' she said quickly.

'Yes, it's the best you can do. So...'

She was listening intently, not wanting to miss a word.

'... so when I opened my account I chose '146' because it's not the best.'

'Almost.'

He nodded. 'Exactly ... and it makes me think twice about things. Nobody gets everything right, all the time. And it's no harm being reminded of that from time to time.'

She nodded. Inspector Danny O'Neill was a complex man alright, she thought, and she liked him a little more.

An hour later they were sitting with Donie Driscoll in Baker's Corner pub. At the end of the bar a large flat screen television was showing horse racing, and a few of the patrons shouted encouragement to the deaf and distant equines.

'Right, Donie, tell me how you know about the pencil' said O'Neill.

Driscoll was sitting at a table in the corner with the two officers opposite. There was to be no escape. He was going nowhere until he answered some questions – he knew the routine. He was nervous and kept his head down a little, looking up fleetingly at his inquisitors. It was subservient, but if it would help to get rid of the coppers, then fuck it. He took a mouthful of lager and his eyes shifted from O'Neill to Connolly and back again before he put the glass down.

'Well,' said O'Neill, forcing an answer.

Driscoll hadn't shaved for a few days and the silvery stubble wasn't helping the cops in their assessment of O'Toole's former informant. He would never contact *The Local* again, not when it brought this shit down on him. Jesus, he was just trying to make a few euros like everyone else, and now look at him, surrounded by coppers in his local boozer. His credibility would be shot to pieces and there'd be no more juicy little snippets of gossip and information to pass on. No money either. It was a bad day, and from the shouts at the television his horse had just lost – a loser. That makes two of us, he thought, and wiped his mouth.

'My niece, Debbie, works in the Body Factory,' he said.

'You mean the Coroner's Office, don't you?' said Connolly evenly, not buying his attempt at humour.

'Yeah, yeah. She works in the Administration Office and sees all the files.' He leaned forward. 'And hears things.'

'Like what?' asked O'Neill clearly.

'Like that those two women were both killed with a pencil. I mean, you couldn't make that shit up,' he said. 'Debbie phoned me about it. So, I passed it on to Tooler, and now you're here. Short and sweet, I'd say.'

'More like short and bitter, Donie,' O'Neill said, not taking his eyes off Driscoll's shifty gaze. If you really needed to trust someone then Donie Driscoll was not your man. He was a toerag who feathered his own nest and like all criminals, was reliably unreliable. 'Right, I'm going to make a call, Donie, and you'd better be telling me the truth, otherwise …'.

O'Neill went outside and called Shelly Tobin. She answered on the second ring and they spoke for just over two minutes. 'Yeah, looking forward to it,' he said finally and hung up.

'Our man here might just be telling the truth,' he said as he sat back down. 'Is that difficult for you, Donie?'

Driscoll didn't respond to the sarcasm and kept his mouth closed. The sneer that crawled over his face was answer enough.

'Thanks for your time, and let's NOT do this again. Okay?'

Driscoll understood. 'That's fine by me. Abso-fucking-lutely.'

O'Neill told Connolly what Shelly had said. Driscoll's niece did work in the office and would be in serious trouble for her breach of confidentiality. And probably sacked.

'Only to be expected,' said Connolly.

'I agree, but it doesn't get us any closer to the Penman.' He tapped the steering wheel a few times, thinking, before starting the car and slipping once again into Dublin's seemingly never-ending traffic.

28

The talking heads on the radio programmes were busy. As the body count rose and peoples' nerves started to fray, more and more listen to criminologists, psychologists and retired police officers discussing the killer's motives and how he might be caught. In a not so obvious way it was still stoking the fires of interest, and kept ratings high. The radio presenters were, after all, performing a 'service to the public' and would keep doing so as long as the punters kept phoning in. At least if the crimes were being discussed then they were not forgotten – and that was good for business. It was June, the 'silly season' for newspapers and news in general, and anything was worth covering. If they gave it enough space it would generate its own momentum and that was what was beginning to happen.

'And you wanted to say something, Charlie?' asked the presenter. The show had been on for nearly twenty minutes and the presenter was in fine voice and full control. 'About Liam Burke, was it?' he added quickly.

Charlie Reynolds, one of the country's leading investigative journalists, was itching to make his contribution. 'Yes, it is,' he said. 'And his involvement in certain property deals.' He cleared his throat with a slightly practised cough. 'It's well known in certain circles that a number of his deals have gone sour and that his one-time partners are not happy. I heard only last week …'.

'In the Horseshoe Bar, no doubt,' quipped the presenter, who was familiar with one of the city's leading watering holes, located in The Shelbourne Hotel.

'Sure didn't I see yourself there last week, Gerry, talking with—'

'Now, now, Charlie, this is not about me, so back to Liam Burke, please,' said the presenter, just about holding in a laugh. Gerry Kenny had been doing interviews for twenty years and there wasn't a trick that he didn't use to get the desired response. He was a slick operator and played the game better than any other radio presenter.

'Of course, of course. As I was saying, I've heard that two bigwigs who were involved with Burke in that property in Irishtown are planning to take action against him.'

'A bit late for that, don't you think?'

'Maybe for Burke, but not for his estate. If it has any money in it, and I suspect that it has, then his old mates may get their hands on some of it.' He paused. 'It's all very nasty, really, and a million miles from the picture of himself that he presented to the public when he decided to stand for election. Did you know that in the property world he was called "The Dog" because he didn't care what he had to do to get a property if he wanted it? He fought dirty and made a lot of enemies.'

'Enemies, or just envious investors?' asked Kenny.

'Hmm. I'd say a bit of both, but his enemies are powerful people with long memories.'

'Wow, Charlie, that all sounds very dark and dangerous.'

'Well, when you're talking millions, sometimes hundreds of millions, and not forgetting the little matter of egos, then anything can happen.' He sniffed. 'It has all the makings of a thriller, and I've no doubt that as we speak, someone out there is writing the bestseller.'

'You're such a cynic,' said Kenny.

'And you'll be interviewing the author in no time. Mark my words,' quipped the investigator before the presenter went to a commercial break.

'That's all I need,' said Inspector Tony Lewis angrily, before switching off the radio. He took a long deep pull on his cigarette and then squashed it in the ashtray. It was filling up rapidly and he pushed it to the edge of his desk, out of sight. He had been off the weed for almost two years now, but Liam Burke getting himself murdered had put an end to all that good work.

'I saw Burke's solicitor and accountant yesterday, and yes, he hasn't always played the game by the rules. He could sail close to the wind and really go for it when he wanted to.' Detective Bernard Reilly was standing opposite Lewis and saw the desperation in his eyes. He looked rough and seemed to have aged years in the last few days. He was under severe pressure from on high and right now he hadn't a clue. Not a sniff. Nothing. The best of the best were on board, and although the crime scene had been examined in the minutest detail, they had found nothing. No expense was being spared, but as Lewis was finding out, if there's nothing out there, then there's nothing out there. And you're fucked.

'Does that help us?' asked Lewis.

'Could do, sir. I have three financial experts examining some of the bigger deals and I'm going to see his main bankers when I'm finished here. Should be interesting to see what they know: what properties he bought and sold and any he may have used as collateral. Maybe he wasn't as open with his property mates as he should have been.'

Lewis listened carefully, leaned back in his chair and steepled his hands. He looked up at Reilly, his number two, and wondered what age he was: thirty-four, or was it thirty-five? It didn't matter. What mattered was that his best man was on the case and maybe he would get lucky. He had cracked tough cases before and it seemed that he was enjoying being involved in this one. It would look good if he managed to catch the killer, but until that happened, Lewis, and everyone else, was under pressure like never before. 'So, Bernard, who do you think did it?'

Reilly sniffed. 'Christ, I don't know, sir, but I wouldn't be surprised if one of the partners were involved.' He loosened his tie and took a deep breath. 'If you've been cheated, tricked or whatever you want to call it, out of a very large amount of money,' he shrugged, 'then I could certainly see something like this happening.' He paused and got a grip on the idea that was floating away. 'You know that there are a lot of boys from up North who are out of work nowadays, and who would find something like this very easy.'

'Jesus, Bernard, we don't need a terrorist angle, for God's sake. This is crazy enough without having to start chasing after those old ghosts.' He paused. 'And I even heard one smartass on the radio calling it Dublin's version of the grassy knoll. For fuck's sake!'

Reilly bit his lip and kept a straight face. 'I know, sir, but we can't afford to discount it. I mean, we do know that some of these old boys are involved in extortion and protection. It's not a big jump, certainly for some of those guys, to take out a bloke when he's jogging. He wasn't high profile and he had no protection. It would have been a no-brainer, if you were so inclined.'

Lewis stood and came around the desk. Through the window he could see the crowds enter and leave Dundrum Town Centre, the city's hottest place for a spot of retail therapy. Bargains were what most people wanted, and maybe a coffee with a friend. And a little gossip.

How he'd like some gossip to help his case. 'I hear what you're saying, and thanks for that. I hope that you're wrong about it, but I'll pass it on to the boys in The Park. They deal with that sort of stuff all the time, so let's see what they make of it. Okay?'

Reilly nodded. 'Fine with me, sir. I'll let you know how it goes at the bank.'

They walked to the door. 'And which bank is it?' Lewis asked as he began walking to the toilet.

Reilly grimaced. 'It's Anglo Irish, sir,'

Lewis rolled his eyes to heaven and kept going. The fact that Burke was a customer of a bank that was under investigation by the authorities for financial mismanagement was all that he needed. 'What have I done to deserve this pile of shit?' he asked quietly, as the sound of his shoes tapped along the hall. Nobody was listening, and he knew it.

★

O'Neill ran hard on Sandymount Strand. It was busy, as walkers, joggers and other less energetic souls enjoyed the early evening sunshine. It was still warm and a light breeze tickled the leaves on the trees that lined the pavement. Dogs barked as they chased sticks thrown high in the air. Further out, on a small sandbank, a group of boys shouted as they attempted to get their kites flying.

Small white horses broke on the incoming tide and he splashed in the water as it slowly came ashore. He felt good, but could only think about what Shelly Tobin had told him earlier, about Burke's fatal wound. She knew that it had been made by someone skilled with a knife, and he wondered if the Penman could be involved. What a crazy idea, he kept telling himself. There was no connection, how could there be?

He eased to a stop and looked out at the incoming tide and beyond to the yachts in the bay. 'I don't have a connection anywhere yet,' he said, and straightened up. So, there's no obvious reason why the Penman should be ruled out of the Burke investigation. It was a scary thought, but one that he felt he should bear in mind. He would keep it to himself for the time being and just see what happened.

Nothing, hopefully.

The weird case could, possibly, get even weirder. Fuck, he needed that like a hole in the head. His demons were coming into focus and he scrunched his eyes, trying to chase them away. It was useless and he exhaled loudly and felt his shoulders drop.

A dog's barking cut through his thinking. It ran, splashing loudly in the water, and retrieved a stick. O'Neill ran again, harder, much harder, and got into a familiar rhythm. Soon he was lost, unthinking, his feet crashing into the bubbling tide.

29

He took a deep pull on his cigarette and then put it out in the ashtray, his index finger pressing down hard. A wisp of smoke slid from his almost-closed lips as he started the DVD player again. The screen showed the police press conference, the stressed look on Tony Lewis's face, and the tension in the room. It was nearly a week since he had murdered Liam Burke, but the case had not progressed beyond speculation and bitchy gossip. He didn't stop the sneer that was growing at the side of his mouth. He liked it and reached for another cigarette. 'And we've heard nothing from Inspector O'Neill either,' he said bitterly, and lit up. When he put out his cigarette he knew it was time to move.

The train slowed as it approached Sydney Parade station, just as the girl opened her mobile phone and dialled. It rang twice. 'I'm at Sydney Parade,' she said.

'Okay, darling, I'm on my way,' her father said and hung up.

The girl put the phone back into her bag and looked around at the other passengers. The carriage was almost empty, with a kissing couple oblivious to the world at the far end and near the rear door, three boozed-up students were telling jokes and laughing loudly.

Otherwise, the carriage was empty.

He leaned closer to the wall with a perfect view of the incoming train and carefully put on a pair of tight-fitting leather gloves. He worked his fingers back and forth until he was happy and then took a couple of slow deep breaths to settle himself.

The train slowed and he could see the rich marsh reflected in the train's windows as it screeched to a halt. The automatic doors hissed open and he felt his heartbeat quicken with anticipation as the blonde girl stepped down into the pool of yellow light.

She walked towards the exit as the train jerked into life and made for its next stop in Booterstown. Most importantly, she was on her own. He felt himself stiffen with excitement.

Behind him, the late night traffic on the Rock Road slid by, eerily lit by the tungsten lights that stretched along the road like giant alien visitors. In the darkness they looked threatening and the traffic seemed to speed past them before it was noticed. A local wag had said that the place should now be called Bogeytown, and many agreed.

The girl took out her mobile phone and flipped the cover open. Her face was lit up and he could see her as she came closer and turned into the ticket hall. She paused for a moment and stepped over a pool of vomit, the sharp smell making her wince. She heard her heels clicking on the tiles of the ticket office and wondered why it was so dark. There was always a light in the corner but now it seemed to be broken. She quickened her pace, pressed the speed dial and held the phone to her ear. 'Hi Dad, I'm at the sta ...' she said, and then the first blow landed.

'Bitch!' he said and hit her again on the back of the head, slamming her against the wall. She dropped her phone and handbag and felt her face scrape against the brickwork. She tasted blood at the corner of her mouth as her attacker kicked her in the side, knocking the wind out of her. She slid down the wall and felt his breath on her neck when he leaned down and spat in her face. 'You're all the same, all the fucking same!' he spat and punched her in the face.

'Stop, please … stop,' she managed through tears and pain as he jabbed a pencil into her neck. The shock to her system was overwhelming and she fell into the blackness.

'Fuck you, fuck you,' he said through gritted teeth and spat on her with all the venom he could muster. He squatted down and looked at the crumpled body, listening. The blood was rushing in his head and his heart was beating like a freight train. He thought he heard a sound close by, and stopped. The darkness outside the station was suddenly cut in two as a car's headlights sliced through it, highlighting the parking signs and a bicycle chained to the metal railings.

'Fuck,' he said, running back towards the tracks. The car stopped, the driver's door opened and he knew who it was. 'Well, my friend, you're in for a big fucking surprise,' he said, and his chest heaved in a silent laugh. He jumped from the platform onto the track, running carefully along the sleepers to a gap in the sea wall. He climbed over the fence and in a few strides was on the beach. The sound of the dark rolling sea was the only thing he heard as he jogged along the hard sand, the granite wall his protector. High above, a cloud slid across the face of the moon, dimming the last piece of light. The only witness, he thought, and grinned. He felt the exhilaration of the moment flood his body. He was complete again and in a few minutes even his footprints would be gone. No trace, just the way he wanted it. He was invisible.

30

A few glasses of Chateau Bellevue la Foret, Liz's favourite wine, helped him to sleep and keep the demons at bay. They were showing up too often now and he wondered whether he should talk to his doctor. He hated feeling so weak, relying on a bottle of wine to ease his pain. I'll see the doctor when this is over, he promised Liz's photograph, and closed his eyes.

And then his mobile phone started ringing.

He reached over and picked it up. 'Yeah,' he groaned and pushed up against a pillow.

'Sorry to call you at this hour, Danny, but he's done it again.' Pat Brady's voice was calm.

O'Neill held his breath, waiting for the bad news.

'the Penman, he's attacked a girl at Booterstown Station.'

O'Neill took a deep breath. 'Fuck … is she dead?'

'No, she's just hanging on.' He paused and O'Neill could hear voices in the background. 'She's taken one helluva beating.'

O'Neill swung his legs over the edge of the bed. 'Okay, Pat. Get a patrol car to collect me in twenty minutes. Oh, and have you contacted Forensics?' he asked.

'I have, and they're on their way already.'

'Very good. See you then.' He rang off and went into the bathroom, and not daring to look in the mirror, turned on the shower. It wouldn't wash away his demons but it might just clear his head. He needed that, and then some.

★

The flashing yellow lights on the two police cars cast an eerie, uncomfortable glow. An officer stretched a roll of yellow tape from a lamppost, forming a secure area. It flapped in the breeze, and behind it the Forensics' van doors were open. Gary O'Connell stepped down and nodded as O'Neill came over.

'Anything?' he asked.

O'Connell raised his eyes. 'A lot of blood, there's always a lot of blood,' he said. 'But ...'.

O'Neill gave him a sharp look. 'But what?'

'Come on, I'll show you.'

The two men walked up the steps into the ticket hall, where Forensics officers in white boiler suits went about their grim work. One was taking photographs while another was dusting down the scene for fingerprints – the usual. Another adjusted a portable light that bathed the small space in a strong antiseptic glow. It highlighted the blood on the tiles, making the place look like an abattoir.

'Jesus,' said O'Neill. 'What a mess.' He wiped his mouth with the back of his hand and slowly shook his head.

O'Connell pointed into a corner. 'Over there,' he said.

O'Neill's eyes followed O'Connell's finger and saw the small dark object. 'What is it?' he said.

'I think it's the girl's mobile phone. And ... I think it was on when the attack happened.' He said nothing more.

'You think that we might be able to get something from it? Christ, how weird is that.'

O'Connell nodded. 'Yeah, we'll take it back to the lab. I'll let you know what we find.'

O'Neill heard footsteps behind him and turned. 'The girl's name is Caroline Dolan,' said Brady. 'Her father is outside. He was here to collect her and ...'.

'So he found her,' said O'Neill flatly. It wasn't a question, and the image of the father finding his daughter filled his mind. He felt the taste of bile creeping up his throat .

'She's been taken to St Vincent's Hospital,' said Brady.

O'Neill nodded. 'Good, we'll go there in a few minutes.'

The traffic on the Rock Road slowed as drivers and passengers tried to get a better look. No news was good news but the scene at the station had all the making of a scoop. It would be on the radio in the morning and the talking heads would be out in force. If this latest attack was the work of the Penman, then the pressure was going to increase even more. With a reduced team of officers, finding this crazy guy just got more difficult, if that were even possible, thought O'Neill. A Forensics officer took another photograph, the blinding flash followed by the whirr of the automatic winder.

'In here,' said the police officer, leading a man who looked as though he had just got out of bed. It was probably true, given that it was now nearly 2:30a.m. and that he was wearing old slippers. His grey hair was unkempt and his eyes were red and nervous. They darted from the young police officer to O'Neill and Brady. 'This is Mr Fletcher, he's the station manager.'

Brady spoke. 'Thanks,' he said to the officer who turned and went back outside.

O'Neill eyed the CCTV camera above the ticket office window. 'I need to get the tape from that camera, can you help?'

Fletcher gulped nervously. 'Yes, I can get that for you.' He fiddled with a bunch of keys and walked to the office. He opened another door into a small cream-coloured room with a sink, fridge, table and three plastic chairs. A calendar with images of motorbikes and scantily clad models hung above the table and had names and times written on it. Must be the roster, thought O'Neill, as Fletcher bent down and pressed a button. A light flashed on the video machine and then a cassette was pushed out. He took it and handed it to O'Neill. 'It only works when there is movement,' said Fletcher. 'It's not on all the time.' It sounded like an apology.

O'Neill looked at the cassette and then at the ticket office. 'Probably not going to be too bright out there,' he said, thinking out loud. 'I hope that we can make stuff out.'

'Maybe we can get it enhanced if we need to, sir,' said Brady. 'There's a professor in Trinity College who is renowned for doing that sort of thing. I read an article about him in a technical magazine recently.'

'Is that what you've been reading lately? I'm impressed.'

Brady was mildly embarrassed, as if a dirty little secret had been revealed. He chewed his lip and said nothing.

'Fine, let's have a look at it first and see what we have,' said O'Neill. He went outside and felt the cool air on his face. It was damp and he shivered in the strengthening breeze. The salty air tickled his nose and he reached for a hankie. 'Right, Pat, I'm going to St Vincent's to see what's what. You handle things here and I'll see you in the office in the morning.'

'Will do.' Brady turned away and went over to speak to Fletcher. He took out his notebook and tapped his pockets as he searched for a pen. What next, thought O'Neill, as he sat into the police car and headed for the hospital.

★

It was almost 3a.m. when O'Neill entered the automatic doors of St Vincent's Hospital and his nose turned in response to the smell, that hospital smell. The large atrium was almost empty, with only a worker sweeping between the rows of empty chairs where patients normally waited. Two young men sat and stared vacantly at the television where footballers moved in silence. It was a strange scene, but then sitting in a hospital at such an hour wasn't exactly what most people did.

The quiet of the place was unsettling.

He asked about Caroline Dolan and was directed to the Intensive Care Unit on the third floor.

When the door slid open it hit him, the smell bringing it all back in an instant. He shivered and had to stop to take out his hankie to cover his nose. All those weeks lying in bed with that stab wound in his lower stomach came back in a rush. He was thankful that he had been in hospital, recovering and being cared for by friendly staff. He couldn't have asked for more, but the smell brought him back to that horrible moment. A few more inches this way or that and he'd probably have died. It was a stroke of luck. He felt his fingers touch the wound.

'She's in theatre at the moment,' the nurse at the reception desk said. 'I've no idea how long it will be. You never know with stuff like this.' Her voice was calm as she held his look.

'So … you can't tell me anything?' he said a little awkwardly.

The nurse pursed her lips and put her pen down. Her brown eyes took him in as she silently appraised him. He reckoned that she was in her forties but she could have passed for someone ten years younger. She wore hardly any makeup, she didn't need to, and the soft pink lipstick was her only indulgence. Her dark hair was hidden beneath a white cap, but a few strands had escaped and hung lazily above her ears.

She had the easy confidence of someone who had worked in the hospital for years and was well used to dealing with anxious relatives. And police. 'Inspector, right now the young lady is fighting for her life and I cannot tell you any more than that. The operation could take a long time, who knows?' A small smile curled at the edges of her mouth. 'I appreciate your concern, but she is in safe hands now. Let the surgeons do what they have to do, and hope for the best.'

He knew she was right, and nodded. 'I understand, thank you.' He handed her a card. 'That's my number, please call when you have some news. It's important.'

The nurse looked at the card. 'Will do, Inspector Danny O'Neill, will do,' she said.

'And you are?'

'My name is Doreen Shaw. And it's Sister Shaw to you.'

He suddenly realised how much he liked this woman. For someone who dealt with distraught families every day, she was one cool customer. She was definitely the right person for the job, and very much in charge. 'Shaw, like the writer,' he said.

She leaned forward an inch or two, a gesture that held his attention. 'He should be so lucky,' she said, and raised an eyebrow.

O'Neill smiled; it was all he could do. 'Indeed,' he said quietly, and left.

31

News of the most recent attack was everywhere, and callers to the morning radio shows were demanding answers. 'What is going on?' an angry voice had demanded. 'The place is worse than Dodge City.' It expressed the sentiment of all the other callers and O'Neill finally turned the radio off in frustration. He banged the steering wheel and shouted 'Fuck!' as the traffic lights changed to red.

The atmosphere in the Detectives' Room was tense when O'Neill arrived. After a quick meeting with Doyle where he brought him up to date, he called all the team together.

'You all know by now that another woman was attacked last night, at Booterstown station. I went to the hospital to see her but she was being operated on. They will contact me, hopefully this morning, with her condition.'

'How badly was she injured?' asked Christine Connolly, her voice edged with concern.

O'Neill shrugged. 'I don't know exactly, but judging from the crime scene she must have lost a lot of blood.' He paused. 'And she was stabbed.'

'With what?' It was Dave Conroy.

'It looks like he used a pencil.'

'So it's the same guy?' said Connolly.

'We don't know yet, but he looks good for it.'

Heads nodded, taking in the information, but nobody said anything.

'So, today I want to find out everything we can about Caroline Dolan: friends, work, hobbies, clubs, boyfriends, girlfriends … everything. There has to be a connection between the victims and we must find it. Otherwise this guy is going to keep on attacking women and …'.

He didn't have to finish the sentence – the team knew what he was saying.

Pat Brady spoke. 'I've updated the board with the details from last night.' He pointed to the three photographs and the information about each of the victims. There were plenty of lines drawn but none intersecting that might indicate a connection. He lifted the videocassette off the desk. 'We still have to check this.'

'Very good, Pat, let's have a look now.'

Conroy and Brady wheeled the television and video player from the corner of the room and turned it on. 'Close the blinds, Dave,' said Brady as the team stared at the blank screen.

A small red light flickered as the tape started and the tiled ticket office was on screen. A counter on the bottom left ticked over as a digital clock on the other corner showed the time in hours, minutes and seconds. It showed 9:05:24 p.m. 'That's when the manager went home, sir. He started the CCTV just before he left. It's what he always does.'

O'Neill nodded without looking away. 'Good, so can you now speed up and get to the attack? There's nothing for us here.'

'If the attack happened at about midnight then our guy might have been lying in wait for her, and we might get a look at him a few minutes beforehand,' said Brady.

O'Neill and Connolly looked at him. 'Very good, Pat, you might be on to something,' said O'Neill. 'Right, stop the video five minutes before the attack and let's see if we get lucky.' The thought that they might see the Penman suddenly lifted the heavy atmosphere and they waited silently as Brady fast-forwarded the tape. It hissed and clicked as the images flicked wildly past, as if in a hurry to catch the killer.

Click.

Brady pressed the handset and the time showed 11:58:24 p.m. The tiled ticket office was empty – but only for a few seconds. From the top right-hand corner of the screen a man entered and stopped, looking around. Was he checking the time of the last train home or was he the Penman? He looked up at the corner of the office, took a few steps forwards and stretched his hand up. Seconds later the ticket office went into darkness.

'He's broken the light,' said Conroy. 'Smart fucker.'

'Can you brighten the picture?' O'Neill said, cursing the bastard and his own bad luck. A great chance had presented itself and just as quickly it had been taken away. It was cruel, but he couldn't do anything about that now.

Brady tried to improve the picture but it was of little use. 'Maybe the bloke in Trinity College can help. I'll take it into him when we're finished.'

'Okay, Pat. Let it roll.'

As the time ticked past 12:03:36 a.m. a ghostly image appeared from the bottom left corner. 'That must be Caroline Dolan,' said Connolly.

In a heartbeat the team could make out moving figures and a small light static against a wall. The attack lasted barely twenty seconds and ended when a stream of light lit up the ticket office.

'Pause it,' shouted O'Neill.

A figure, crouched and ready for action, turned his head. The team could see his long hair and what looked like white trainers. It was barely a profile but it was the first time that they had seen the Penman. They all looked long and hard at the quivering image.

'Fucker,' said Conroy again.

'Yes, but not an invisible one. Not any more,' added Christine Connolly.

Brady hit play and the tape continued, as the figure appeared to move to the platform. 'That was how he escaped,' he said, thinking out loud, and the others nodded their agreement.

'So there is probably no evidence there now, but Christine and Pat can check it out while I visit the hospital,' said O'Neill.

'Have we any help with the door-to-door work?' asked Conroy with little enthusiasm.

O'Neill shook his head. 'You can get a couple of officers downstairs, but with the Burke case taking up all the spare staff, I'm afraid we're down to the bare bones.'

Brady shrugged at the expected answer. 'By the way, is there any news on how that case is going? Lots being said on the radio.'

This time O'Neill shrugged. 'From what the boss told me, they've absolutely no idea, and no leads. There's some speculation about property deals gone sour and one or other of Burke's partners taking revenge. Seems a bit far-fetched, but they've got nothing else to go on. I know Tony Lewis, and if there's anyone who you would want to lead the investigation then he's the man. He's a fine investigator.'

'A bit like our case, sir, no clues,' said Christine Connolly and left it at that.

Nobody said a word, but the silence in the room was deafening.

It was an uncomfortable few seconds before she spoke again. 'And what was the light on the ground?'

'That was the light from Caroline's mobile phone, which the Forensics Unit is now examining,' answered Brady.

O'Neill suddenly realised that Brady was wearing a new suit and shirt with a colourful silk tie. That was different, and his shoes were polished and shining. Was he trying to impress Christine Connolly? he thought. He liked him for even trying.

'So you mean that we might be able to *hear* the attack?' she said. She shivered at the idea.

It was sick but there it was, out in the open.

'Jesus, that's really sick,' said Conroy, wincing.

'Not as sick as what that fucker did,' said O'Neill, 'but … if we can get something useful from it, then it may help us catch the bastard.'

★

When the meeting was over and tasks assigned, O'Neill went to the restaurant and then made his way along the coast road to St Vincent's Hospital. Had they just got a break or was it a teaser that would come to nothing? He didn't know and hoped a crack would appear that would give him a glimpse, a clear one, of his enemy. He knew from previous cases that small things led to bigger things, and he said a silent prayer as he pulled into the car park.

'Good Morning, Inspector,' said Sister Shaw as he approached the desk. In the cold light of day she looked even more prim and proper, and ready to deal with anything.

'Hello, Sister Shaw. Have you any news for me?'

She tapped her keyboard and looked at the computer screen. 'Yes,' she said. 'Caroline is out of danger, but you will have to speak with Doctor Magee first. Nobody is to see her without seeing him first.' This was not open for discussion.

'That's great news, excellent. And may I have a word with the doctor, if he's available? I'd appreciate it.'

Sister Shaw picked up the phone and dialled. She looked at him and he knew she was checking him out. 'You look tired, Inspector. Not sleeping well?'

'Well, when you've been chasing a crazed killer for the past couple of weeks, it's not easy to get a good night's sleep. Too much going on up here,' he said, tapping his head. 'It's ...'.

'... a dirty job, but someone has to do it. I understand,' she replied. If anyone knew it was dirty then she did. 'Oh, Doctor Magee, I have Inspector O'Neill here and he would like to speak with you about Caroline Dolan.' She listened for a few seconds. 'Okay, I'll tell him,' she said, and put the phone down. She looked over the desk. 'He's on his way down, Inspector. Take a seat.'

Magee stepped from the lift and, following Shaw's eyes, went over to O'Neill. 'Inspector, good to see you.'

They shook hands.

'And you too,' said O'Neill. 'I was wondering how Caroline Dolan is and if, maybe, I could have a word with her?'

Magee nodded his head but said nothing. He slipped his hands into his pockets and O'Neill reckoned that the young man had been up all night. He had that midnight shadow around the cheeks and his hair was tousled. Maybe he had just woken up, he thought, understanding the medic's demanding job. Either way, he looked as though he needed a rest and he could certainly empathise with him on that score.

'If Caroline had not been so fit, we might have lost her. She's a strong young woman and that most certainly helped her to stay alive.'

'That's great news, really great.'

Magee turned and O'Neill followed him. 'She was stabbed with a pencil, but thankfully it missed her vital organs and hasn't caused too much damage. She was also kicked and has been badly bruised, but she has no broken bones.'

O'Neill felt relieved. It was the first time since the case began that he felt marginally hopeful and wondered if the tide was turning. Hopefully it was coming in.

They stopped outside a door where Caroline's name was noted in large black letters on a white card.

Magee turned to O'Neill. 'I want to see how she is, Inspector, so do not say anything unless I say so. Is that clear?'

'Yes, Doctor. I'm just delighted that she is alive.'

Magee pushed the door open and O'Neill saw a young girl lost behind a bank of cables, lights and machines that clicked and showed numbers rising and falling as she breathed. A plastic tube exited her nose and was soon lost under the blanket that touched her chin. Her breathing was easy and the blanket moved slowly up and down while he stood at the end of the bed looking at her.

Magee looked at her chart and then checked the readouts from the machines on a small screen. He nodded happily. Then he leaned close and spoke softly. 'Caroline, this is Doctor Magee. How are you feeling now? Any better?'

She let out a moan, but not one that he took as being painful. It was like what you'd expect from someone who has just woken up from a deep sleep.

'Good, that's good, Caroline.' He looked at O'Neill. 'I have someone here who would like to ask you a few questions about what happened. It's Inspector O'Neill, Okay?'

Another soft moan was her reply. Murphy again checked the small screen and waved O'Neill forward.

'Caroline, can you tell me anything about what happened to you last night? It would be a great help.'

Her head moved on the pillow.

She moved again but she didn't say anything. She didn't even moan.

Magee waved for O'Neill to stop. 'Thank you, Caroline. You go back to sleep and we'll talk later.'

Outside the two men walked to the lift. 'Sorry about that, Inspector, but she is obviously too tired right now. Come back tomorrow.'

'I will do, Doctor. And thanks for your efforts in keeping her alive. You did a great job.'

Magee smiled, his eyelids even heavier now. 'Thank you, and I hope you find the man responsible. He must be a very sick individual indeed.'

'He's all that and more, no doubt about it.'

Magee nodded and they shook hands. He turned and headed back along the corridor when O'Neill called out. 'Doctor, what happened to Caroline's clothes when she was brought in? Were they thrown out, or are they …'.

Murphy rubbed his chin with the back of his hand. O'Neill noted that his eyes seemed brighter. 'A good question, Inspector. That's a very good question indeed. Let's ask Sister Shaw, she's the fountain of all knowledge around here.'

'I can certainly believe that.'

The two men walked purposefully to the reception desk.

Thirty minutes later Caroline Dolan's clothes were located in a storeroom in the basement. They were in a black plastic bag and somebody had thankfully tied a label showing the time they had been removed from the operating theatre. 'They could have some of the attacker's DNA on them,' O'Neill said, holding the bag by the thick knot.

'There's a lot of her blood on them, Inspector, it's not going to be easy to get anything,' offered Magee.

That was obvious, but O'Neill wasn't put off. 'I know, but our Forensics boys love a challenge.'

'Best of luck.'

'Thanks, and I'll call in tomorrow.'

An hour later, O'Neill was sitting in Gary O'Connell's office, the plastic bag on a chair beside him.

'It's all yours, Gary. The doctor will send on Caroline's DNA profile so that you can eliminate hers from your testing.'

'Okay, Danny.'

'And the mobile phone, anything there?'

'O'Connell checked his computer screen and tapped it with his finger. 'It was sent to our electronics boys in The Park and they're working on it now. They have to contact the service provider, but as it's part of a possible murder inquiry, all doors are open. They should have something by tomorrow.'

'That's fine. And do let me know as soon as …'.

'Don't worry, Danny, you're sadly at the top of my list.'

O'Neill grinned. 'Thanks. It's nice to know that someone's thinking about me.'

O'Connell shook his head. 'Get out of here. Hey, maybe the Assistant State Pathologist might be thinking of you too. What a lucky boy you are.'

'Okay, enough of this, I'm off,' he said, and left the grinning Head of Forensics to his bloody work.

Outside, the day was warming up and he drove back to the police station without the radio on. He didn't need any more bad news. He thought of Caroline's clothes and hoped that the attacker had mistakenly left a mark. He had to be positive, and right now, for some unknown reason, he was more positive than he had been in weeks, even if it was only in a small way.

As he pulled into the traffic he remembered Christine Connolly's words earlier and frowned in concentration. It was surprising, almost unbelievable when he thought about it, that neither case had shown any progress. Considering the resources thrown at both cases it was surprising, if not unbelievable, that nothing had turned up. He decided to call Tony Lewis and have a word. It couldn't do any harm, and anyway, he hadn't seen him for at least two, or three years. Time flies when you're chasing shadows.

32

A game of cricket was in progress when Pat Brady walked past the pavilion. Small groups of students sat on the grass and cheered on their friends as a gentle warm breeze rustled the leaves above. Around him was the constant chatter of students relaxing and tourists taking in the sights of Dublin's oldest university. The words of the song 'Summer in Dublin' came into his head and he sang it to himself, enjoying the temporary escape from the tension of the police station.

The Audio and Visual Arts office had a view of Nassau Street and he looked at the bustling crowds all the way up Dawson Street to St Stephen's Green. It was a novel view and one that he wouldn't mind swapping for the one he had each day in Dun Laoghaire. The view from the Detectives' Room was nothing like this, with the old clock tower on the main street the only relief. Maybe it was deliberate, he thought, to keep staff at their desks. Was it a control thing? Probably not, but either way, right now, the view was just fine.

He turned when he heard someone say his name.

'Detective Brady, I'm Niall Bailey, Head of Visual Studies. Good to see you.'

They shook hands and Brady was surprised at how young the man looked. Bailey wore blue corduroy trousers, a white shirt and his dark hair fell well below his collar. A pair of desert boots completed the casual look. His face was tanned and his blue eyes bright and alert.

Brady smiled. 'Sorry, but I expected someone older to be in charge. My mistake,' he offered, and held his hands up.

Bailey laughed. 'Don't worry; you're not the first person to be surprised. The department is fairly new and the university wanted someone young, well, youngish, to run it, and I was recruited from Berkeley, across the bay from San Francisco.'

'That explains the tan.'

He nodded. 'I'd been over there for ten years and was keen to come home. I jumped at the opportunity when it came. Now I'm just back from a month's work over there, so this is the result. I get invited back there every year for a series of lectures and to do some research, so I'm not complaining. It's also good PR for the university, so everyone's a winner.'

'Sounds good to me.'

Bailey led the way to his office where he offered Brady some coffee.

'White with one,' Brady said, putting the videocassette on the desk. He tapped it with a finger. 'This is what I would like you to have a look at.'

Bailey noted the tape and sat down opposite. 'Can you tell me something about it, and what you need?' Bailey asked, taking a sip of coffee.

Brady explained about the attack in Booterstown station and what they could see on the tape. He said that he had read the article about Bailey's recent work and that was why he was sitting here.

'Good to see that you have a scientific interest, Detective; it's commendable. If you are happy to leave the tape with me overnight, I should have an answer by tomorrow.' He put his cup down and picked up the tape. 'I wonder what little gem of information I can extract from you, eh?' he said, a row of pearly white teeth showing.

'Anything would be better than what we have. So, yes, you may keep it. But I'll have to ask you to sign for it, as it is the DART's property and it's evidence in an ongoing police investigation.'

'No problem,' said Bailey. 'Glad to help. I just hope that we can entice whatever little snippet of information that's inside.'

He put the tape down. 'One of my colleagues in America did something like this before, so I've already put a call into him.' He winked at Brady. 'Fingers crossed?'

'Yeah, fingers crossed it is then.'

★

By the time the officers returned to the police station after hours of house-to-house calls, they were none the wiser. They confirmed that Caroline Dolan lived on Pinehaven, off Cross Avenue, not more than a few minutes walk from where Barbara Ryan had lived. And not more than a six or seven minute walk to Angie Murphy's front door. All the victims lived within a stone's throw of each of each other, but still no lines intersected. It was just more frustration and nothing useful was added to the murder board.

Caroline Dolan worked in advertising and was a keen middle distance runner. She had represented Dublin in various national championships and her strong body and constitution had helped her to survive the attack. '*Mens sana in corpore sano* – a healthy mind in a healthy body,' said Christine Connolly as she taped a picture of Caroline Dolan to the board.

'Very profound,' said Conroy.

She looked at him but didn't see any cynicism. 'Well it's true, isn't it?'

'Yeah, and long may she … run. It saved her life?'

She stepped back and looked at the board. 'All three victims are from the same neighbourhood, that much is clear. But we can't find any connections between them. They are of different ages, *blondes*, but aren't friends. A mother, a lecturer and someone who works in advertising, who somehow crossed the killer's path – but where?'

'That's the million dollar-dollar question, Christine,' said Conroy. 'But in all the years I've been working on murder cases I've never seen anything like it. Not a clue in sight.'

'I spoke with someone in Quantico yesterday and he was at a loss,' she said, and rolled her eyes.

'Jeez, if those boys can't help, well …'.

'They did say that the killer must appear as presentable, very presentable, and non-threatening, otherwise Barbara Ryan would not have invited him inside,' she added.

Conroy unfolded his arms. 'Okay, but what about the other attacks? He wasn't being very presentable then, was he?'

Connolly shrugged. 'Fair point, Dave, and I don't have an answer to that.'

'If the same man is responsible for all three attacks, and it looks like he was, then it's surprising that he was most exposed just before he killed Barbara Ryan. His first attack, agreed?' said Conroy.

'Agreed,' said Connolly.

'Maybe because the first attack did not go according to plan, whatever that was, he now attacks in the dark. He's safer there.'

Connolly nodded. 'Go on, this is good.'

Conroy wasn't sure where to go. 'As you said before it appears that his actions are escalating. He thinks that he'll never be caught and he can do whatever he likes, when he likes. So, if that is the case, then his next attack is coming in the next few days and, more than likely, at night.'

'I hear what you're saying, but it's not getting us any nearer.'

Conroy exhaled loudly. 'No, nothing's getting us closer.' Connolly shook her head back and forth, trying to get the pieces of the puzzle to somehow fall into place. 'I'd give anything to know what it is that we just can't see. I'm not saying it's staring us in the face but we must be close. We've turned over so many stones, and still there's nothing.' She was stumped.

'Maybe when we see the video, we may get a good look at the bastard.'

She nodded. 'Hopefully … but I'm not so sure.'

'And why do you say that?'

She faced Conroy. 'This guy is very clever, and to date, he has given us nothing.'

'There's a blood sample from Barbara Ryan's home, and the spit,' he offered.

'Yes, I'll give you that, but since then, nothing. And that may tie-in with what you just said about why the second and third attacks are different from the first one. When he set out to attack Caroline Dolan he was probably wearing a baseball cap or beanie. He knew that there was a CCTV camera in the ticket office but couldn't put it out of commission, hence the head cover. We'll see the lab boys do their stuff.'

'I see where you're coming from, Christine, I sure hope that you aren't right.'

'So do I,' she said, but with little conviction.

★

Over dinner, O'Neill brought Shelly up to speed on the case.

'With a bit of luck you will get something from the video and maybe even the mobile phone,' she said, and swirled wine in her glass.

He was doing the same but there were no answers at the bottom of his glass. He looked up. 'We've done so much work but got no further since day one. I think we'll have to get lucky. I see no other way forward.'

Shelly took a sip. 'And I hear from John Boyd that there's no progress in the Burke case either. Strange, eh?'

He put his glass down. 'Are you suggesting there's a connection with Burke and the other attacks? A bit unlikely don't you think?'

'I agree it's unlikely, but crazy things happen. If we are looking for only one guy then this really complicates a very complicated story.'

O'Neill leaned forward, his elbows on the table. 'Why do you think the cases might be connected? I mean we have no evidence to suggest that they might be. In fact, we have no useful evidence *at all.*'

'I know, and that's what makes it possible. The killer has left no trace,' she stressed, 'so that's consistent. If you really wanted to kill Burke, why not shoot him? It would be much cleaner and more definitive. But no, the killer slashes him with a knife. Once! And that, believe me, takes some doing.'

'Go on,' he said, topping up their glasses.

'If you were hired to kill Burke, surely you wouldn't just bring along a knife. No professional killer would be so casual, if that's the right word. I just … just feel there's something there.' She took a long sip. 'That's all.'

He smiled. 'I'm impressed, Miss Marple. Maybe you should join the police force. It could do with someone like you!'

She raised her brow, teasing. 'And what can *you*, Inspector, do with me?'

O'Neill came around to the other side of the table, leaned down and kissed her. 'Why don't I interview you now and we'll see what …'.

Shelly placed a finger on his lips. 'You might be surprised at what I know, Inspector,' she said softly and they kissed again.

'I can't wait,' he said, pleased at how his investigation had taken such an unexpected and pleasantly demanding turn.

33

Pat Brady took the call from Niall Bailey. 'I have something for you, Detective. Do you want to come in and I can go through it with you?'

Brady agreed and said that he would be in Trinity College within the hour. 'Good, I'll have the coffee ready. Bring some doughnuts,' he said and put down the phone.

'Who was that?' asked O'Neill.

'My man with the video, says he has something for us.'

'Good stuff, Pat. Get back as soon as you can. I know Doyle is anxious to see it. He wants to let the chiefs in The Park know if it's useful or not.'

'Will do,' Brady said as he picked up his jacket and left.

O'Neill noted that he was wearing another new tie, one with abstract colourful images that certainly made a statement. Pat was definitely putting his best foot, or tie, forward, and he reminded himself to watch for Christine Connolly's reaction.

After a meeting with Doyle he went to the restaurant for coffee. Outside, beyond the heavy glass windows, the silent world went about its business. Traffic passed by and people walked in the sunshine.

A bank of white cloud hung high above Howth looking down on Dublin Bay. It was an image that an artist would like to capture, but sadly O'Neill never painted anything other than doors and garden gates. He appreciated the skill involved and he also appreciated what Shelly had said last night. And how

Christine Connolly had hinted at the lack of progress in both cases. Was she thinking what Shelly had said? Coincidence! He hadn't passed it on to Doyle yet, but there might come a time. This case was weird from the beginning, so there was no point in trying to anticipate where it was going next. It was a waste of time and energy that he couldn't afford. Especially after last night, he thought, his lips curling in a mischievous smile.

Back at his desk he flicked through the latest edition of *The Local* and noted its restrained coverage of the recent attacks. That's more like it lads, he thought, as his mobile began ringing.

It was Gary O'Connell. 'Morning, Danny, and have you had your coffee and cake yet?' He knew the routine.

'Hey, are you spying on me or what?'

O'Connell laughed. 'You are just so predictable.'

'I must remember you the next time I need a psychological assessment. I didn't know that you dabbled in that dark science as well. You're full of surprises, Gary!'

O'Connell laughed again. 'And I have another one for you.'

O'Neill was suddenly listening very carefully. 'Go on.'

'I've got two in fact.'

O'Neill sat down and reached for a pen. 'Okay, shoot.'

O'Connell coughed, readying himself. 'Firstly, we found DNA that does not belong to Caroline Dolan, and we are trying to match it with the unidentified blood sample from the Ryan attack, and the spit from the second attack. I'll have an answer after lunch.'

'Excellent. And two.'

'Well, we were able to retrieve some of the recording of the attack from her mobile phone.' He paused and his voice dropped. 'It doesn't make for easy listening, Danny, but it's there alright.'

O'Neill was surprised. 'Wow, Gary, that's … great news. When can I have a copy of it?'

'I have to go to Greystones after this call, so I'll drop it in to you.'

'Excellent, see you then. And I might even buy you a coffee.'

'It's a deal,' O'Connell said and hung up.

With the phone still in his hand O'Neill called Tony Lewis, and after a minute or so of small talk they agreed to meet away from any prying eyes in a place they both knew well.

★

The sun was beating down and Garda McEvoy was sweating. He could feel his shirt sticking to him and his hankie was damp from wiping his brow. He stepped under the canopy of a pharmacy to take a breather.

'Looks like you're melting.'

McEvoy turned and saw a postman pushing his bicycle along the pavement.

'You're not joking, it's murder out there.'

The older man nodded and continued on his way.

McEvoy suddenly called out to the man. 'Can you tell me what your route is?'

People moved around the two men as they stood in the middle of the pavement.

'I deliver to Trimelston Avenue, Trimelston Park and Woodbine. And the hotel, but there's not much for that place now that it's closing down.'

McEvoy's eyes narrowed. 'You must have delivered post to Barbara Ryan's house?'

He nodded his head and looked down at the ground. 'Of course; have done for years. She was a nice woman, always had a smile. A good person, you know.'

McEvoy nodded. 'I know what you mean. I wonder if you can remember seeing anything strange around the house.'

The postman was confused. 'Strange?'

'You know, out of the ordinary, around the time that she was killed. Anything at all. It doesn't matter how small it might seem to you, it might be useful.'

The postman wiped his face with a bare elbow. He moved to the kerb and left his bicycle against a lamppost. McEvoy was again mopping his brow and wondered if this had been such a good idea.

'I remember seeing a bloke on a bicycle acting funny near her house. That was a few days ago, before she was killed.'

'Funny, how?'

The postman thought for a moment. 'I remember coming around the corner and this cyclist suddenly turned, in the middle of the road, and headed off in the opposite direction. It was like he was startled. Know what I mean?'

McEvoy nodded.

'He leaned forward, keeping his face hidden. I thought that was a bit odd.' He shrugged his shoulders. 'It was an uncomfortable position to cycle in, that's all.'

'And what did he look like, can you remember?'

The postman scratched his head and grimaced. 'I think he had dark hair. And it was long.'

'How long?'

'Like a student's – long!' He tapped his shoulder to indicate length.

McEvoy had heard enough and had forgotten about the sun. 'I think that my boss would like to have a word with you, if you don't mind.'

The postman picked up his bicycle. 'That's fine by me. Anything to get out of this heat.'

McEvoy grinned. 'I couldn't have put it better,' he said, and they headed through the pedestrians to the cool comfort of the police station.

Patrick Stopman had worked in the neighbourhood for nearly twenty years and knew it like the back of his gnarled hand. He told his story to O'Neill who listened without once interrupting.

'That's very useful, very useful indeed. Thank you for your time.' He paused. 'One last thing.'

'Yes?' said the postman, leaning forward in his chair.

'I would like you to talk to our sketch artist so that you might give us a description of the man you saw. Every little bit helps,' O'Neill said calmly. The information that this man had just given could be very useful and he didn't want to make him any more nervous than he was. Sitting in a police station on a hot summer's day wasn't anybody's idea of fun.

The postman made a face. 'Sure, I can give it a go.' He licked his lips. 'Any chance of a drink? I'm parched.'

O'Neill sat up quickly. 'I'm sorry about that, Mr Stopman. How careless of me. Garda McEvoy can take you to the restaurant and get you whatever you want, and then you can meet the sketch artist.'

O'Neill was updating the murder board when Gary O'Connell knocked on the door. 'You look like a teacher,' he said. 'What's new?'

O'Neill told him about the postman's story and the videocassette that Pat Brady was collecting.

'Seems like there's a lot happening all of a sudden. That's good. Maybe the tide is turning,' added O'Connell as he fished in his briefcase and took out Caroline Dolan's mobile phone and a disc. 'These are for you,' he said and closed his briefcase. 'We've transferred the call onto the disc so you can listen to it. It's not good, Danny.'

O'Neill looked at the table and felt a cold shiver run up his spine. 'Thanks for that.'

'No problem. I just hope it's useful, that's all.' He swung his briefcase off the table. 'I'm under pressure, so I'll pass on the offer of coffee. I'll get you again.'

O'Neill looked down at the mobile phone and saw his reflection in the small screen. 'What did you see and hear?' he said quietly, tracing a finger over the keypad. The inanimate object, a silent witness at the attack on Caroline Dolan, sat on the table but offered nothing. But Gary got you to talk didn't he, he thought. He went to see Doyle.

By mid-afternoon Brady had returned from Trinity College with an enhanced copy of the videocassette. The images were clearer now but it still wasn't possible to identify the attacker. He was wearing a beanie, as Christine Connolly had suggested, and Bailey had reckoned that he was about five feet eight inches tall.

'How did he work that out?' asked Doyle.

'I don't know, but I wouldn't argue with him. He's a very clever guy, and God only knows what equipment he has access to.'

'Fair enough,' said Doyle. 'So where does all this leave us, Danny?'

O'Neill stood in front of the murder board with the grainy image of the killer and the work by the sketch artist. They seemed to show the same guy but nobody conclusive. And certainly nothing a defence barrister would worry about.

It was just more frustration.

'But we did hear him shouting "… you're all the same" on the audio clip, just like Margaret Power's attacker did. So, it must be the same guy, but who is he?' He drew a line from Caroline Dolan's picture to Margaret Power and added the 'all the same' comment. 'Okay, first of all, this news stays in this room.'

The team agreed.

'We could be close to our guy, but as you can see … or not, he's still invisible to us. Next, how to use this information? I don't want to scare this guy into another frenzied attack, especially if he thinks we are getting close to him. We continue as we are but with his image in our minds.'

Paul Grant spoke. 'If we have this information why not just get it out there, sir? Someone might recognise him from the audio clip or the CCTV image.'

Doyle stood. 'Your concerns are noted, and I appreciate them. But right now we are withholding this information. For the time being at least. Our masters agree that the killer's details are not clear enough to release to the public, and that we would not be helped by getting a flood of erroneous prank calls.'

Everyone knew about that.

'That would waste time and resources and we all know that they are very limited commodities right now,' O'Neill added. 'Rather than leaving this information to gather dust, I will be having a word with our friends in *The Local*.'

Connolly sniffed.

'They will say how the investigation is moving forward, that the police are happy with the progress in the case, and that the public should know that they are doing everything they can. All avenues are being investigated and …'.

'… because you are putting such a positive spin on things, our guy may start looking over his shoulder,' said Christine Connolly, 'and make a mistake.'

'Exactly,' said O'Neill. 'Our guy feels … knows, he's invisible. Invincible, even. So with this statement maybe he'll feel a little less so. He knows that we are not going to reveal our hand and we need to keep him guessing.'

★

The meeting ended and, after assigning work for the next day, O'Neill left and headed off to meet Tony Lewis. He drove to the campus at Belfield, parked his car, and took off his jacket and tie, leaving them on the back seat. He rolled up his sleeves and put on a pair of sunglasses and headed past the Science Block to the coffee shop by the lake. The late afternoon sun sparkled as it bounced off the glass and steel of the modern buildings, making him smile. Nobody paid him any attention and that was exactly how he wanted it.

He spotted Tony Lewis beside the lake watching the swans and ducks paddle about in the late sunshine. He had put on a few pounds since they had last met and his hunched shoulders seemed to be carrying the weight of the world on them. He looked older than his years, and O'Neill was happy he wasn't chasing Burke's killer. He smiled when they shook hands. It was firm like he remembered and he held it a little longer than normal. 'Good to see you, Tony,' he said and nodded gently.

'And you too, Danny. You're still looking pretty good. What are you taking? – nothing illegal I hope,' he joked.

O'Neill grinned. 'No, I go running on Sandymount Strand every morning, or at least as often as I can. You know that old phrase about "a healthy mind in a healthy body"? well I'm starting to believe it.'

'And no doubt Shelly Tobin approves, eh?'

'Jesus, is there nothing secret any more?' he said, his voice cracking before the pair of them laughed.

'So it's true then,' said Lewis. 'Good man.'

O'Neill put his hands up. 'Okay, enough of this. I didn't come here to be questioned about my sex life, and certainly not by you of all people.' He turned to the café. 'Come on, let's go and get some coffee. I'm treating you.'

'Still the big spender,' Lewis teased.

After they got their drinks and sandwiches they walked around the lake and sat on a seat well away from any eavesdroppers. Sunbeams danced on the water and all around them there was a quiet stillness. Off to the side two students dressed in cut-offs and T-shirts expertly threw a Frisbee. It was a perfect summer evening for getting up a sweat and, of course, talking murder.

They talked about old times in the university and the crazy things they had done. It all seemed so innocent and long ago, especially after all the crime they had each seen and experienced in their professional lives. Some gulls swept down looking for crumbs and O'Neill tossed the last piece of his sandwich into the air. It was snapped up immediately.

Lewis wiped his mouth with a napkin   'So, Danny, what's on your mind?'

He had thought about this and wanted to make sure that he wasn't going to sound like an idiot. 'It's like this, Tony: I think it's strange that neither of us has made any progress. None at all. That strikes me as odd, very odd indeed.'

Lewis lit a cigarette, let out a long stream of smoke but said nothing. He nodded for Danny to continue.

'I know that your case is very high profile, a politician has been murdered after all, and I have two women dead, but we are no wiser now than we were days ago. We know absolutely nothing.' He turned and looked at his old college friend and noticed the tiredness around his eyes and the grey hairs above his ear. 'In all the years that I've been investigating murder cases I've never seen anything like it, Tony. Never.' He hunched forward and watched the swans fight over scraps that a student was throwing to them.

Lewis took a long pull and then crushed the cigarette under his foot. 'I agree, Danny, it's hard to believe. My team has been going over this with a fine tooth comb, no expense spared, and we've got nothing. Sweet fuck all.' He leaned forward and put his elbows on his thighs. 'I hate to admit it, but right now, we're stuck.'

O'Neill turned his head.

'I'm getting grief from the government, from his family and his constituents, but we've not found anything to point a finger at anyone.'

'I thought that you were looking at some of his business partners?' said O'Neill.

Lewis sat up and ran a hand through his hair. 'Yeah, we did too, but it's a dead end. We've done all the financial checking and there's nothing missing or smelly.'

'Hmm.'

'And we've put the squeeze on the drug dealers that Burke was going to target when he got into government. They're not involved and it wouldn't be good for their business if you know what I mean? That would just bring down so much shit on their heads. And believe me, those boys aren't that stupid.'

O'Neill nodded. 'I see. So what are you going to do now?'

Lewis held out his hands. 'Don't know … just don't know.'

They sat in silence for a while and watched as more gulls splashed down and joined the fight for the crumbs that were on offer.

O'Neill sat up and sighed. 'I know this is going to sound stupid, but...'

Lewis looked at him and raised an eyebrow 'But ...?'

'But I'm wondering if there is any connection between the two investigations. I know it sounds crazy … but that's what I'm thinking. And the craziest thing is, I don't know why.'

Lewis let the words sink in, crossed his legs and stretched his arms onto the back of the seat. 'I agree it's crazy, but what's really nagging you? And remember that Burke was slashed to death with a long knife and that's not what happened to your women, is it?'

It wasn't what O'Neill wanted to hear, but he knew his old friend was right.

'I know, I know … but the attacks were so clinical and carried out within a few days of each other. It could be some sort of escalation ...'.

'Or you could be talking shite, Danny. That sounds very CSI to me.'

O'Neill shrugged. 'Agreed, but it's just that the two women who were murdered had nothing in common except that they lived near to each other. In fact, not more than half a mile from here. And no matter how hard we try to establish a connection we still can't find it. It's a real mystery.'

'And you think what?'

'I don't know, Tony. I just don't know. But I'm desperate and open to all suggestions. And I was hoping that if I knew something of Burke's background and movement then ... well you never know.'

'It's good that you are thinking outside the box, because I think that's all that's left now.' Over the next twenty minutes, Lewis gave a résumé of the investigation and of what they had established about Burke and his business links. Also, he explained about the affairs Burke had, but that no leads had been developed.

'And what about his campaign manager?' asked O'Neill who was listening intently.

'Maurice Kavanagh. He's a former high flyer in PR and worked closely with Burke for the last eighteen months or so.'

'He ought to know where any skeletons are buried, Tony.'

'I've been down that track, Danny, but we got nowhere.'

O'Neill took off his sunglasses and rubbed his nose. 'I know that Burke didn't live near these women, but I'm wondering if their paths ever crossed. Just looking for a connection.'

Lewis nodded and grinned. 'I know you are and you're bloody right. I don't know any more, but I'll have another word with Kavanagh and see if he's more helpful this time.'

O'Neill clapped his hands. 'Good stuff ... and make sure to find out Burke's movements around the election. It may well be that some nutter doesn't like politicians.'

Lewis laughed and slapped O'Neill on the back. 'And God knows, that's most of us.'

The two men shook hands and headed off with nothing new added to their investigations, only O'Neill's crazy idea that Tony Lewis would follow-up. He felt he already knew the answer – and it was negative.

O'Neill went home, changed into a T-shirt, shorts and running shoes and had a long hard run on the strand. It had been quite a day in a series of many big days. He felt that the wheels were moving and a few more rolls might get things really moving to an end. It would be a bloody end, as the Penman, Clipboard Man, or whoever the bastard was had spilled enough blood already, but his own would be the final drop. It didn't bother O'Neill what the killer thought as long as he was caught, dead or alive. 'It's your choice mate,' he said to the tumbling waves. 'I don't give a fuck.'

34

The room stank, the smell of stale cigarettes and empty takeaway cartons strong and sharp. He paid it no attention as he listened to the radio, a cup of coffee on his chest. He was thinking about the attack in Booterstown and how the arrival of the car had messed things up. It was a slip, he knew that, and how close he had come to being spotted. He didn't have everything under control, and that made him think hard.

The radio announcer broke for the news.

It was the fourth item that pricked his ears. 'Police today have said that the young woman who was attacked two nights ago at Booterstown station is off life-support. She was seriously injured and hospital staff are continuing to monitor her progress.'

'Lucky bitch,' he said. 'If that car hadn't come along you'd be dead like the other two. The next one won't be so lucky.' There was nothing about Liam Burke or the other women's investigations. The police had no ideas, and he grinned with deep satisfaction.

He sat up and looked at the pictures on the wall. There were plenty to choose from and he wondered who was going to be next. After the Booterstown affair he knew that he would have to prepare even better than before, and as he slowly touched each picture a tingle of excitement danced up his spine. He loved this moment the most – his choice. He was in total control and his girls were waiting for him to call them forward. 'Choose me,' they said to him, but he let them wait. A little teasing, they all liked that! He closed his eyes and the tingling intensified.

His breathing quickened when he picked up the long knife that he had used to kill Liam Burke. He touched the blade, drawing a drop of blood from his finger. He licked it clean and looked closely at the small wound. What a deep one a pencil must make, he mused, and again sucked his finger.

He scanned the pictures again – 'Eeny-meeny-mine-mo,' he whispered, and suddenly plunged the knife into one of them, the blade quivering for an age before coming to a stop. He touched the handle with his palm and slowly moved back and forward, feeling the pressure and loving the resistance. He closed his eyes and took a deep breath. 'Ahhh! I guess we have a date, darling, just you and me.' He stepped back, lit another cigarette and squinted through the spiralling smoke at the next lucky girl.

He ran his tongue along his lips, the edges of his mouth twisting into an evil grin. 'Soon, darling, real soon.'

35

The traffic was light when O'Neill drove along Strand Road, the sea blue and calm beyond. Early morning windsurfers, their colourful sails rippling joyously, were making the most of the rising breeze. They cut swathes in the water and leapt high off breaking waves.

To his right, two men, one on a ladder, the other holding it still, were putting up posters for the forthcoming Dun Laoghaire regatta. A pile of posters lay on the ground and an idea came and went in an instant. He scrunched his eyes trying to get a hold of it but it was gone. What was it? he wondered, hitting the steering wheel in frustration.

Christine Connolly was talking to Pat Brady when O'Neill came into the office. They stopped when they saw him and he knew that he had been right about the pair of them getting chummy. They seemed almost embarrassed, and Brady slunk off and sat at his own desk, pretending to be busy.

'Any news?' O'Neill said, taking off his jacket.

'No, nothing,' said Brady.

'I have a few follow-up house-to-house calls to make near the Dolan home,' said Connolly, 'after I finish these notes. But that's it, sir.'

'Good, just keep at it.' There was nothing more to say, so he went to see Doyle.

'Morning, Danny, alright?'

The boss was, as usual, deep into a mountain of files.

'I'm good, but this case is really proving to be a pain. We have what we believe is useful information but it's not enough. At every turn the killer is a step ahead of us, and it's hard to see any way of catching him.'

Doyle sat back in his chair. 'I understand. So do the big boys in The Park. This sort of thing is never easy and that's why it's on your desk. You're the best I have and you're doing a fine job. These things take time. We are always responding to events, always behind. It's what happens, Danny, you know that better than anyone.'

The two looked at each other for a few moments but said nothing. There was nothing to say and O'Neill didn't want to broach the idea of a single killer with him yet. There was a huge team working on the Burke case and they would surely crack it soon. There was no advantage in suggesting his 'crazy' idea now, so he kept it to himself. They discussed re-examining all the evidence and then O'Neill went back to his desk.

'Where's Dave?' he asked after a few minutes.

'Oh, some man called and wanted to speak to a detective so he's gone to see him, sir,' explained Connolly.

'About what?'

'A theft of some sort. Didn't sound very serious.'

★

Dave Conroy decided to cycle to Blackrock and enjoy the fresh air along Seapoint Avenue. The view out to sea was spectacular. A handful of small white clouds, delicate and unthreatening, broke up the endless blue and reminded him of school holidays in the country. Life was so easy then, playing football with his cousins, swimming in the lake near his aunt's house in Roscommon and collecting the hay under a hot sun. They were the best of times and he told himself that he should visit soon. His Aunt Rita, his favourite aunt, was now in her late seventies and he knew she would enjoy the surprise. Yes, he would do that as soon as things got sorted out here. But the way things were going, that could be a while.

He passed the long alley at Seapoint station where Margaret Power had been attacked and wondered about her attacker. the Penman was elusive, and why he did what he did was anybody's guess. Who knew what was going on in anybody's mind? Nobody, that's who. It was all speculation and theory, at least until he was caught and the shrinks could get to work on him. Most importantly, the public wouldn't care what made him do what he did as long as he was locked away for a very long time.

He swung right onto Main Street and freewheeled down to the library where he chained his bicycle to one of the new metal parking racks.

The place was busy and he spotted the shop between a newsagent and the old chemist shop that had been there for years. Above it the windows were white and looked as though they had been recently painted. Probably set in flats, he thought, and waited for the pedestrian lights to change.

The door was heavy when he pushed it in and he realised that he had never been in a pawnbroker's shop before. His father had said that only people on their uppers went to them. It was a short step from moneylenders, he had warned.

He looked up and noted the red light of a security camera. And then another one. The place was secure and the owner was taking all the right precautions, especially with all the high-quality goods around: televisions, DVD players, cabinets full of cameras and silverware. All would be of interest to any thief. These items were like instant cash and there was always someone who was willing to take a chance. In these difficult economic times that type of crime was on the increase. 'The Celtic Rat' effect, as one commentator so cleverly put it.

A voice from behind surprised him.

'Can I help?' it asked.

Conroy turned and saw a silver-haired man behind a desk at the end of the shop, looking over the top of his spectacles. He was wearing a dark suit, white shirt and silk tie, and a handkerchief in the top pocket. Very smart, thought Conroy, reaching for his ID.

'Detective Conroy. I took a call earlier. Was it from you?'

The man smiled and the creases around his eyes stood up a little. The skin was tight and Conroy knew that it had been exposed to a lot of sunshine. Months of it, thought Conroy, offering his hand.

They shook hands. 'David Jackson, I'm the owner. And, yes, I did call you.' He opened the drop-down counter and waved Conroy in. 'It's quieter inside,' he said. 'We don't want to be disturbed.' He bent down and flicked a switch under the counter and the front door clicked. Red beams of light criss-crossed the shop and Conroy knew that they would not be disturbed.

Jackson led Conroy down a long corridor that was crammed high with expensive white goods, from computers to stereos. Everything had a price and Jackson knew that better than most people.

Jackson sat at his desk and beckoned to Conroy to sit opposite him. Against a wall was the biggest television that Conroy had ever seen, and he couldn't help but smile.

Jackson noticed. 'Yes, it's all of seventy inches. Something else, eh?'

Conroy laughed. 'It wouldn't fit into my flat; it's like a cinema screen. Need a big house for that.'

Jackson considered the massive screen. 'Yes, the man who brought it in had some, how should I put it … bad luck on the business front. Cleaned out, I believe, is the phrase he used.'

'Wow, you couldn't miss that monster in any room.'

'Sure wouldn't, Detective. It's impressive.'

Jackson opened a drawer and took out a folded red cloth. He pulled back the corners and revealed a silver necklace.

Conroy leaned forward and put his hands on the edge of the desk. 'Is this why you called, Mr Jackson?' he asked and looked up at the man. He must have been in his late fifties or early sixties, but he was in good shape. No double chins and his skin was pink and healthy.

'Yes, that's right. I bought it from a man yesterday, a man I have to say, that I have done plenty of business with.' He lifted a small letter opener and slid it under the necklace and flipped it over. He pointed. 'There, can you see the letters?'

Conroy stretched over and saw the two letters on a disc that hung from the centre of the necklace. 'C. D.' he said softly.

'Yes, Detective, C.D. And then I remembered Caroline Dolan. The woman attacked a few days ago.' Jackson took off his spectacles and rubbed his eyes.

Conroy was stunned, but he couldn't take his eyes off the small disc. 'In that case, Mr Jackson, then I'd like to know who sold it to you. It could be very important.'

Jackson picked up a remote control and zapped the massive television into life. There was a deep buzzing sound and then the screen lit up in glorious Technicolor.

'Wow,' said Conroy. 'What a picture! It's crystal clear.'

'I love it,' Jackson said. 'It's so over the top. Listen.' He held the volume button down and the sound in the small office was deafening, and pitch-perfect.

On screen a surfer was riding a tumbling wave and Conroy felt that he was right there with him. The colours and sounds were incredible – better than anything he had ever witnessed. 'Must have cost a fortune.'

'With a suitable surround sound system connected to it you'd have little change from, say, fifteen, maybe even twenty thousand.'

'*Phew*, you're not joking. I'll have to win the Lottery to get one of those.' He waved the dream away. 'Later.'

Jackson scrolled through menus and clicked on 'DVD player'. The screen went dark and Conroy recognised the shop interior. Jackson fast-forwarded and the time indicator in the top corner became a speeding blur. He stopped the player and looked at Conroy. 'This is the man I bought the necklace from. As you can see the image is pretty good.'

Conroy took in the shop and the silverware that glinted in the glass cabinets. There was nobody else in the shop and he could see pedestrians walking by the shop window.

'His name is Clarke and he …'.

Conroy held up a hand. 'Sorry, Mr Jackson, have you got a first name?'

'It's Nobby, and he lives at 13, Patrician Gardens …'.

'Stillorgan,' said Conroy, finishing the sentence.

'You know the place then, Detective?'

Conroy looked at the desk and felt bile gurgle in his stomach. The memory was still raw and without thinking he touched his head. 'Sure do, Mr Jackson. The last time I was there I ended up in hospital when a guy hit me with an iron bar while I was trying to stop a thief from escaping. It's a long story.'

Jackson was sitting forward with elbows on the desk. 'And did you stop him?'

He was gently rubbing his head while recalling the incident. The robbery of an off-licence in the Stillorgan Shopping Centre had gone wrong and he and another officer were the first to respond. His partner managed to tackle one of the criminals with a flying rugby-style tackle and pull him down. Suddenly, a youth with a bag of money jumped him and knocked him out. He fled in a small hatchback sports car, but only yards away the car mounted a kerb and crashed headlong into a wall. The fight was over. So, yes, he knew Patrician Gardens very well.

Jackson shifted in his chair. 'That was very brave of you, Detective. Well done.'

Conroy nodded and turned to the screen where Nobby Clarke was held in electronic aspic. 'Can I have a copy of this? We'll need to see it at the station. It will be quite safe, Mr Jackson, I can assure that.'

Jackson hit a few buttons and in moments Conroy could see that a copy of the DVD was being saved to a computer that sat below the massive screen. When it was finished the tray opened and he handed the copy to Conroy who put it in his pocket.

Jackson stood up and straightened his tie. 'Detective Conroy, let me make myself perfectly clear.'

'Fine, Mr Jackson.'

'I have been in business here for seventeen years. I have seen good times and bad times. In the good times, business is not so good for me, and in the bad times, business is good for me. Understand?'

'I understand.'

'I have dealt with all sorts and all their predicaments, but I have never been in trouble. Not with the law, at least.' He raised his voice. 'I am not going to start now.' He folded the red cloth, put it into a metal box, and pushed it across the table.

Conroy picked it up and snapped the clasp.

'If this man had anything to do with the attack on that young woman, well I hope that he gets what he deserves.' He stepped from behind the desk. 'I have two daughters and I don't know what I would do if anything happened to them. Now take the necklace and do something good with it, Detective.'

'I'll do my best, Mr Jackson, you can be sure of that.'

They went to the front door and shook hands. 'I'm sure that your best will be good enough, Detective,' he said, and quietly closed the door.

★

Half an hour later Conroy was putting the DVD into the machine and looking at Nobby Clarke. He had dark hair to his collar and he was wearing white trainers. The scientists in Trinity College had calculated that the man on the Booterstown CCTV was approximately five-eight. Nobby Clarke, sadly for him, seemed a good match. Now all they had to do was catch the bastard.

O'Neill took over. 'Okay, this might be our lucky break, so let's all pay attention. Dave, you can confirm the address and who lives there. Check council registers and whatever else you can get your hands on. Paul, I want you to check with the electricity and water companies and find out who's paying the bills there. And see if you can get any details of mobile phones.

'Christine, see what you can find on Nobby Clarke; any previous arrests and what he might do to earn a few quid. He may even have a proper job and a Social Security number.'

That got a laugh. It was needed.

'Pat and I will check the local maps and get a plan together for Mr Nobby Clarke.'

The glum mood that had been hanging about the room was gone like an early morning mist, and O'Neill wanted to make the most of it. This might well be the chance that he was looking for, but he was too much of a cynic to totally believe it. He'd seen officers blindly follow one 'obvious' path and then regret it. It sapped the team and, without saying anything directly, their credibility was questioned, with negative consequences for everyone.

He was determined not to go down that route. He was as keen as any of his team to catch the killer but he couldn't jump too soon. A mistake at this critical time could be disastrous and he couldn't let this bastard slip away.

36

In less than an hour they had confirmed the address and that a Norbert (Nobby) Clarke lived there. The house was rented and another man's name popped up: Jack Kelly, who Brady knew by reputation, bad reputation. It looked like they had come upon a den of thieves and O'Neill wanted a watertight plan.

'I want the first two cars, that's Dave and Pat, to go straight on; myself and the last car will follow the road around left. That should be able to cut off any escape.' He looked at the anxious faces. 'Can you imagine the press if this guy gets away? It's not going to happen, is that clear?'

'Crystal clear,' said Doyle from the doorway.

All the heads turned.

'Carry on, Danny, and keep me informed.'

'Right, let's get ready – we'll be off in twenty minutes. No sirens or screeching brakes. This is not a TV show. These guys will have their antennae up, so be prepared.'

Brady put up his hand. 'I know Jack Kelly from a few years back. He was involved with a biker gang that ran drugs in South Dublin. He wasn't a big player, but he was the muscle. So this guy will definitely not come easy.'

'Twenty minutes, everyone,' said O'Neill over the sound of shuffling feet.

The four unmarked cars set off without drawing attention and headed towards Stillorgan. Nobody talked, all keeping their thoughts to themselves. They were completely focused and wanted the action to be quick and decisive.

All four cars headed along the coast, past Seapoint, Blackrock and Monkstown before turning inland at Newtownpark Avenue. A few hundred yards later they turned right and were on Stillorgan Park Road. The plan was for O'Neill and Connolly to walk by the house and see how things looked before he ordered any assault. Even the word seemed heavy: assault. That's what soldiers did, not police in South Dublin on a quiet summer's evening.

Brady radioed that they were in place and ready. The uniformed officers in the last car had removed their jackets and ties, rolled their sleeves up and could have passed for boys heading home after work.

'I'm going to have a look,' said O'Neill into the radio. 'Nobody do anything without my say so. Leaving the car now.'

Connolly got out the other side and they walked like any couple out for a summer stroll, glancing at houses as they went along. Some houses were in need of attention, with cracked windows and uncut front lawns. No. 13 was much like they had expected, with a wheel-less car up on blocks in the garden and two motorbikes beside it. An old sheet, torn and stained with oily blotches, lay on the ground, covered with tools and a roll of toilet paper. O'Neill reckoned that repairs were being carried out on the big Kawasaki.

At least someone was at home.

Brady and his team were already making their way towards the house when O'Neill spoke into the walkie-talkie: 'Someone's inside, so I guess we'll just have to knock on the door.'

Brady grinned.

'Remember that Kelly is an animal and he'll do anything to get away. Be careful,' he said, and he waited for Conroy to call. Two minutes later he called; he had the back entrance covered.

'Good work, Dave,' said O'Neill. 'I'm moving now.'

A few casual strollers gave them a second glance but kept going. Close looks were not encouraged.

The two casually dressed officers followed a few yards behind, sharing a laugh and a cigarette.

O'Neill and Connolly walked to the front door like local councillors soliciting votes. His finger was almost on the buzzer, when Jack Kelly swung the door open. His long hair was lank and greasy, and his moustache was out of control. A missing upper front tooth and a spider's web tattoo on his neck completed the hard man image. He didn't have to try very hard to look mean, for Jack Kelly it was a genetic trait.

'What the fuck do you want?' he spat, and leered at Christine Connolly. That leer said what he would do to her and he stuck his chest out.

O'Neill stepped closer. 'Nobby, is he in?'

Kelly stared at O'Neill and didn't hide his suspicion. 'Who the fuck are you?' It took a few seconds for him to realise what was going on and he shouted. 'Nobby it's the filth, get the fuck outta here!' He swung a punch at O'Neill but hit only fresh air. He staggered, his target gone, and lashed a kick at Connolly. It missed her knee by an inch. 'Fuck!' he screamed and swung a punch at her head. To his astonishment the pretty woman landed a perfectly placed foot between his legs. The pain was gut wrenching, and he shot the contents of his stomach on to his boots. He swayed and fell to his knees, another withering surge of pain shooting through his body, and collapsed, head on the ground, his damaged, precious jewels throbbing like never before.

'Back door, back door!' shouted O'Neill when he heard the kitchen door fly open. Connolly and the two officers ran around the corner where Nobby Clarke was fighting. One officer had a bloody nose and another was on the ground holding his stomach. In a few steps Brady hit Clarke in the kidneys and he went down screaming.

'Bastards!' he shouted and swung another punch. 'Bastards! You're all fucking bastards!'

'Got some mouth on him,' said Brady, getting his breath back, 'and he can certainly hand it out.'

O'Neill saw the dark hair, white trainers and nasty look on Clarke's face. 'Get this piece of shit to the station, and that big fuck in the front garden. He's going to the station as well.'

'That bastard has had everything at the public's expense,' said Brady through gritted teeth. 'He's a fucking leech – take, take, and more fucking take. We're better off without his sort. Fucking pond-life.'

'Calm down, Pat, we've got him. Let's get O'Connell over here and then we can go back and have a word with Nobby.' He grabbed him by the shoulder. 'Isn't that right, Nobby? I've been really looking forward to this ... honestly.'

'You're breaking my fucking arm, you bastard. It's me fucking arm.' Clarke twisted on his knees; sweat ran down his face, dropping off his chin.

O'Neill leaned into Clarke's ear. He whispered but the words were clear: 'Believe me, Nobby, if I want to break your precious fucking arm then you *will* know about pain. So *don't fuck* with me.'

He and Connolly got into the car and headed back to the police station. 'That was interesting,' she said and sat back as the world passed by.

★

The sky was darkening by the time Nobby Clarke was brought into the interview room. Two uniformed officers stood over him and hoped that he would do or say something offensive. After breaking one of their colleague's noses and hospitalising another they were itching to hit him. His head was stooped and his shoulders hunched as he cowered beneath the mountain of shit that was waiting to drop on him. Telling stories in the pub about hitting coppers was one thing, but sitting here in front of them in a darkened room was something else. What had he done? he wondered, and kept his head down. Sell a little dope, but that was hardly a reason to send squad cars and senior coppers. What the fuck was this all about? he asked himself silently.

O'Neill had cleaned up before the interview. They both looked smart. They were good and he was bad; it was part of the psychological game that Connolly suggested they play.

Nobby Clarke had a few scratches on his face, his eyes were tired and nervous. His hair hung below his collar and his height was what O'Neill was expecting. Nobby was looking like the suspect in both the Booterstown station and the pawnshop clips, but O'Neill was beginning to have a bad feeling. He looked at the man across the table; a quiver of doubt came into his mind. It was unexpected, but when he looked closer at Nobby Clarke, his gut instinct demanded attention.

It was just another hurdle, another blip in a case that had been weird from the start. Doubt itself was no bad thing, as it forced you to make absolutely certain of the facts – that really was the point of it all. No doubts, no regrets, no problems.

'Do you know why you're here, Nobby?' O'Neill asked, taking a sip of coffee.

An ankle chain kept Nobby locked to his chair, but his hands rested on his lap. 'Can I get some coffee?'

O'Neill turned to Connolly and they both looked at the suspect. 'No, you fucking can't have coffee,' snapped O'Neill. 'You answer the questions in here. You must at least understand that bit?'

'And what's going on?' Nobby asked carefully.

O'Neill grinned, but it was a nasty grin, full of suppressed anger. 'You're a slow learner, Nobby, real fucking slow. Maybe that's why you're in here.'

Nobby kept quiet, he didn't like the way the copper spoke.

O'Neill drank some more. 'For the second and last time, I'll ask the same question: Do you know why you're here, Nobby?'

Nobby's scared eyes flicked between O'Neill and Connolly but saw no comfort. The bitch, he certainly wouldn't mind shagging her, looked like she might be even more deadly than the guy asking the questions. 'I don't know, I've no idea!'

Connolly spoke. 'You pawned a woman's necklace in Blackrock, remember?'

The necklace, shit. He knew it was too good to be true. There was no point in denying it, as he knew he was probably on the shop's security camera. 'Yeah.'

'That necklace belonged to Caroline Dolan, the woman who was attacked in Booterstown station, and who is now in St

Vincent's Hospital fighting for her life. Does that mean anything to you, Nobby?'

His head dropped and he sighed. 'What the fuck are you talking about? I never hurt anybody, never.'

O'Neill stood, walked to the door and then slowly turned around. 'You really are stupid, Nobby. Really fucking stupid.' He shook his head. 'I've had some real beauties in here over the years but, fuck me, you're something else. What did I say a few minutes ago, Nobby?'

No answer.

'Right. For those in the "hard of hearing gang", it goes like this: I ask the questions and you answer them. I can't make it any simpler, Nobby. Understand?'

Nobby nodded his head and stared at his lap.

'Answer the question.'

'I don't know nothing about no attack in Booterstown or wherever. I don't do that shit.' He was still looking at his hands. They were shaking now.

'What shit do you *do*, Nobby?' O'Neill asked.

Clarke scrunched his nose and breathed deeply. 'I sell a bit of dope, grass or hash, nothing heavy. I don't attack people. I couldn't do it. Jesus!'

'So where did you get the necklace?' Connolly crossed out a question in her notebook.

'I found it.'

O'Neill laughed. 'Jaysus, Nobby, you can do better than that. That's the sort of a thing a child would say. "I found it on the street". Try again.'

He lifted his arms and awkwardly wiped his mouth with the sleeve of his shirt. 'I was drinking in The Punchbowl and it was on the ground beside my car when I was going home. It was in the car park.'

'So you drink and drive, you sell drugs and you hit police officers, that's quite a list, Nobby, and we've only been here a few minutes. What are we going to find out over the next two or three hours? This should be interesting.' O'Neill turned to Connolly.

'Yeah, this should be something else. I can't wait,' she said, and opened her eyes a little more – in mock anticipation.

Nobby Clarke's tough image slipped quickly. The fact that he was in the frame for an attack on a woman who might just die was a long way from dealing some soft drugs. They've got something badly wrong here, but how the fuck do I convince them?

Over the next hour he answered all their questions as quickly and honestly as possible. Whatever happened to that woman, he sure as hell wasn't going to take the rap for it. He'd never carried a knife, ever. It was the truth. They had to believe him.

'So, Nobby, where were you last Monday?' asked Connolly, her eyes fixed on him.

Last Monday, shit. How the fuck do I know where I was? he thought, his brain scrambling for an answer. A little voice kept saying Booterstown. Think, you stupid fuck, just think or else.... He was thinking hard; so hard that he was beginning to feel dizzy. A click. 'Yeah, I was in Galway delivering stuff,' he said .

O'Neill raised an eyebrow. 'Stuff?'

'Yeah, stuff. You know stuff: televisions, beds, fridges and that kinda stuff. I do it regularly; it pays well.'

'That's nice to know, Nobby, and I suppose you declare your earnings to the taxman, eh?' O'Neill took a big sip and emptied his cup.

No answer.

'Just another pack of lies, eh, Nobby? How many more laws have you broken, or do you care? You don't even know how to give a fuck.' O'Neill stood up again, the chair legs scraping angrily, and Nobby visibly tensed.

'It's the truth, honestly!' he cried, expecting a thump.

'Nobby, Nobby, Nobby, you wouldn't recognise the truth if it bit you on the arse. You're a liar, a genetically programmed one at that, and I'd have difficulty believing The Lord's Prayer coming from your lips.' O'Neill shrugged. 'What am I going to do with you?' He walked to the wall and leaned against it. 'I know, Nobby, I know exactly what I'll do.'

Connolly saw fear in Clarke's eyes, and waited.

'Shall I tell you what that is?' He stepped forward. 'I'm going upstairs now to call my reporter friend in *The Local* and tell him that the police have just captured Dublin's most wanted man. He will be charged tomorrow morning and then the world can feast their eyes on you and abuse him from a great height. Should be a day to remember.'

Nobby began to wet himself and he couldn't stop it. 'I was working with Des Hennessey. He has a business delivering stuff around the country and I help him when he needs another pair of hands.'

'That's better, Nobby, much better. And where do I find this Des Hennessey?'

Nobby coughed and a bead of sweat dropped onto the table. 'He's got a warehouse off Sallynoggin Park, in the old industrial estate. Know it?'

'Know it?' O'Neill laughed. 'The place is full of scumbags, of course I know it. I've made plenty of *social calls* in there, not always welcomed though. It's a shithole, if ever there was one.'

Connolly left the room and went upstairs to start checking on Des Hennessey and his business.

'Between you and me, I've had it up to here,' O'Neill placed his hand to his nose, 'and I'm not in a good mood. That's as honest as I can be. So here's the deal. I'll check out this Des Hennessey tomorrow and find out what he has to say. I hope that he's not gone away delivering *stuff*; that would be very unfortunate.' He tapped the table with a finger, the sound short and sharp in the stuffy room. 'And if he tells the truth then you'll be fine, Nobby. If he doesn't …'.

O'Neill called out for the officers to take the suspect away. 'I hope that Des is as good a friend as you think he is. Honour among thieves and all that. Take him.'

Upstairs the lights were on and O'Neill realised how late it was. Interviewing scumbags, what a way to spend a summer's evening.

'I've got a Des Hennessey where Nobby said he would be. I'm checking how his business stands with the Revenue, any outstanding taxes or whatever.' Christine Connolly was sitting in front of her computer carefully studying the onscreen information.

'Looks like Des has forgotten to pay his VAT since last year. That's definitely a reason to make a social call, sir. But ...'.

O'Neill was looking at her, waiting.

'Des Hennessy, otherwise know as "Tats" because of his many tattoos, has previous convictions.'

'Great stuff, for what?' he asked, suddenly feeling a little less tired.

She leaned closer to the computer screen. 'Well, he's been inside twice: for burglary, and for receiving stolen property.' She looked up and smiled. 'Last year he was let out of jail early because of prisoner overcrowding. So he's ...'.

'... so he's supposed to keep out of trouble.' O'Neill grinned. 'Tut, tut, Tats, but some guys just never learn, do they?'

Connolly smiled. 'Thankfully, no.' She hit the print button and collected the reports.

'Good stuff, but right now I'm going home. Get a swab from Clarke and send it to O'Connell. That will rule him in *or* out. Update the board, will you? I'll see you in the morning. We'll take a couple of officers with us as backup. That neck of the woods is dangerous, and I want Des to get the right signal. I'm tired of wasting time while that crazy fuck is out there.' He picked up his jacket and left. The air outside was fresh and clear, but his mind was agitated with doubts that wouldn't go away.

37

O'Neill wasn't enjoying his breakfast as caller after caller vented their spleen about the lack of progress on the Penman and Burke cases. The radio host was stoking the fires of anger and interested only in the vitriol pouring in. It was populist stuff and he egged each caller on. 'Are you as disappointed as Valerie was? Call me now, and have your say. God knows we need to hear from you, people are scared. Call me on …'.

He turned the mouthy radio jock off, wondering what made these radio guys tick. For them, everything had to be in chaos, and they had a willing audience who just wanted to vent their frustration. If the presenter had nothing to bitch and rant about then he didn't have a show. While O'Neill was trying to catch the callous bastard, a radio presenter, paid by the same taxpayer that paid his wages, was stirring up the mob. And making his job even harder. Would they be as mouthy if their own daughter had been a victim? Stupid question.

Brady and Connolly were talking when O'Neill came in. They were getting on and it was good to see the positive influence she seemed to be having on his team.

He rang down to the cells. 'How were our guests?'

'Good as gold, sir,' said the gaoler with undisguised contempt. 'There wasn't a word out of either of them. Big girls when that metal door is closed. They're all the same.'

'Thanks, I'll be down later.'

He walked over to Brady's desk. 'Anything I should know about?'

Brady shrugged. 'No, nothing new overnight, apart from more irate callers shouting down the phone.'

'They'll soon run out of steam, it's always the same. The cranks will always be with us, always wasting our time. And God knows we've wasted enough of it already.' He turned to Connolly. 'Did you send Nobby's swab to O'Connell?'

'Yes, sir. I did it as soon as I got off the phone last night. O'Connell said he'll have a result with us by the afternoon.'

'Good, and in the meantime, why don't we go and have a word with Des Hennessey? Pat, get another officer – that should send the right signal. Dave, you mind the fort.'

O'Neill looked at the board with all the names and dates they had gathered so far. There were photos stuck with tape, red lines showing timelines, pictures pinned up, but nothing made sense. All the help from the public and the contribution of the profiler hadn't pushed the investigation along any further. The information was like scattered pieces from a jigsaw waiting for the big central piece to fall into place.

They left to interview the man who delivered stuff and O'Neill wondered what answers he would give. Could he deliver an alibi for his friend, Nobby Clarke? He would soon know.

The car climbed Lower Glenageary Road and O'Neill watched the bay disappear in the rear-view mirror. The roundabout at the top of the road was blocked so he and another officer got out, and went to have a look. A white van and a bus had collided and there was a lot of shouting and finger pointing.

'So who's at fault? And please don't waste my time.' O'Neill said, stepping between the shouting men. The van had lost a rear light and received a small dent, but there was very little damage. The officer went between the two vehicles and took some photographs on his mobile phone. He then phoned the traffic control unit and requested a review of the videotape for the roundabout. Two minutes later the drivers shook hands and went about their business with a salutary warning from O'Neill ringing in their ears.

The industrial estate was even dirtier than he remembered. A burnt-out shell of a car and broken glass welcomed him. He turned to Brady. 'I want you and the officer to stay back. I don't want to scare this guy, but if I need to intimidate him then Christine Connolly will call. Keep a close eye on things.'

O'Neill and Connolly walked around the wrecked car. 'I see what you mean about it being a shithole, sir.' She smiled.

'It's a shithole alright; even a blind man could see that. Know what I mean?'

'I know exactly what you mean. In fact I can even smell the place – not on any Michelin guide I bet.'

O'Neill stopped. 'You stay behind, but close. And keep your radio on.'

Connolly knew that she had acquitted herself with Jack Kelly, but O'Neill didn't want to put her in the line of fire again. She was a guest on the team, and a valuable one at that. 'I'll be fine, sir. Don't worry.'

'I'm not worried about you, Christine; I'm more worried about what you might do to one of these scumbags.' He winked, then turned and headed for a line of three dodgy warehouses where broken windows seemed to be the norm.

A scruffy sign, hand-painted and worn, declaring 'Hennessey Transport,' made O'Neill grin. It was on a wall above a metal door that was seven or eight feet from a folding garage-door. Both doors were covered in colourful graffiti.

A man was wiping the windscreen of a well-travelled van in front of the garage door. He stopped when he saw O'Neill and rubbed his hands in the dirty rag.

'I'm looking for Des Hennessey. Is that yourself?' asked O'Neill, stopping about six feet from him.

The man was wearing a T-shirt with 'Led Zeppelin' written across the top. It was old, the letters faded and O'Neill also noticed a tear on the right shoulder. Both arms bore tattoos; a long sword on the right arm and a curling green snake on the left. He even had tats on individual fingers – the letters 'L O V E' loud and proud on his rag-holding hand. His hair was short and his eyes darted between O'Neill and Connolly, trying to gauge what was coming.

'And who's looking for him?'

O'Neill smiled. He'd played this game many times, but not today. 'Like I said first time, I am.'

A creaking movement to the right drew O'Neill's eyes away. The rusty door was pushed open and a man stepped out. He was tall, dressed from head to toe in black, and his most distinguishing feature was a unibrow. He might have been the missing link but O'Neill didn't have time for a discussion on anthropology. The guy was holding a baseball bat that was chipped and marked. He looked like he had used it before. O'Neill had seen enough.

He pointed to the Neanderthal and took out his ID. 'If you make one move you will regret it for a long time. That much I promise you. I am having a *really* bad day and the last thing I need is someone like you getting in my way. Do I make myself clear?'

The man with the rag swallowed hard. 'Leave it, Horse, go back inside,' said Hennessey evenly.

Horse grunted and did what he was told. At least he was a trained horse, thought O'Neill, and turned to the Rag Man.

'I'm Des Hennessey ... what do you want?'

Connolly came over and checked him out from head to toe as she walked. He felt as if he had been stripped naked, and in a way he had. He'd just become another entry in her profile book, but not one that would stand out. In fact, he barely registered.

'Tell me about Nobby Clarke.' O'Neill put up an index finger. 'And please, don't insult my intelligence by saying that you don't know him. Okay?'

'Yeah, I know Nobby. Why, is he in trouble?'

'I ask the questions.'

Des Hennessey was nervous. Connolly could see sweat on his brow and his tightly knit fingers.

'What does he do for you?' O'Neill asked and looked about at the other units. It must have been four or five years since he'd been here and that operation had gone well. His boss, Joe Dixon, had been tipped off that one of the units was a chop shop for stolen cars and they had raided it. There was a lot of shouting and fighting before the boss decided that it had been a good day's work. It had been a 'result'.

'He's a strong boy and I use him when I need extra help. Especially when I have to deliver in the country. Dodgy roads, sometimes no roads ... know what I mean?' Hennessey was trying to sound helpful.

'And where were you on last Monday?'

O'Neill and Connolly stood shoulder to shoulder, like one big pain in the arse.

'I think ...'.

'You think?' snapped O'Neill. 'You can do better than that, Des.'

Hennessey was beginning to redden and his voice thickened. 'I think ... we were in Galway. Stayed overnight and came home the next day.'

Connolly spoke. 'Can anybody vouch for you?'

'We stayed in a guesthouse near Salthill. It's called The Valparaiso. Ask for Deirdre Salmon, she's the owner. It's where I always stay when I'm in Galway.' Hennessey wiped his mouth with the back of his hand and didn't realise how dirty it was. He spat on the ground and immediately apologised. 'Sorry about that,' he said, and looked at Connolly, who was already dialling a number on her mobile.

O'Neill came closer. 'I hope for your and Nobby's sake that you are not telling me lies.'

He shook his head.

'Because, Mr Hennessey, if I have to come back we will not be having a friendly conversation like we are having now. I know that you were let out of jail because of overcrowding and that means that you are technically still "locked up". So, if what you've told me is wrong, then ...'. He didn't need to say any more and walked away.

In a moment, the fight was gone from Hennessey, and he cut a sad figure with the dirty rag hanging in his hand. He felt useless and shakily lit a cigarette, watching O'Neill's back get smaller as he moved away. He was going to clean up his act most definitely, and that was a promise. Because he knew, as sure as night follows day, that the cop with the tired eyes would enjoy calling on him again. 'Bastard,' he spat, but low enough so that the cops wouldn't hear it.

★

Dave Conroy was still handling the barrage of calls from the cranky and nervous public. Worst of all was Councillor Whitehead, who was known to have a rather high opinion of himself. What an arsehole, he thought, as the councillor ranted on and on. Conroy didn't know anybody who had a good word for him.

'Get off your fat arses and find this mad man!' he shouted, and Conroy held the phone away from his ear. What an arsehole, he said to Grant.

'Don't be unkind to arseholes, Dave, they're good things to have – but he's not one of them,' Grant said walking back to his desk.

Back at the station, Conroy told O'Neill about Whitehead's call and that he intended to inform Doyle. 'He's already spoken to him, as far as I know, Dave. Don't worry about him.'

'He's a greedy bastard,' added Conroy.

'I know, Dave. Money first, as always.'

Connolly put her phone down. 'I spoke with the woman in Galway, sir, and she said that Hennessey and Clarke were there at the time of the Booterstown attack. Sorry.'

'Damn,' said O'Neill, making a fist. Another dead end, but he had felt it all along.

'What about Clarke's DNA? That may put him in the frame?' said Brady.

O'Neill leaned back in his chair and stretched his hands behind his head. 'I don't think it's Clarke. He's not the type.'

'Not the type. What do you mean?' asked Brady. He suddenly realised how wrong he had been about David Ryan and regretted what he had said. Too impulsive, he thought, and bit his lip.

'This killer is organised and you certainly can't say that about Clarke. He's a waster dealing a little dope here and there, scratching about for a few quid, and sharing a house with a thug like Jack Kelly. I can't imagine him being able to keep a secret, let alone plan and carry out murders without leaving a trace behind.'

It was clear that they had the wrong man and the DNA would confirm it. There was nothing else to do.

'We'll wait for O'Connell and then we'll let him go. For now, him and his greasy mate can rest up,' said O'Neill in a tired voice.

Connolly updated the board and stepped back. There was so much information – but still nothing. She started at the top and worked her way along the names, places and lines but couldn't see a thing. She stopped and her eyes went to the bottom of the board. She saw a name and wondered why she hadn't heard from him. Dano, the guy from DropIt Deliveries had not got back to her and she wrote down the phone number.

She phoned the delivery company and remembered Kathy when she heard the young voice. No, Dano was not in but she would pass on the message.

There really was nothing more to do.

38

Gary O'Connell phoned and his report ruled Nobby Clarke out of the investigation. Whatever he was guilty of, attacking Caroline Dolan was not it. His DNA was not a match to the sample retrieved from either Booterstown station or the Ryan house. He was in the clear, except for his assault on the police officers during his arrest. He could still be in trouble but Doyle agreed with O'Neill that there was no point in proceeding down that line.

'You're free to go,' O'Neill said and told the officers to remove Clarke's handcuffs.

Clarke looked warily at O'Neill as he lit his first cigarette of the day and sucked in a bellyful of smoke. 'You spoke with Des?'

'Yeah, we spoke. You should do something better than hanging around with him or Jack Kelly. They're trouble, and you know it. You can do better.'

Clarke nodded. 'What about the coppers I hit? Are you going to prosecute me for that?'

'No, we're not.' He paused. 'But let's put it this way. It's on ice, and if you are in trouble again it might resurface and ...'.

Clarke knew what he was saying. 'Thanks, nice one.'

'Go on, get out of here, and stay out of trouble.'

Clarke left quickly, giving O'Neill a thumbs up.

It was just another dead end in the investigative life of Inspector Danny O'Neill. If that arsehole, the Penman, was writing about him, what would he say? O'Neill hated this sort of dark, negative thinking but it wouldn't go away. He thought of all the nasty jibes and names that people use against one another to score points. 'waste of space', 'useless', 'rubbish'. They were too numerous to go through, but the one that stuck didn't sound bad, didn't seem to hold the spite of others, but it's meaning was clear – for as far as the the Penman, was concerned, runner-up said it all. After all the effort by him and the team, he had to face the painful truth: that he, Inspector Danny O'Neill, was a runner-up. A fucking loser!

He got a coffee in the restaurant, took it outside and went for a walk on the harbour. All around him carefree people were casually walking in the sunshine. Children ran up and down the granite slabs, chasing each other as seagulls cawed noisily at them. Boats drifted in the clear water of the marina where a giant ferry was preparing for another swift trip to Holyhead.

He felt alone and a cold shiver rippled across his body. On a warm summer day, in broad daylight on the pier, he was alone. He knew that it was wrong but the feeling of failure was biting deep. He hated letting Barbara Ryan, Angie Murphy, Caroline Dolan and, of course, Helen Murray, down, but he was stuck. Stuck in a maze of dead-ends with no sign of a fresh clue. He would have a word later with Doyle. The investigation needed a new perspective and he sadly wasn't the man to provide it. He made up his mind to talk with Doyle tomorrow.

He noticed a missed call and dialled Shelly.

'You sound down in the dumps, Danny,' she said, concern obvious in her voice.

He told her about what had been happening and how the investigation had stalled.

'That's terrible. I'm very sorry to hear that, Danny, I really am.'

'Thanks, but I'm sorry to be laying this shit on you. It's got nothing to do with you, Shelly.'

Shelly sniffed. 'Well, I identified the murder weapon. And I carried out the post mortems, so I *am* involved. Maybe we can talk later?'

'Yeah, that'd be nice, really nice. Would you like to come over for dinner tonight? You have a key, haven't you?' He closed his eyes, hoping fervently.

'Hmm, sounds good to me. And yes, I have a key, thanks. See you at seven, and make sure that you're hungry, as I'm cooking, okay?' She rang off before he could say a word. He stood up and walked back to the station, thinking about how Doyle was going to act. He felt sick.

★

Tony Lewis angrily crushed his cigarette into the ashtray and let out a long low sigh, the smoke streaming across his desk. Another meeting had turned up nothing and the Minister for Justice was getting more rattled. His job was on the line and he had let Lewis know it. It was a fight for survival and he was determined to do whatever he could to preserve his position, and if that meant replacing Lewis, then so be it. He would be seen to have taken action – it was about deflection, and he was good at deflecting shit away.

Lewis picked up the phone and called O'Neill, who answered on the second ring.

'Morning, Danny, how are you?'

'Okay … probably better than you, I suspect.'

'Too bloody right,' said Lewis. 'You must be a mind reader.' He sniffed and tapped his fingers on the desk.

O'Neill could feel the desperation in his friend's voice and said nothing.

'Anyway, I've had a word with Maurice Kavanagh, you remember Liam Burke's PR agent, and he's willing to talk with you. Hush-hush and all that.'

'What do you mean, Tony?'

'He'll meet you in an hour as he's going away later. Somewhere neutral would be nice and won't draw any attention. I told him what you were thinking about and he's happy to follow any line of enquiry that might lead to catching Burke's killer.' He gave O'Neill the telephone number.

'Thanks, Tony.'

'And do let me know if you find anything.'

'Of course, consider it done.'

Forty minutes later O'Neill and Brady drove into town along the coast road, which for once was relatively quiet. 'So how are you getting on with Christine?' he asked.

'What?' Brady replied quickly.

'From what I see you two seem to be getting on pretty well. Hey, there's nothing wrong with that, in fact, it's very good.'

Brady blushed and tried to look straight ahead.

'She's a very attractive woman and as sharp as a tack, you know that.'

'Yes, I know that, and so does everybody else.' He wasn't sure what to say and wondered what O'Neill was *really* on about.

'It's just that I've seen a change in you over the last few weeks and I must say that I'm …'.

Brady closed his eyes, waiting.

'… I'm impressed, really impressed.'

Brady turned. 'Thanks.'

'You're welcome.'

'I like her and there's no harm in putting myself in the frame, is there?'

O'Neill shook his head. 'None at all, none whatsoever. It's all you can do … and the best of luck with it.'

Brady realised, and not for the first time, that O'Neill missed nothing, even with all the pressure of running a high-profile investigation. He was never to be underestimated and Brady felt deep down that if anyone was going to catch the Penman, then O'Neill was the one. 'Dan the Man' was considered the station's top officer and he realised, if somewhat begrudgingly, that it was indeed true. He would not challenge him so quickly in future – he had been so wrong about David Ryan. Just because he was older didn't mean he was better, and watching O'Neill this closely certainly brought that home.

They parked on Upper Mount Street near Kavanagh's office but didn't go in. O'Neill phoned Maurice Kavanagh and they arranged to meet across the road in Merrion Square. 'Near the Joker's Chair,' he said, and hung up.

O'Neill and Brady strolled into the park where beds of flowers were in magnificent bloom, their scent drifting and teasing. Sun worshippers were stretched out on the grass, while two young mothers with young children sat and chatted on a large striped blanket.

The two policemen walked past the Joker's Chair and sat at the nearest bench. Above the tall trees rose the flat redbrick Georgian terrace of Merrion Square; its windows glinting in the sunlight.

'So what is Kavanagh going to tell us?' asked Brady, sitting back on the warm bench.

O'Neill drew a hand across his mouth. 'I don't know, Pat, it's just a shot in the dark.'

'But sometimes you might hit something.'

O'Neill grinned. 'That's exactly how I see it. Nothing ventured, nothing gained.'

Two minutes later, Maurice Kavanagh walked around the hedge and spotted them. He was tall, over six foot, and his fair hair was immaculately cut. His black trousers were pressed and he had a mobile phone in his hand. He walked with confidence and O'Neill saw one of the young mothers eyeing him closely.

O'Neill nodded a hello and Kavanagh sat down casually between the two policemen. 'So, how can I help?' he asked, and slipped his sunglasses into his shirt pocket.

'I don't exactly know yet,' said O'Neill, 'but maybe you can tell me about Liam Burke. You were close to him, obviously, and anything you can tell us may help.'

Kavanagh nodded. 'Okay, but I only got to know him in the last year or so when he decided to get into politics. He had made enough money from his property deals and was keen to do something new.'

'And why politics?' asked O'Neill.

Kavanagh shrugged. 'Why not politics? It's high profile, important and pays well. It's got the lot.'

'And which was more important to Burke? The high-profile part I assume?' asked O'Neill.

Kavanagh smiled. 'Tony Lewis said you were sharp, and I can see why. And, if the truth be told, I reckon it was the high-profile aspect that appealed to him. He fancied himself, and after making his millions he wanted, no, he needed, to be seen as a success. It was his nature. Too much testosterone ... you know the type.'

'Cock of the walk,' said Brady.

Kavanagh turned and sniggered. 'Spot on.'

O'Neill said nothing for a few moments. 'And have you any idea as to the reason why he was killed? Any resentment in the party about him being put on the ticket so quickly? Are there any skeletons in the closet that we should know about? Angry business partners, for instance? Anything at all?'

Kavanagh leaned back on the bench and twirled his phone in his hand. 'Nothing that I know of. I asked him this at the start of our relationship, and he swore that there was nothing in his past that I should be worried about. His death is a complete mystery to me.' He shrugged. 'I'm dumbfounded, I've no idea.'

The three men sat in silence until the sound of someone playing music made them turn their heads. Across from the flowerbeds a young guy was sitting in a lotus position, oblivious to the world, playing the clarinet while his girlfriend sipped a cold drink.

Brady spoke. 'So far as the politics were concerned he needed to get himself elected, so what did that take?'

Kavanagh again turned to Brady and took in his clear blue eyes and their intensity. 'It meant going to meetings and more bloody meetings, and then on the day of the elections visiting polling stations. You know, to put his face in the shop window.'

'Why polling stations? Surely at that point in the game voters will have already made up their minds?'

'Not necessarily,' replied Kavanagh. 'Some people may see him and decide to vote for him. It happens. He was a sharp looking man, you know.'

'And what polling stations did you go to on the big day? Can you remember?'

Kavanagh shrugged. 'Not off the top of my head, but I can fax a copy of the day's itinerary to you.'

There was nothing more to be said and Maurice Kavanagh headed back to his office with his mobile firmly placed against his ear.

'A shot in the dark,' said Brady as they walked to the car.

'Yeah,' said O'Neill, but his mind was elsewhere, trying to focus on an idea that teased him before again slipping away in the sunshine.

39

By the time they arrived back at the police station, Maurice
Kavanagh's fax had arrived. It listed all the polling stations
that he and Burke had visited on the morning of the election
and the times of arrival. There were nineteen addresses on it and
O'Neill gave it to Brady. 'Here, Pat, have a look at this and see
what you can make out of it. I'm going to see the boss.'

The bell in St Michael's Church was ringing for five o'clock
when Christine Connolly's phone rang.

'Detective Connolly, can I help?'

'Of course you can help, and you sound so good and official,'
the voice said.

'Hey, who is this?' she snapped and heads turned.

'You sound even better when you're annoyed. How cool!'

'Do you have a name or are you just wasting police time?'
Her voice dropped. 'One of my techies is running a trace, so
you'd better be quick. You sound like a guy who's quick.' It was
cutting and meant to provoke a reaction.

It did – from the others in the room.

'Hey, it's me, Dano, and what's with the hostility? Cool it,
it's not good for you,' he said evenly.

Dano was one cool customer and she grinned when she
realised it was him. 'So what have you got for me, Dano?'

He laughed. 'Are you always like this? Straight into it, no
dancing around a little? Sizing things up. Getting to know …'.

Christine butted in. 'I don't have the time, Dano, and I
could do you for wasting precious police time. So, if you have
something to say, then say it.'

She wasn't playing any games, and he knew it.

'Well, I played football the other night with some guys who used to work at DropIt.'

'And?'

'One of them remembered that we did a survey about eighteen months ago, and that one of the lads left shortly afterwards. He was a good worker, too.'

Connolly waited for a name and could feel her pulse rate increase.

'Why did he leave, if he was that good?' she asked.

'He got some government or local government job, paid well. Much better than here.'

'Government job? Can you be any clearer, please?'

'One of the lads, Bertie, who knew him best, thought it was something to do with elections. That's as much as I know, sorry.' He paused a moment. 'He was working for me one day and then he collected his money at the end of the week, and that was it. I was hoping that he'd show up again, but ...'.

'And tell me, Dano, did he fit the picture. You know – dark hair, about five-eight?'

'That's him alright; that's Ned Wilson.'

'Ned Wilson,' Connolly said and wrote the name on a yellow Post-It note.

'We called him Ned the Head because he likes his music a lot ... and is never off his bike. And he has a motorbike as well, always dressed in black. Real Goth-like.'

Christine sat down and started writing. 'Dano, what sort of bicycle did he have?' O'Neill and the others had all gathered around her desk.

'One of those fancy racing bikes, spent all his money on it. Thought he was Stephen Roche.' Dano laughed at the memory.

'That's great, Dano. And do you know where he lived?'

'I think in Dun Laoghaire or ... maybe Glasthule. I can't be sure as nobody ever gives their real address. They don't want to be traced by the authorities. People who work in my line of business tend to move around, know what I mean?'

Connolly grinned. 'I understand ... and thanks a lot.'

'Anything for the nice lady.' He laughed and hung up.

Connolly's eyes were bright and excited as she told O'Neill what Dano had just said.

'Right, check this bastard's name through every computer you can. Now,' he said firmly.

He went to the toilet, relieved himself and washed his face. 'Was this another false lead?' he asked the mirror, but didn't wait for an answer.

Paul Grant was in front of his computer with the phone to his ear. 'Say again,' he said and tapped his keyboard. The screen changed and a list of names appeared in alphabetical order. He leaned closer and ran the tip of his pen against a name. 'I have a Ned Wilson in No. 26, Summerhill Parade, Glasthule,' he said, and O'Neill ran over to have a look.

'Where is this coming from, Paul?' he asked, nervous tension tingling the back of his head.

'This is from the Revenue. It has all the data tied to Social Security numbers and the last known residence available. It was updated over a year ago.' He looked out the window, thinking. 'So where has he been working since then?' he said.

'Doing odd jobs, I bet. All off the record, exactly like your man Dano just said,' offered Conroy.

'And has he ever been arrested? I want to know,' said O'Neill.

Connolly was tapping her keyboard before he was finished his sentence.

O'Neill walked around the office, oblivious to the noise and chatter around him. He was looking yet again at the board, pleading for it to share its secret. It was tantalising to be so close and not to be able to see it. He walked over to the window and looked down at the normal world as it carried on its business.

One of the officers who Nobby had hit was standing on the other side of the road talking to a young man who set a ladder against a lamppost and climbed up. The officer held it while a woman handed the young man a pair of scissors. He snipped a plastic cable and passed down another old poster. It was from the recent election with the dull slogan 'You Deserve A Job'. The woman put it into the back of a white van, and the young man then slid the ladder in on top it.

Something began nagging at O'Neill. It was like a familiar itch, but he couldn't quite get to it. He looked around the office, his eyes not seeing anything, until they spotted the poster leaning against the wall. It was still there, the politician still grinning. O'Neill closed his eyes as the idea slowly began to make itself clear. It had slipped away before, but now he felt he could grab it.

Suddenly he felt as if he was having an out-of-body experience as images, names and lines began to merge and make sense. He saw it, saw how it happened … saw how Ned Wilson met his victims.

'Someone contact the Election Office, now!' he shouted.

'What is it?' cried Connolly.

All the others in the room were looking at O'Neill, waiting.

'It's where Wilson meets his victims – at the elections.' He clicked his fingers excitedly and began pacing up and down the office.

Brady looked at Grant and Connolly and put his phone down. 'The election?' he said, a look of bemusement on his face.

O'Neill instructed Conroy to phone the Election Office. Conroy enquired to confirm Dano's claim that Wilson left for a job in the election office; to find out when Wilson worked there; and whether the victims would have had any contact with him. Conroy did as told.

The tension in the room was palpable.

'Well?' said O'Neill from the far end of the office.

Conroy looked at his note. 'You're right, sir, Ned Wilson worked as a Polling Clerk at the elections.'

'Where?'

'He was based at the National School on Booterstown Avenue.'

'Which is only around the corner from where the victims lived,' added Connolly, thinking aloud.

'And I bet that our victims all voted at his table.'

Conroy had to grin. 'Yes, sir, and all the victims voted at table eleven.'

O'Neill rubbed his face in his hands, and looked at Connolly. 'Think about it. You go to the Polling Office and what do you do?' It wasn't a question.

Connolly answered. 'You hand in your voting card with your name and address on it. Christ,' she said, suddenly realising the importance of her own words.

O'Neill clapped his hands. 'Exactly. You actually give your most private information to the Polling Clerk. It's checked against the register and you're marked off.'

'Marked off for murder,' added Paul Grant, his fingers paused over the keyboard.

'So simple, so bloody simple,' said O'Neill. 'Who would ever have thought of it?' These women were doing what they were entitled to do, and they ended up dead.

Conroy spoke again. 'And before working in Booterstown, Wilson worked at the Polling Office in Seapoint. And, no doubt, that's where he met Margaret Power.' He looked up. 'Coincidence, eh?'

'No coincidence, Dave, no way,' said O'Neill, staring at the murder board.

Brady stood up, holding a sheet of paper. 'This is the list of the Polling Stations that Burke and Kavanagh visited on the day of the election and, surprise, surprise they were in Booterstown in the morning.'

'So Wilson must have seen him there,' said O'Neill, his hands over the back of his head, thinking. 'And, of course, the new ballot papers have the candidate's photo and address on them. He probably stalked him and … we know the rest.' Connolly tapped a finger against her lip. 'And you can see why Barbara Ryan might let him in. She knew him, at least knew his face. And he may well have been friendly when she came to vote. No point in scaring the prey.'

How cold it sounded. How calculating and devious, but then who knew what was going on inside Ned Wilson's head? It was simplicity itself. Innocent women, without realising it, had all but invited him into their lives. It was sick, but an opportunity too good to miss for someone with a deadly scheme in mind. 'Marked off for murder', how very well put.

40

O'Neill called Doyle and told him what he had and what he planned to do. It was agreed that O'Neill should check out where Wilson lived and approach it with two teams from both ends of the road. This would stop any escape attempt and protect the neighbours if things got messy.

'He's a crazy man, Danny, so watch yourself. Best of luck,' said Doyle.

Pat Brady updated the board and the confusion that had plagued the investigation was almost gone. They finally had a lead. Wilson was the thread connecting all the women. He was probably the cyclist seen by the postman near Barbara Ryan's house, and he fitted the description of the man from the Booterstown attack. This was no coincidence – they now knew who the Penman was.

'I know that place,' Brady said. 'A school friend of mine used to live on that road. His father was a bit of an inventor and he had a shed at the back of the garden. There was a door that led onto a lane behind so we should make sure that's covered. It backs onto the DART line.'

They looked at the map. 'Good, that limits his options. Pat and Dave, take two officers with you and gain entrance to the lane through one of these first houses, and make your way down to the back of No. 26.'

Brady and Conroy nodded.

'Christine and I will come from the other end.' He turned to Christine. 'Are you ready for some more action?' He couldn't help but grin.

'Can't wait,' she said. '*This* is going to be exciting.'

'And dangerous,' he said. 'I don't want any heroes, do you all hear me?'

They heard him.

'Are we using walkie-talkies?' asked Brady.

'Yes, and you let me know when you're in place. Everybody clear?'

Everybody was very clear and itching to go.

Less than ten minutes later the cars pulled out of the police car park and began the short trip to Summerhill Parade. They drove along Windsor Terrace where people were enjoying the view of Dublin Bay, the fresh air and an impromptu jazz band that had set up on the wide grass space. A boy was throwing a frisbee to a girl whose long blonde hair danced in the sunshine. Nobody paid them any attention, thought O'Neill, as they turned into Islington Ave, and stopped.

They had one last team talk and headed up the road and right again onto Summerhill Parade. Brady, Conroy and two officers went to the first house, knocked, and within a few moments were inside.

'We'll give them a minute or so to work their way down to No. 26,' said O'Neill, a swarm of butterflies fluttering madly in the pit of his stomach.

Connolly and O'Neill walked casually down the road where the smells of cooking drifted from open windows. He could hear a radio playing but couldn't recognise the song. In another garden a man was washing his car, but paid them no attention as they passed by, talking.

'We're in place,' said Brady.

'This is it, then. Ready?'

The fire in Christine's eyes told him she was. 'You bet,' she said, gripping a can of pepper spray.

The ordinariness of the place, the plain houses with neat tiny gardens and hedges were at odds with the mayhem brought by the Penman. Hide in plain sight so as not to get noticed, isn't that what the experts said? If that was the case here then Ned Wilson had learned well.

Number 24, 25 … 26.

A tall hedge blocked the house from view and the gate was unpainted unlike all the others. The place was scruffy and uninviting. The grass needed cutting and a bin was bulging with refuse. Beside it he saw a red–coloured racing bike chained to the fence. It was a good sign.

'It's got to be him,' said Connolly quietly.

O'Neill nodded and took a deep breath. 'I'm going in,' he said into the walkie-talkie and pushed the gate. It creaked and he winced.

He took two steps into the garden and saw the curtain move. It was followed by a loud crash as something hit the floor inside. 'The bastard's at home!' he shouted.

The front door was unpainted and had a cracked window that was held together with strips of black tape. The porch was unswept with a stack of old newspapers yellowing with age. He knew that nobody ever came to this house and that was just how the Penman wanted it.

He lifted the knocker and hit the door, hard. 'This is the police, open up!' he shouted.

There was no response and he stepped back and hit the door with his shoe. It didn't give, but a second, more determined lunge saw splinters fly as the lock exploded and the door swung open. It swung back violently, and Connolly followed O'Neill, pepper spray at the ready.

Out back, Brady the others were shouting and clambering over the wall.

O'Neill ran into the back room as a black cat dashed between his legs and out onto the street. He stepped in a pool of spilt milk and lost his balance for a moment before reaching for a chair and staying upright. 'Fuck!' he shouted and looked around at the empty, untidy room where an unmade bed dominated. Above it a poster for the film *Hannibal* hung, with a bottom corner rising like a sneering grin.

Wilson wasn't here but he'd have to come back, thought O'Neill, as Connolly called to him. 'Better see this, sir,' she said from the front room.

Brady was now in the kitchen and the other officers were guarding the front door. 'What happened?' he shouted.

'The bloody cat jumped down from the window and disturbed the curtain,' said O'Neill. 'I though the bastard was making a run for it.'

'Fuck, so he's not here,' said Brady letting out a loud sigh.

'Look at these,' said Connolly again, pointing to the photographs above the fireplace.

O'Neill's eyes followed.

'That's Barbara Ryan ...' she said.

'... and that's Angie Murphy,' said Brady, stepping closer. 'Fucking murder gallery, can you believe it?'

He turned slowly and saw a crazy look in O'Neill's eyes. He looked at the photographs again and saw one with a long knife stuck in it. There was something familiar about it, but that couldn't possibly be her. How could it be her? He squinted and told himself to concentrate. And then he knew.

O'Neill took a step closer. 'Oh, sweet Jesus, it can't be!' he cried out and turned for the door. 'It's Shelly, he's going to kill her next. He's been stalking her from the start. Fuck!'

The photograph of Danny and Shelly outside Barbara Ryan's house was beside one of her leaving the Coroner's office, and it had a black drawn on it.

It meant only one thing. O'Neill's heart was in his mouth.

'She's at my house!' he shouted. 'I have to get to her.' He paused, his brain trying to work out what to do. 'Pat, you and the lads stay here in case the bastard comes back. Dave and Christine come with me.'

They ran from No. 26 and sprinted to O'Neill's car as neighbours came out to see what all the commotion was about.

Conroy stuck the red flashing light on the roof before the car screeched away with its siren blaring. O'Neill threw his mobile to Connolly and told her to call Shelly.

She dialled the number as the car raced through traffic lights, almost clipping a bus. Pedestrians stood transfixed as the Audi flew past them on the wrong side of the road. It was a matter of life and death – and O'Neill had to get to Shelly. He couldn't, wouldn't let her down. Not another victim who would lose her life because of him. It had all came down to this – it really was that simple.

'Get the fuck outta the way!' he screamed. The car swung across the road before he managed to regain control again.

'There's no answer!' Connolly shouted and started dialling again.

'Keep at it!' he shouted and zoomed past a line of cars.

41

Wilson parked his motorbike around the corner from O'Neill's house and took off his helmet. It was quiet and there was nobody on the street. Perfect, he thought, and ran his hands through his hair.

Killing the coroner, he liked the sound of that, it was going to be fun, and necessary. It would halt O'Neill in his tracks, and give himself time to consider what he was going to do next. This would be his biggest achievement and make everyone realise how good he was. But more than that, the coroner was almost the image of his mother. She had to die. He closed his eyes for a few moments and knew that this was the one. He was going to enjoy this more than any of the other attacks. He knew it, felt it. He started walking to O'Neill's house.

★

The traffic on the Rock Road moved over as O'Neill sped past Booterstown station. He was doing almost 120 kilometres an hour, and in the back seat Christine Connolly was still trying to contact Shelly. 'There's no answer, sir.'

'Just keep trying, I know she's there,' O'Neill shouted and braked hard for the turn on to Strand Road.

'Get outta the way,' screamed Conroy as the Audi rounded a slow-moving van; its driver's eyes wide open in surprise.

★

Shelly opened a bottle of wine and poured some into the mince, stirring continuously. She poured a little more and smiled. 'That's better,' she said and hummed along to the song on the radio. She was enjoying herself and looking forward to a pleasant evening. A *very* pleasant one, she thought, and smiled again.

She looked up when she heard a knock at the front door. She wiped her hands and cursed the interruption. 'Damn, that's all I need.'

She ran a hand over her hair and opened the door.

The man pushed the door back and knocked her against the wall before she knew what was happening. He swung a fist and hit her above the ear. She screamed with pain and surprise and stumbled along the hall.

★

'Come on, come on,' O'Neill shouted and pressed his hand to the horn. People walking on the beach looked up and saw the police car with the flashing light speed past and then swerve into St John's Road. The sound of screeching tyres got more attention as O'Neill just missed a parked car before straightening up and slamming his foot to the floor.

★

'It's your turn, bitch!' Wilson cried and wrapped an arm around her neck and forced her into the kitchen, her feet barely touching the floor.

Shelly struggled and flailed, her arms trying to hit her attacker, but he was too strong. Her hands clawed at his face, making him only angrier.

'You're mine, bitch. All mine,' he spat in her ear and tightened his grip. He bit her shoulder, and she could only manage a muffled cry. She was gasping and her chest was on fire. White dots were floating in front of her eyes – she could feel herself slipping away....

'We're going have some fun, bitch,' he hissed in her ear, his tongue licking her as he twisted her neck harder. 'Bitches like you need to be taught a lesson.' He squeezed her breast roughly.

'You're all the fucking same,' he said quietly and pushed her down on the kitchen table.

She could feel the life running out of her as her eyes began to bulge. The pain was excruciating. She had to do something. She tried vainly to reach for the bottle of wine.

He saw it and yanked her up straight so that she was on her toes. 'No fucking way, bitch, no fucking way.'

She gasped, the room spinning in front of her. He eased his grip a little, trying to get a better hold and she knew it was her last chance. She lifted her foot and brought the heel of her shoe crashing and scraping down on his ankle. She could feel it tear into his leg and he screamed and let her go.

She slipped sideways and then made for the front door.

'You cunt, you're dead! Fucking dead!' he roared. He hobbled, holding his ankle, cursing her with each breath. He picked a knife up off the counter and chased her into the hall.

Shelly staggered through the front door as O'Neill rushed past her. He had a metal torch in his hand and swung at Wilson when he came into the hall. He hit him a glancing blow and Wilson banged into the staircase. O'Neill swung the torch again but Wilson was quick and cut O'Neill across his face, drawing a spurt of blood. O'Neill stumbled with blood in his eye and Wilson went in for the kill. 'Fuck you, copper, you've ruined everything!' he shouted and thrust the knife at O'Neill's chest.

Dave Conroy screamed wildly and dived at Wilson, his hands reaching for the knife. He crashed into the killer who was knocked sideways and collided headfirst with the doorjamb. It made a dull sound, like an exploding melon, and he was down. And out.

O'Neill gasped, his chest still heaving as the blood from the cut flowed onto his shirt. 'Jesus, Dave, you were like Superman. I didn't know that you could fly. That was some move. Thanks.'

Conroy lay on top of the pile of bodies, breathing heavily. 'Phew,' he said, blowing hard. He checked that Wilson was unconscious and offered O'Neill a hand.

Outside, Christine Connolly had an arm around Shelly, comforting her. Minutes later the first ambulance arrived, and soon the house was surrounded with police cars and onlookers as Wilson was taken way.

O'Neill hugged Shelly tightly. 'This was never meant to happen, I'm sorry. So very, very sorry.'

She put a finger on his lips and shook her head. 'It's not your fault, Danny.' She looked him straight in the eye. 'And thanks for saving me.' They kissed briefly before getting into the ambulance and heading off to hospital.

42

The next few days passed in a blur as the media went into overdrive with their coverage of the Penman's arrest. There were stories from people who knew him, or at least claimed to, and the usual pieces by psychologists about the killer's upbringing and motive. O'Neill watched it all, detached, but pleased that it was finally over.

Gary O'Connell's team had carried out a rigorous search of Wilson's house and found notebooks and diaries detailing his activities. They described the abuse and hatred of his mother that sparked everything. It was a sad tale.

It was ironic that Caroline Dolan was released from the same hospital that Wilson was brought into, where he was now under armed guard. He wasn't talking much, but O'Neill, Doyle and the top brass in The Park weren't too concerned. A vicious killer was off the streets and that was the main thing.

And Dave Conroy picked up the phone and kept a promise. He called Margaret Power and told her about Wilson's capture. She thanked him, then hung up. There was nothing more to say.

Doyle held another press conference and cleared up a few points for the hungry journalists. The biggest surprise of all was that the Burke murder was now also solved. It was known that Burke had visited the Booterstown Polling Station and that Wilson had killed him to divert police and resources from the Penman cases. The chiefs in The Park sent their congratulations to the team on a job well done.

It rained hard the day that Ned Wilson ambled into court to face sentencing. He showed no remorse and didn't say a word as he was led away. 'Fuck you, too,' said O'Neill under his breath. He would remember him every time he looked in the mirror at the long scar below his left eye.

The sky was reddening, the dying sun an orange ball sinking fast, as he ran along the strand. The seagulls followed him, cawing as they swooped. He stopped and panted loudly, feeling the sweat drip from his face on to his damp T-shirt. He was feeling good, and enjoying the wind on his wet face. His phone rang – it was Shelly.

'Hi, dinner at seven, Inspector?'

'Yes, like I said.'

'Good, I'm looking forward to it. See you later.'

He grinned. 'So am I, Shelly … so am I.'

He turned and sprinted hard down the beach, the air tangy and clear in his nose. He had been given another chance and this time he was going to make the most of it. He was now running for his life, not from it. He was free.